The Forest Of Eternals

The Scrolls Of Tralatitious

A Novel

by

Patrick Clermont

Jor
Thanks for the music
Support...
Good luck with the music
Look forward to hearing
Mike

Library and Archives Canada Cataloguing in Publication

Clermont, Patrick, 1969-

A Novel

ISBN 978-1-7776504-3-8

To my wife Sharla, thank you for encouraging me every step of the way, and fixing all my grammar and spelling mistakes and for inspiring most of the good stuff in here.

To my daughter Pebbles, thanks for all the artwork I get to look at. It inspires me to write better so this story can one day be as beautiful as your work.

To my daughter Ravah, thanks for telling me what I need to hear, not what I want to hear. Your input has changed the way I write and has made me not only a better writer, but a better storyteller.

Prolog

Prologue

The Prophet Of Peace

The fables of the Rubicon Forest were considered old and wise; the stories were known to everyone and the fear of entering it or being forced to enter it, was a most terrifying dreadful thing.

There was not a soul alive who knew of even one person who had entered and returned to tell about it; at least not in the last thousand years. No, not even The Old Lady knew of anyone, and she was said to be over eight hundred years old.

The legends chronicled in the Scrolls of Tralatitious tell of a time when the Rubicon was known as the Forest of Eternals and this place had the power to feed everyone on Eternal. It was an endless harvest of edible flowers, mushrooms, fruits and vegetables. Food was abundant and plentiful. The Forest of Eternals was a magical place. However that name had not been spoken since *The Absconding*.

The Old Lady was in possession of The Scrolls of Tralatitious. Manuscripts written thousands of years before her birth by her ancestors, *The Longevite Tribe*. She was the last known member of her tribe and she alone was in constant possession of the Scrolls.

The ancient documents told the stories of five tribes who were led by the Patriot of Peace who wore magical garments known as The Armor. It was written that the mystical Armor gave the possessor unimaginable wisdom and a prolonged almost endless existence. For six thousand years the Patriot of Peace or "Pop" as the tribe's people affectionately remembered him, kept the peace in the city of Eternal.

Throughout Pop's reign there were no wars, no famines, no disease. Peace, joy and unity thrived. One night Pop had a prophetic dream, he would soon be crossing the great divide. He left the city and traveled deep into the forest where he spent forty days and forty nights meditating and searching for insight on what he should do.

Rumours quickly spread that Pop had gone to the forest to die and everyone wondered what would become of their city without his guidance.

Upon returning, he gathered five people, one from each tribe. "I have chosen to divide the armour among four of the five tribes."

He foretold of a day, when the armor would be reunited by *The One* who could bear its weight.

Pop chose leaders for the five tribes, he gathered them together and in a somber and magisterial inauguration he presented them with the Armor.

"From this day forth, you will be a representative of the armor and its distinctive hallmark and attributes. Verily I say that only through a genuine manifestation of humility and modesty can the possessor be endowed with its full potential."

He removed his helmet and called forward the first leader. "Bravo, I bestow upon you this Helmet and the leadership of the Casque Tribe. Surrender your mind and thoughts to all that is good, virtuous and honorable. Teach your people to be noble, send them throughout the city that they may be mentors of wisdom and forgiveness."

Pop placed the helmet into Bravo's hands and left him with this warning. "When the shadows of the day become long and wisdom is clouded, stand firm as the advocate and judge of all the tribes. Be prudent. Deliver your decisions with exceptional discernment."

He removed his arm from the straps used to hold the shield. He held it out to Beria; he would now lead the citizens of the Eastern part of the city. "Beria, be a wise and gentle leader to the children who have been bestowed to you. Just as a shield is used for protection and safeguarding, you also must be a refuge and shelter to all of Eternal."

With gentleness he admonished Beria. "When you see the arrows of iniquity descending upon Eternal, lift your armor and gather her people under your shield. Let your conduct and service be a guide to all. Let all of your decisions and statutes be made using soundness of mind."

Pop then made his way to a woman named Purdah. She instinctively raised her arms in the air that he might lower the breastplate onto her. "Wear this Breastplate and honor it. Be upright, honest and virtuous."

"When the nights become long and arduous and temptations arise to darken the spirit of the people, remember the power of this breastplate. Let it protect your heart so it may not be damaged. Utter words of peace, unite the children of the city. Even the smallest amount of light will shine in the darkness. Let it be your guide."

He turned and faced the fourth leader. He held out his sword to Demorg. One hand held the grip, the other the point. Demorg reached out and grabbed hold of it. The Prophet of Peace held it, as he uttered the following words.

"Demorg, I have chosen you as leader of the Sword Tribe. The sword has two edges, one can be used to defend and the other to subdue; it has the power to bring forth light or darkness. Therefore, let your desire and zeal always lean toward sympathy and understanding. Silence the siren song, overcome temptation. Lead my children at all times toward the light of peace forever into all eternity."

When he finished presenting the armor to the four, he made his way to Mater, a giant of a man. "Mater, with my life, I give you life. You and your tribe have been bestowed with the gift of longevity. The gift of a thousand year existence if it is possible."

He placed his hand on the man's shoulder. "Write the stories and history of the people. Never let them be forgotten, pass on your knowledge from generation to generation. Serve and be served. Protect and be protected."

He concluded with these final words. "Those who have gifts and powers should always protect and serve those who don't. I say to all of you standing here that without meekness and humility all hope is lost; listen to my words when I say that the true power of the armor lies in those two things. May peace continue to reign until the armor is once again reunited."

After a long and somber silence, the five stood watching as Pop made his way to his final resting place, somewhere in the Forest of Eternals.

The Rubicon

For a period of time everything went well and the people lived in peace. They all worked for the betterment of the other. That is until, one day Demorg was spotted returning from the forest with a large number of his tribe's people.

There was an electrifying and somewhat disconcerted buzz felt with the sound of his return.He led his people home, arms filled with large objects. Their cheering grew louder and became more aggressive as they approached the city. Eternals from the west gathered to see what all the commotion was about. When Demorg came into plain view, the people saw clearly the item he held above his head.

The people were shocked and dismayed. He had returned with dead animals to feed them. The other leaders who were there to share in the harvest were appalled.

"What is this thing you are doing?" they asked Demorg.

"I have found a way to use the sword to bring more food!" He exclaimed boldly, so that all the city could hear him.

"We can work less and have more to eat."

"Flesh does not eat flesh," said Purdah.

"The Patriot of Peace said that we would surely die if we ate flesh," added Bravo.

"Look at me you fools." He raised his arm up and turned around, smiling and nodding in agreement with himself, making sure everyone gathered could see him. "Not one of us has died from eating this animal."

Filled with rage, Demorg furiously spat out, "The Patriot lied to us when he told us we would die the day we ate flesh. I am here to show you that this is not so."

He shoved his way through, pushing and thrusting people side to side. He stopped abruptly and yelled from the center of the people. "Are these ghosts that surround me? Did I pass through them or did I have to make my way through with force? As you can see we are alive and well!"

He grabbed his belly and laughed. "Full and satiated bellies, that's what we'll die of." he spoke with a mirth that made him sound mad and his words derisory. His tribe joined in the laughter and began to clap and cheer in unison.

The others did not approve. "Flesh does not eat flesh." repeated Bravo.

The tribes discussed the issue among themselves and quickly came to a unanimous decision.

"Demorg, we can not in good conscience accept or tolerate this action. You must cease this madness." Beria continued. "We live in peace and are well fed by the Forest of Eternals. Let us remain at peace. If we begin breaking our traditions where will it end?"

Demorg was incensed. "Do you dismiss me so easily?"

He shouted at them. "We must develop and change these old and rotting traditions! All of you can see with your own eyes that we are alive. The lies of death did not come upon any of my people."

"The opposite is true, eating flesh has opened our eyes and made us stronger and wiser."

He made his way through the crowd halting in front of the leaders. "Are you all fools?" He shouted in their faces.

He turned to face the crowds. More and more people gathered. "Do you wish to remain entrapped and blinded by your old and dying ways?" He cried out to the crowd.

He paused for a long moment. In frustration, he pointed at the leaders and howled, "If you make this declaration, I swear with my life and the lives of those who follow me," he raised his weapon, "my sword will not stand idly by and watch this world decay because of your fear!"

"Flesh shall not eat flesh!" cried out Beria.

"Flesh shall not eat flesh!" Purdah shouted. She could see the crowd was becoming feverish and agitated.

As the multitude pressed closer to Demorg, he could sense that he was beginning to command the situation and that his dominion was fast approaching. He declared his hostilities toward the other leaders. "Flesh can eat flesh!" he shouted at the now frenzied throng.

"We did not die! You will not die! The time for change has come. Let the old traditions die with these muggins. Do not tolerate their lies any longer. Join me and my clan if you want to live forever. With me you shall be free of all *their* useless rules! Come with me, or stay and live in shackles and bondage!"

Many in the crowd started to chant his name... "De-morg, De-morg" soon thousands upon thousands were chanting in unity.

"Leave with me, embrace freedom; together we will make a new city where abundance will reign. No one will ever be hungry and all will taste the nectar of independence. Let us build a place where lies, deceit and plans made under the cover of darkness have no place." Demorg's voice rang out like thunder. "My sword will be used as a tool to feed you and as protection against those who would see you starve and keep you blind." Many people from all tribes were persuaded and embraced a union with Demorg and his clan.

Word of Demorg's promises traveled quickly. Talk of building a new nation and of newfound freedoms and liberties traveled throughout the land. Over the following weeks the procession out of the city was over a million strong.

There were but only a few handfuls of people from the Sword Tribe who chose to secede. Some chose to be absorbed by other tribes while others chose to remain leaderless in the west end, while others chose to live as gypsies.

Demorg gave the signal and led his new found kingdom into the Forest of Eternals. They were never seen again.

Soon after Demorg and his people had vanished deep into the forest, people began to notice that the Forest of Eternals was losing its ability to feed the masses. Food became scarce. Eventually there was so little to harvest that people stopped entering the forest. Then it was discovered that those who did enter it in search of food, were never seen from again.

It was then that the council of leaders decided that Purdah should proclaim that Demorg had brought death and destruction with his choices. They gathered the citizens and Purdah spoke.

"The Forest of Eternals is no longer safe for us. I decree from this day forth, the forest will be known as the Rubicon Forest; because Demorg and his people have cursed the land. A line has been drawn and it is forbidden by all to enter it. Those who cross it will be damned and salvation from its curse will be unattainable."

The Armored tribes agreed to build a protective wall around the city to protect themselves from Demorg's return.

Three Tribes Go To War

With all this unfolding, struggles and conflicts between the remaining three armored tribes began. Beria and Bravo began arguing over who should have rule over the western portion of the city now that Demorg was gone.

Soon Beria was going mad trying to gain power and Kingship over the whole of the city. He believed that he was *The One,* who could protect the people from the coming onslaught that would surely soon be ushered in by Demorg.

His words and actions began to worry and strain relationships with the others. His demands to be the sole possessor of the remaining pieces of armor were so worrying that one night on the way home from a briefing, he was assassinated. It was Bravo of the Casques, who believed it was his duty to resolve and administer judgment against Beria and the precarious situation he was creating.

When the Shield tribe discovered Bravo's involvement in the murder of their leader, an insurrection ensued. Those who supported Beria, planned to assassinate Bravo in an act of retribution in an operation they called the *Rebellion of Sagacity.* Their success created a series of vendettas.

As these battles were occuring between the Casques and the Shields, there were also struggles for leadership within each of those tribes. Multiple splinter groups began to form. For three and a half years there were battles both within and between them. A time known as *The Cabal.* A period of murders, suicides, assassinations and massacres. As quickly as a faction was formed it would fall. Discord and distrust were rampant amongst all.

For all their fighting and disagreements, the leaderless Casques and Shields were united on one matter, the belief that Purdah of the Breast Plate Tribe could not be trusted. Her constant contact with both sides began to be worrisome. It was understood by both the Shields and the Casques that Purdah should be removed from her position lest she join forces with one side and give them the advantage.

Hearsay and rumours spread throughout the two rudderless tribes. Confabulation took hold of the masses. Every type of paranoia and hysteria was put on display, and it became natural for them to behave in these manners.

"She's preparing to take control of us!" they cried out from the windows.

In the gin mill they would whisper "She's plotting to hold all the pieces of the armor. She will be invincible if she's not stopped."

On the city streets they cried "Purdah will kill us all!"

An agreement was reached by the two distrustful groups during a covert merger. "We agree that on the morning of her 75th Jubilee, she will be purged." said the acting leaders.

True to their words, Purdah was ambushed on the way to her jubilee. All of her entourage was killed. Her body was found slashed in two. The tribes were so deep in their misgivings they believed (falsely of course), that by slicing her body in half, her followers would believe that Demorg was somehow responsible for her death. Of course Purdah's tribe did not even consider this.

All three tribes were now without leaders. Panic was followed by hysteria, which soon led to lawlessness. Leaders rose and fell by the week and sometimes the hour. Eventually this led to chaos, disorder and anarchy. All three armored tribes were at war, and their efforts to build truces between one another to try and gain an advantage in their power and position fell apart before the ink dried.

The feuds turned to all out war. This brought with it famine and an immeasurable amount of gore. Blood flowing from the city at its most wicked period of combat was said to be waist high. After three and a half months of combat, and extinguishing thirty percent of the population, an armistice was created by the Longevity tribe. It was subscribed to by all.

A pestilence soon followed as a result of the interment. Four more years of slow, painful and feverish death followed. Another forty percent of the population was lost. The survivors had no other option but to help each other out. It wasn't enough not to be at war. If they didn't ban together soon, not one soul would be left alive.

During the war, the Longevity tribe had been a neutral party. However, neutrality was not an option during the time of the plague. They were hit the hardest. When the blight finally ended, only twelve could be accounted for.

The Prophecy

The night of the last death from the plague, all twelve members of the Longevity tribe received the same prophetic dream.

The next morning the twelve gathered together and summoned the newly elected leaders of the three tribes. They instructed them to unite all the people from all tribes and bade them to go to the western portion of the city nearest to the Rubicon. It was mandated that all who were able, must attend.

On the first day of the week an ocean of people had gathered to hear from the Longevites. The people stood motionless and soundless; an unprecedented calm filled the air; it was a sea of tranquility.

The twelve stood on pedestals at great distances apart and surrounded the gathered masses.

"I was standing in the darkness. It was a lightless and dreaded night." The twelve spoke in unison.

The people were astounded at the thundering sounds of their proclamations. The words spoken by the Longevites echoed over the crowd.

After describing their dream, they went on to explain their vision and how the armor must be removed from the city and concealed in the Rubicon forest.

"Our shame has been exposed and we have been shown that not one of us is worthy of the armor. But know this, there is a day and an hour when the Armor Of Peace will be reunited.

"Your children will be delivered to the forest and many calamities will come to fall upon them. But know this, that after a time they shall conquer and suppress the beast that tortures them. On that day the Armor of Peace will be once again reunited and true peace shall be restored."

The crowd was silent. Their thoughts turned to themselves and they began to whisper, "Who will go? Who will bear this tragedy that befalls the whole world? Who will give up another brother or sister?"

The Longevites knew what they were thinking and spoke up. "We understand your fears. We will not ask any of you to sacrifice a life. Three of us were anointed in our dream. They will die, so that we all may live."

The three remained silent as their names were pronounced. "Paladin, Patron and Protag will make their way tonight."

That evening everyone bade them farewell. Hands were laid on the chosen as they made their way out of the city gate. Not a word was spoken. Only the somber sound of tears and mourning could be heard as they made their way toward the Rubicon Forest. When they entered, each went in his predetermined direction. Paladin with the Shield, Patron carried the Helmet and Protag the Breastplate. They were never to be seen again.

After the three vanished into the Rubicon, the nine who were left called to everyone.

"Today we start a new chapter in our lives. Let us never forget all the tragedies that we have withstood in the recent past. The brothers, sisters, mothers, fathers and children we have destroyed, because of our lawlessness. Our transgressions have doomed three blameless souls to the Rubicon. This day in our history should never be disregarded or overlooked. Every year at this time, we shall celebrate for three days the lives of those who died for us. Tonight and for the next two nights we shall unite in peace and friendship in the *Celebration of Liberation*."

These and hundreds of other stories that were penned by the Longevites are all held in The Scrolls of Tralatitious. They are constant reminders of all the events of the past, the joyous, the dreaded and all the hopes for the future.

Chapter 1 The Window

"Murder!" yelled the troublesome minor. Upal was pointing toward the western horizon. He turned to face the door that led down stairs and shouted once again. "Murder!"

The cries startled his old bewitched Keeper who was sitting at the kitchen table swilling her daily allotment of wine. His howls made her heart sink and instinctively her head fell into the palm of her right hand. She gently yet firmly massaged her temples trying to knead away the sound of his wails. To no avail.

She quietly whispered to herself. "Precious."

All children are precious, she thought as she struggled to take in a deep breath. She hadn't fully convinced herself of that yet (in Upal's case anyhow).

Her mind swirled with misgivings about *some* (she looked up at the ceiling) of her recent life choices. She lifted her glass up to the sunlight beaming through the north facing window. She looked deep into the remaining burgundy ounces, "No amount of wine can cover the stains and pains of the past." she said soberly. "It's only noon." she grumbled as she picked up the bottle of wine to see what remained. The bottle was still half full; she'd be fine.

Her eyes made their way across the small house to the stairs and on their way they caught a glimpse of a small mouse making its way out through a crack in the door. Oh to be that mouse, no troubles, no worries… The thought ended there. She took in a breath and held it. She did her best to elevate her aged and bibulous body from her decrepit and fragile old chair.

Mrs. Nibbledent was not one to be kept in the dark about the latest gossip or scandal, so she slowly and painfully made her way to the broken, crumbling (and upon closer inspection... one might add), filthy and rotting clay stairs.

By the time she reached the third step she was exhausted. She took a break and tried to catch her breath before attempting to continue. I can't remember the last time I climbed these stairs, she thought to herself. But she did remember, and as she looked up the stairwell a haunting, distant memory flashed through her.

It was about a child who might have lived up there, a lifetime ago. She took hold of a key that hung around her neck and squeezed it tightly in the palm of her right hand as she tried to force the somber memory from her mind. She chose instead to focus her attention on a crack she spotted on the fourth step. It looked like something, she was sure of it, but her damp, blinking, wine filled eyes had a hard time focusing on it.

She felt something rolling down her cheek; she used her index finger to carefully catch a tear. She looked at it for a moment, then brought the drop to her lips. In it she tasted the pains of past memories, memories she didn't want to think about, but even more than that, they were memories she didn't want to lose.

She bowed her head and breathed out, "I am not young, I have never been young."

She redirected her attention to the next few steps, trying to distract herself from the previous images. She pointed out to herself how years of grating, scratching, grounding, and eroding had taken their toll on the staircase. Regrettably, she concluded that time had not been much kinder to her. It was true. The stairs were as old and broken as the wine drinking dipsomaniac making her way up; she could feel it in every crack, snap and pop that came with each step.

After a long sigh, she worked up the courage to continue the journey, and as she took on the fourth step, she heard Upal's cries. She shouted up at the teen, "If I come up there and there is no bloody murder," her shrieking voice echoed up the staircase to the boy's room, "there will be!" She forced her leg up the fifth step, "What kind of a Keeper takes in a demented and bothersome child like this one?" She gaspingly shouted up the stairs again. "I must be crazy!"

A handful of steps more and she stopped to take a few breaths. Holding herself up against the wall she shouted up to the bad hat who was screaming bloody murder. "I tell you this," she struggled to take in a breath. "If I didn't need the money", she paused to take in all the air her aged and smoke damaged lungs could, "... and could find another less inconvenient discard..." she coughed and hacked, "I would do it in a second. I would make you disappear." She spit out these last words between chokes and wheezes, "Whereby you could never bother anyone again."

Mrs. Nibbledent was old, if sixty is old? She looked well beyond her years. Her sagging neck complimented her droopy and flaccid eyes which only helped to accentuate the face fungus hanging from her feeble chin. Those who crossed her path thought her to be close to a hundred, if not more. Her badly washed out hair did nothing to cover up any of her ripening and aged faults.

Upal would have described her personal perfume as a rancidity of smoke and wine. The three garments she owned, two of which were hanging by the window in an effort to be refreshed, smelled much the same.

As for being Upal's Keeper? He told anyone who asked, that she was the only one crazy or disinterested enough to tolerate his rebellion. He claimed that she did it solely for the money. After all, those funds kept her glass of wine full.

Well, actually, empty.

His self-proclaimed rebellion wasn't that far off. In his sixteen years (about five of those spent as an orphan), Upal had been discharged by well over twenty Keepers, sometimes spending less than a week with them. His reputation was well documented. No Keeper in their right mind wanted to take him in. Therefore, the C.R.U.C. (Counsel of Refused and Unwanted Children) had no choice but to leave him with anyone they could find who was desperate enough to take him in, no matter how unqualified or incompetent that person might be. And make no mistake about it, Upal believed Mrs. Nibbledent to be both those things.

"Murder! Murder!" Upal shouted again. He was starting to get bored. He took a quick glance back at the stairs. What is taking her so long? he thought to himself.

"Where?" he heard her shriek as she tumbled up the last two steps. Finally, he thought as he watched Mrs Nibbledent's momentum bring her crashing unpleasantly onto the floor of his bedchamber.

He could hardly hold himself back from laughing. He watched as she struggled to get herself off of her hands and knees. It was almost too much for him to bear.

"Who's being murdered, you foolish hob?" she gasped as she pulled herself up with the help of the nearby wall and Upal's sleeve. She stumbled forward toward his window and the boy instinctively reached out to catch her.

Shaking herself away from his grasp, she braced herself against the ledge and peered out. She could see nothing strange going on. "What are you looking at, you imbecile?" she screeched in Upal's face and a few pinkish strands of saliva left her lips and landed on his cheek. The warm slimy feeling made him gag and he quickly wiped his face with his sleeve.

"Right out there your hideousness." He pointed to the distant sky. "A murder of crows!" Upal erupted with laughter at his senseless joke.

25

Her face went red with rage, "Why you little…" she took on the arduous task of bending over to grab hold of her old worn slipper and began to beat him with it. He raised his arms to shield himself, but he wasn't fazed by her weak attempt at a thrashing. It only made him explode with laughter. After multiple swats, the aged old hag was exhausted. She reversed her course and walked away, all the while mumbling to herself.

She stopped at the doorway for a moment and glanced at the old wooden chest that made its home at the edge of the bed. She took note that the old rusted lock was still intact. She clasped her pendant, turned back and made her way down the stairs.

Upal observed Mrs. Nibbledent floundering her way back down the stairs, hacking, coughing and scrambling for air the entire way. Old hag, he thought to himself. You'd get to your wine quicker if you rolled down.

Upal hated her as much as he did his room or *the dungeon*, as he referred to it most times. Upal hated all his keepers. His situation was just like his room; it was a dark, damp unforgiving hole.

The dungeon was on the top floor of the house. It was filled with cobwebs, cockroaches and mice. The bed was a burlap bag stuffed with hay, that sat on the uneven wood floor. An ancient and tattered wool blanket was used for a covering on cold nights, not that it did much good. Next to the bed leaning up against the wall was a large wooden paddle. It was used to *hit the hay* before bedtime. By doing so (at least in theory), one could dislodge some of the bugs and mice making their home inside.

At the edge of the bed was that old wooden chest with the rusted lock. He'd thought about opening it a few times. He even thought about stealing the key from Mrs. Nibbledent's neck when she was passed out at the table. But he thought that not knowing what was inside was more exciting than knowing. After all what could possibly be in there? The woman had nothing of value.

Upal rarely used the bed for sleep, and if he did, it was only when he found the nights outside too cold or too dangerous. He knew that as long as the hag received her monthly stippen, she didn't care if he came home or not. To be honest, she probably preferred the quiet nights his absence created.

Upal turned his attention back to the window and stared out into the distance. He was suddenly stirred by a peculiarly crisp zephyr; the mild westwardly breeze took hold of him and sent a chill up his spine. It meant something. Well, he wanted it to mean something. He thought about it for a moment; maybe it was a sense of fear? No, it wasn't that. Maybe it was optimism? Optimism? He chuckled. As if, he thought to himself. Maybe, just maybe it was just a chill.

His gaze returned to the murder of crows. Squinting he strived to get a better view of what he was looking at. Little black dots flying to and fro. "They look to be at the edge of the Rubicon." he muttered to himself.

The Rubicon. With that name spoken, absent of any provocation, he heard the ghost of a voice that might or might not have been his own, whisper... "From where no one ever returns."

Chapter 2 Distracted

His mind wandered as he thought about the legendary tales told by The Old Lady. Upal's persistent distractibility turned from the fables and back to the morning sky, where he (for a moment) immersed himself in the pinks, light blues and crimson colored clouds; they were a sharp contrast to the black winged dots in the distant horizon. "I wonder…"

An alley cat caught the corner of his eye and his thoughts were redirected to the crumbling walls and streets below. He looked up, then down, then up and down again. He contemplated the antithesis that was the heavenly colored sky and the unholiness of the neighbourhood he happened to call home. The earth and the sky were so far from each other, complete opposites. If only he could live in the clouds.

Regrettably he lived in reality. His home was not overhead in the soft fluffy cotton filled clouds; it was below in the thoroughfares. The hard streets were covered in dust and loose flying debris. The walls were stained and soaked with urine that trickled down to the ground. Dozens of small musty-smelling ammonia mud puddles were scattered up and down the streets and as if that wasn't enough, it was all topped up with the moderate aroma of other bodily excretions. The scent made its way to up to his dungeon window burning and lingering in his nostrils.

He thought it odd that he actually noticed the smells today. He was so used to it. Somehow, today it was different. It was as if for the first time his eyes were open to the inescapable sadness of it all. No, it wasn't sadness, it was despair, an endless drought of inescapable despair.

Life was colorless.

He closed his eyes and desperately tried to dream of something more. He let his imagination carry him to what life must have been like thousands of years ago. To live in the fabled world described in the Scrolls of Tralatitious (the good parts anyway). A world where the Rubicon was still the Forest of Eternals, a magical place that fed the whole world, a world where no one ever worried about food, health, loneliness, sadness or whatever it was that he had to deal with on a day-to-day basis.

He fantasized about a place where one didn't have to suffer through the daily onslaught of swatting flies and smacking midges. Yet here he was, slapping, smiting and striking swarms of mosquitoes on an ongoing basis. It was exhausting. How unfair it was that he should be trapped in this time of history instead of the *good one*.

He clenched his fist and shook it at the sky in belligerence crying out, "Why me? Why have I been forsaken to this wretchedness?"

"Oh, shut up and be happy you have anything!" came Mrs. Nibbledent's screech from the ground-floor.

He turned his head toward the stairs and groaned quietly, "You shut up."

Life. (What life?) Existence for the modest citizens of Eternal was hard and unforgiving. With only a modicum of food and water obtainable, it was a constant struggle to stay alive, especially in the West Gate.

It's true there were some worse off than he was. The truly unfortunate people were those who stayed hungry for days on end. There were many who slept in alleyways, doorways and on rooftops, wrapping their famished bodies in whatever cover they could find. He sighed and lowered his head and shook it slowly.

A full belly, a warm and safe night's sleep were as hard to find as a warm heart in this age of hopelessness.

He whispered to himself "Look at this."

29

His eyes caught a bunch of deplorable, filthy, unwashed, flyblown children running the streets. He could easily commiserate with them, because just like many of them, he was a parentless and forsaken child, abandoned to a miserable life. Stuck in the system known as C.R.U.C., jumping from Keeper to Keeper (at least until he turned eighteen).

He lifted his eyes to the heavens once more. He wondered again, how this sky and earth could exist in the same place and time. How could you have such a peaceful and calm looking sky, then, look to the ground and see a torn and shattered world where so little peace of mind existed?

"Oh, yeah!" he exclaimed. His focus returned to the flight of the crows. "What are they doing?"

From what he could make out, there looked to be dozens of them and they seemed to be diving towards the ground and back up again. "Maybe..."

"Oop!" A voice cried out from the street below.

Chapter 3 Meet Preet

Upal looked down to see his best friend Preet standing beneath his window. Preet, who was way too big for his fifteen soon-to-be sixteen years, stood seven feet three inches tall. He was however, not used to his newly found body. It seemed that he sprouted two feet overnight, and like magic, he became this high-pitched, squeaky sounding man-child. It was a funny thing seeing a giant with a mouse's voice. The only person bold or maybe just boneheaded enough to laugh and make fun of it, was Upal.

For some unknown reason today seemed different, maybe even a little strange. Today, Upal was seeing things in a different light and he found himself staring at Preet. I mean really looking at him, possibly for the first time.

How was it that he never noticed that Preet had the face of an angel? A tiny smirk came across Upal's face. Look at him, he thought to himself. Preet had a beautifully rounded face with titan sized eyes. Bright azure colored eyes that popped out against the contrast of his chestnut brown skin. His hair was almost as big as he was. He carried a massive mess of an afro. A coiffure full of debris that could be hiding almost anything.

"Hello? Oo-oop?" Preet was waving his arms trying to bring his friend out of his daydream.

"What?" Upal was shaken from his daze.

"Why are you staring at me like that?" He yelled up to the window.

"What are you talking about? I'm not staring at you?"

"Yes you were. You were all like..." Preet looked up with his eyes bulging and his mouth wide open.

Preet was staring at someone who was his polar opposite. At sixteen Upal had a muscular five foot six inch frame. His wavy shoulder length jet black hair surrounded his face like a frame. He had soft blue eyes with a hint of green. He was a good looking lad with an air of ruggedness.

Upal's physical abilities were unmatched by anyone in the West Gate. He was able to bounce and pounce like a cat and somersault like a trapeze artist.

Being friends with Upal had more than a few downsides; his big mouth and attitude were just *two* of them. If there was any trouble to be found, Upal could easily find it, if he wasn't already the one creating it.

Ever since Preet's magical mushrooming, Upal's attitude seemed to have gotten a little worse. It wasn't that Upal couldn't take care of himself, he could. He was as proficient with his feet as he was with his fists; the scars strewn across his body could attest to that. As of late, his troublesome nature had increased. Now that he had constant access to a giant, he took it upon himself to agitate more and more people at once. The problem for Preet was that he was opposed to using his new found size to scare off those Upal would enrage. Nonetheless, Preet's loyalty always stood firm.

"Quit looking at me like that you weirdo." Upal said to him.

"You started it." Preet responded.

Leaning out his window Upal wondered if he would ever leave the house. He shouted down to his friend. "Hey Preet, what do you imagine those crows are doing out there?" He pointed west toward the Rubicon.

Preet turned to look at the splendor of the sky. It took his mind away from his present reality for a brief, almost inconceivable instant. He didn't see anything.

"Hey genius, I'm tall but not that tall." He paused and turned to look again, "I don't see anything."

He looked up at Upal, "Who cares anyhow? Maybe they're feasting on a dead body." he said sardonically.

"You think it's human?" the curious voice from above asked.

"It will be if you don't get down here." came the reply. "Come on, I don't want to stand here all day waiting for you." And with that, Upal was finally leaving the house.

Chapter 4 Getting Out

Upal vaulted out of his dust covered window. He descended the side of the building and seized hold of a frail and weather worn, flagless, flag post, pirouetting and whirling around it with acrobatic beauty as he had done on countless occasions.

He went for one final loop. He envisioned himself releasing the pole, flying into a swan like flip and landing perfectly on his feet (as per usual).

For the last few months this flagpole had taken a regular dose of abuse from him. This time was no different. He was a mere half second away from letting go, when *creaks* and *cracks* were heard. The spinning had finally taken its toll and the rod snapped.

Preet was standing directly below watching the action go down. Seeing that Upal had lost all control and not one to stand in anyone's way, he quickly took a step to the side and watched as Upal came smashing down to the ground.

Upal landed on his back. Preet looked down at him, his face grimacing with sympathetic pain. "That must have hurt."

He was used to Upal doing nitwitted things like this. He watched calmly as Upal displayed the typical signs of panic. "Try to breathe." Upal was trying.

Seeing that his friend had survived the fall and most of the landing, he bent over and brought his face in close proximity to the boy's and whispered in a slightly mocking tone, "Was it worth it?"

Upal grunted and gave a short painfilled nod. "Always." he tried to breathe out. He raised his arm slightly and produced his index finger.

Preet looked at it. "Oh, you think you're number one?" he smiled, knowing that wasn't it.

"Need... minute" Upal gasped. The pain subsided a little and he was able to take a few shallow breaths and purred, "Not my best landing."

"You're gonna have to speak up." muttered Preet, "I can hardly hear you through the pain."

Preet stood upright, put his hands on his hips and looked up and shook his head disapprovingly. He looked down at Upal and kicked him gently. "Look, I know you were a little busy falling and all, but did you see my quick reflexes?" Preet gently nudged him again with his foot.

"Man, I was like a cat. It's like I saw you coming down and *swish*..." He made a side step motion and almost tripped over his own feet. "One second slower and I would have been breaking your fall. *Swish*." he repeated the sound and motion. "Like a cat I tell ya."

He paused for a second and rubbed his chin. He waved his index finger at Upal who was still in recovery mode and said, "You know what Lashra would say to you right now if she were here?"

"Ugh." Upal grunted out with disapproval.

Preet ignored his friend's obvious objection to his going on. "She'd say," and doing a decent impression of his sister, he continued.

"You know Upal, that pole is very much like the average person. This little mishap could go a long way to teaching you a life lesson. What kind of life lesson might you ask?"

"I wouldn't." he chirped.

Preet, I mean, Lashra ignored him. "Well, let me tell you. People like that post can only take so much abuse before they break. Stop trying to break things."

Upal, who was looking up from the ground, was not amused in the slightest.

"Upal, you need to seize the moment. Learn from this, become a better version of you."

"Hey Lashra, can you send your slow-witted brother back?" His breath was finally returning to his wounded body.

"Ha, ha, ha!" Cough, cough. Mrs. Nibbledent's head was sticking out the window. She was happy to have partially witnessed the pain that she had so hoped to inflict on the little missfit, just a few minutes earlier. "Your bizarre friend is right, you little..." she didn't finish her sentence, she just shook her head.

"I have to say... I did enjoy witnessing the swiftness of Karma working its magic on you. I haven't felt pleasure like that in years." she said with a rotted laugh. And just as she spoke the words, a loose piece of wreckage fell from the sky and pounded her on the back of the head. Upal and Preet simultaneously broke into an uncontrollable laugh.

The look on her face was so stormy it scared Preet. He reached down and picked his friend up by the arm so fast and hard that Upal was barely able to land on his feet. The two began to run before Mrs. Nibbledent had the chance to reach for her infamous slipper.

Preet was trying to keep up to Upal. As they took the corner at top speed, Preet tripped over his feet. On his way down, he instinctively reached out to seize onto something that would slow his descent. That something just happened to be Upal's pants.

Preet hit the ground with Upal's pants in his hands. With Upal's pants now down around his ankles, he unexpectedly greeted the dusty pebbled street with his knees, followed quickly by his elbows and just as swiftly his face. The sounds uttered were those of pure pain.

Thankfully the humiliation of having his pants around his ankles, got him up instantly and angrily. Pulling his pants up he frantically started looking for the rope he used as a belt, somehow it was nowhere to be found.

He looked over to Preet who was still trying to get to his feet and furiously yelled at him. "What's wrong with you? Are you trying to kill me?"

Preet sat on the ground looking at his bruised and scraped elbows. "I was going down. It was a reflex." He gestured sorrily.

"I can't find my rope. Now what's going to keep my pants up you half-wit?" he said angrily.

"Seriously Oop? Coming from a tiny person like you? If anything, I'm a *full*-wit. You're the half. I'm the full."

"So?" Upal asked firmly, "What am I gonna do? You should give me your belt." He now had a portion of his pants bunched up in one hand.

Preet looked at him slightly perplexed. "First of all, you don't have enough strength in that little body of yours to carry this much rope and secondly, NO! I'll be more careful next time Oop."

Upal grunted at his friend's attempt at an apology. "You better be, if not, I'll just quit wearing pants, then you won't be reaching out for me."

"You're right Oop, I'd have nothing to hold on too." Preet said as he walked away trying hard not to laugh.

"Ya, ya, real funny." Upal said as he tried to clean some of the dust out of his bloody scrapes and scratches.

Upal caught up to Preet and both walked slowly, trying to shake off the recent tragedy.

"Let's make our way to The Old Lady's house." said Upal, "I'm sure your sister will be there. Maybe she can help me with my pants." he said with a leering smile.

Preet put his hand on Upal's shoulder and brought him to an abrupt stop. In a rigid and unforgiving tone he stated, "If Lashra even comes close to your pants, I will sit on you, killing you instantly. It's that simple." Preet was very protective of his little sister.

Upal shook himself out of Preet's hold. "Well, maybe you should've thought of that before using my pants as a safety net." he responded. "I just meant she can find me a rope." He began to walk away. He looked back to Preet and said, "You're sister can do almost anything. After all, Lashra is very *pul-chri-tu-di-nous*?"

"What?" Preet said dubiously. He shook his head and sighed. He could see that it took every brain cell Upal had not only to remember, but say a big word like... well, the word he had just said.

"You are a desperate boy, Oop." he patted him on the head. "How long did it take you to memorize that word?"

"I told you not to pat me on the head like that."

Preet continued, "You do realize that my sister will not be impressed because you memorized a big word. And you know you'll just embarrass yourself by using it wrongly."

Upal unsuccessfully tried to shove his friend away. "I'm not as dumb as I look Preet."

Preet stopped in his tracks. "How could you be?" He rubbed his forehead with his hand. "Let me try and make this clear for you. Lashra doesn't like you. I mean she likes you but she doesn't *like* you, you know like *that*. And I know you want to kiss her, but ugh... kissing her would be like kissing me. But, if you're that hopeless," he said as he closed his eyes, puckered up and blindly reached out for Upal. "Go ahead, if you want to kiss me I'm right here waiting for you."

"Enough already!" Upal shouted. "You're ranting... calm down. I don't want to kiss your sister and I definitely don't want to kiss you. I just do it to mess with you."

Preet could see that Upal was plainly lying. "You know what would help Oop?"

"What?"

"If you could just shut up once in a while." Preet said quietly.

"I wish it were that easy my friend. I wish it were that easy."

They continued walking in silence.

Chapter 5 The West Gate

The entirety of the city was surrounded by a wall. A wall that was forty feet high and ten feet thick. The construction of the wall began after Demorg's departure. It seemed everyone was convinced by the rumours that Demorg was about to seek his revenge on the people at any moment. Many thought that he would seek out the armor and kill its leaders. Then he'd have rule over the whole of Eternal.

Saudj, Preet's friend and a boy Upal considered his nemesis, had been ranting about that very subject a few days earlier.

"Think about it, it took them a thousand years to build the wall and all that time they think Demorg is coming to kill them? The guy has been gone for five hundred years and no one thinks… Hey! Maybe he's not coming? Maybe, just maybe this story might not be true? I've got an idea. Why don't we stop wasting our time on this wall? No, they just keep building, brick on top of brick, *for a thousand years. A thousand years!* Now it's been thousands of years on top of that… and they still think he's coming?"

Saudj shook his head in disbelief. "I'm not saying we should tear down the wall, but come on, enough with the nonsense. Why are they still trying to sell these fables to us as if they're real? The way my father tells it, Demorg tried to save Eternal by offering an easier way to feed the people. The other tribes were jealous of him."

Preet put his arm around Saudj's shoulder and pulled him in tight. "You're over thinking the whole thing."

Saudj pulled himself away from the giant boy as he picked up his pace.

"I guess what I'm trying to say," Preet continued, "is, I don't care. Wall or no wall, Demorg or no Demorg, I'm hungry. I want to eat. That's the only thing *I* believe in right now."

"Fools!" Saudj said as he turned the corner and headed home, "You guys are just a bunch of pushovers for old stories." he shouted back to the boys.

"Ya, well if none of it is true, then why doesn't anyone ever return from the Rubicon?" Upal added. But it was too late, Saudj was already gone.

The West Gate was the poorest of all the gates. Most kids who lived there had one parent. If they were lucky, their parents cared about what they were doing and where they were going. Kids in the West Gate spent the daylight hours playing, fighting and chasing each other around. The nights consisted of thievery, looting and looking for a safe place to hide and maybe if you were lucky you'd find a few hours of sleep.

Preet was born in the West Gate. Upal started life at the edge of the East Gate. It was a working class area of the city. The East Gate had an almost unlimited supply of Dendrocalamus Asper, a long fast growing plant that was both strong and durable. The Dendro was used to build furniture, houses, utensils, paper… almost anything could be made with it. This made life a little better there. It was less violent and most had enough money and resources to buy food and lodging. The East Gate had access to schools, apothecaries and had safer streets.

The Patrol in the West Gate tended to bend the rule of law for a stippen. Whereas the Patrol in the East Gate was much more restrained and disciplined and so, the nights were relatively quiet.

When Upal was seven, his family was forced to move to the West Gate, after Upal's father, a drunk who hated having children, found himself a young mistress. He left Upal's sick mother with two children to feed and support; it wasn't long before things fell apart and she could no longer afford housing. She and her two children were forced to move to the West Gate; she did the best she could under the circumstances.

Moving there was not easy on Upal. He didn't have much experience with fighting or bullying. He found it quite terrifying, but he managed to stay alive. As time went on, he acquired the skills he would need to defend himself and survive.

Upal's brother who was four years older spent most of his days and nights thieving. He eventually snuck back to the East Gate where all his friends were. He rarely came home and when he did, it didn't take long for him to get into trouble. Within a few years he simply stopped coming home. Upal hadn't seen or heard from him in over five years. He simply assumed he was dead.

Soon after his brother left, Upal's mother died. He always believed she died of sadness. He found himself alone and before long he was being bumped from house to house, Keeper to Keeper.

He quickly learned to trust no one and found that being alone was the best alternative. That was, until he met Preet and Lashra. Or should I just say, Lashra?

Chapter 6 Lashra

"Hey Oop." Preet gave Upal a friendly shove.

Upal was still lost in his thoughts. His friend's gentle nudge was enough to push him aside and make him momentarily let go of his pants. Startled, Upal caught them before they went too far down. "Hey!" He leaned in the other direction and rammed Preet with his shoulder hitting him hard enough to get a reaction from him.

Preet rubbed his side. "Wake up dude. You haven't said a word in ten minutes." He was all bug-eyed. "That's pretty spooky." He chuckled.

Preet unexpectedly stopped in the middle of the road, closed his eyes and took in a deep long breath through his nostrils. A peaceful, dreamy expression came over him. "Mmmm, I love the smell of that baking bread."

Yes, it was a good smell, a tasty smell. An aroma so delicious and wonderful that it had the power (if you were close enough to the Old Lady's house and focused your senses), to camouflage the stench of the city.

"I could easily find my way to her house in the dark." he sighed with delight.

"I can actually taste the flavors in that smokey perfume. It smells like magic." Upal said with a pleasant smile.

They found their way to The Old Lady's house. Upal quietly stuck his head in the window. His eyes were immediately drawn to the girl sitting on the floor next to The Old Lady. Her exquisite frame was flanked by dozens of books. His heart raced uncontrollably. Every time he laid eyes on her, it was as if he'd never experienced her beauty before. She was a vision, she was an overwhelming feast for his eyes. Upal gazed passionately at the pulchritudinous redhead.

She was sitting next to The Old Lady, leaning back against a library of books that had been produced and reproduced, written and rewritten and handed down from generation to generation. The library was created by the Longevites and consisted of hundreds if not thousands of books and scrolls that depicted the history of the people and chronicled the fauna and flora that was contained in the Forest of Eternals.

Lashra beamed like the sun. This was her favorite place to be, surrounded by these books and scrolls. She had surely read everyone of them not once but twice and some, maybe more. This is where she liked to spend most of her days. From sunrise to sunset if you were looking for Lashra, odds were you could find her here. She was brainy and known to be wise beyond her years.

No one could have guessed in a thousand years that she was Preet's fraternal twin. People could hardly believe they were related. She stood six feet tall with a thick curly head full of ringlets. Her crimson colored mane was filled with rays of strawberry blonde strewn throughout. When the late day sun hit her head, it lit her up and it gave the impression that her head was on fire.

Her lips were full and cherry red, which contrasted her pale white skin that was lightly mapped with freckles. Her large absinthe colored eyes were stormy and hypnotizing. Every part of her being was a piece of a puzzle that added to her beauty and majesty. Lashra was mystical and Upal believed there wasn't a person alive who could resist her allure.

She was kind, considerate and tenderhearted. She was always ready to listen and truly cared for people. All those things didn't stop her from being strong willed and persistent in everything she chose to do.

Upal loved her. More than that, he wanted only happiness for her and there was nothing he wouldn't give or do to see that through.

Preet caught Upal longingly admiring Lashra. "Can you please stop looking at my sister that way?"

"What way?" said Upal clumsily. "I was just thinking about how your sister is very... uh... how she uh... looks so much like you." he blurted out in desperation. "It's kinda scary." His smile was questionable and his eyes were wide and wary.

Preet, who was easily deluded when it came to compliments, smiled and nodded emphatically. "It is kinda spooky isn't it?"

Upal turned away immediately before his face could give him away. His eyes ran across the room; it was filled with happy children. At this moment in time The Old Lady was part way through one of her stories from the Scrolls of Tralatitious and even though they'd heard it a thousand times before, it still captivated everyone.

The only person smarter than Lashra, was this eight-hundred year old lady.

Chapter 7 The Old Lady

The Old Lady's abode was situated only a short distance away from the outside entrance of the West Gate. Her chimney seemed to billow bread scented smoke day and night. Her homemade bread fed all those who walked through her door and the many who passed by it. If there was any place in this forsaken world that could bring some sense of contentment and a little peace of mind, it was this one.

On her head was a long achromatic intertwined weave of colorless horse hair. Her large dark chocolate colored eyes were surrounded by plump rosy cheeks. Her smile was sweeping and her face was cordial and inviting. It had the power to comfort and settle any situation. Even though she was almost a thousand years old, she somehow managed to hold on to her beauty in a most inexplicable way.

As for her size? She was huge. A mountain of a woman, standing over nine feet tall. She was the only one who could embrace Preet and make him feel like the little boy he truly was.

Even with her large size and the fact that she was over eight hundred years old, she moved like someone... half her age? She was still very agile.

"The Old Lady"; it was obviously not her given name. No one had ever known her to go by any other name. It had always been *The Old Lady this and The Old Lady that.*

Now understand this fully, there was no disrespect meant whatsoever. She was a well loved and most cherished treasure in everyone's world. Children young and old would sit and listen to her stories day in and day out. There was so much to hear and listen to. Of course there was, after all she was over eight hundred years old.

The Old Lady was the last known living member of the Longevity tribe. She was the only person who could travel from gate to gate and be welcomed by all. Some did find it a little strange that she chose to make the West Gate her home, but, she would always say to those who asked, "Those who have much should serve and protect those who have little."

The Old Lady was also a Keeper and of all the Keepers in Eternal, she was the most loving, caring, kind, gentle and generous soul that the universe could have provided.

The law of the land stated that all Keepers should love and care for the orphans in their charge like they were their own, and she did.

There were some Keepers who kept children more as slaves or house servants. If you were lucky enough to have a Keeper who was even just kind to you, you learned to keep your mouth shut and be respectful. Otherwise you might be traded in for someone better and then you would simply be shipped out to a more desperate Keeper who was not as kind. Upal knew this situation very well.

The Old Lady had survived seven husbands. She was never able to have children of her own. For some unknown reason (she kept to herself), she always kept five children at a time, not one more and not one less.

She would never ask or tell a child it was time to leave her care. One person she tended to was *Timmy the Beautiful*. He was twenty one years old and was known to everyone in this area of the West Gate. He would ride around on his tricycle and collect debris which he would place in a big basket on the back of his trike.

He was never difficult. If he stopped and talked to you, he would never leave without first reaching into his pocket to retrieve his locket. He would open it, so he could show you a picture of his mother. He would then give her a kiss and gently return her to his pocket.

Once the locket was safely in place, he would sing you the well known song of the people *We shall live in peace.* When he finished he would say "Live in peace." like it was a command, then he would go on his way.

His special needs somehow made him a shining light of hope. The Old Lady used to say, "If we could all love each other the way we love Timmy the Beautiful, this world would be a noble one."

The Old Lady loved to tell and teach her stories. It seemed that in the last few months she told one particular story over and over. Almost with a sense of urgency. It always started the same way.

"My great-grandmother told this to my grandmother who told it to my mother who told it to me and now I tell it to you".

She was already deep into the story when Upal and Preet arrived at her window. Her smokey, gravelly voice delivered words in a melodic rhythmic fashion. Every sound she made seemed sacred.

"...the day will come when *The One* will unite the armor..."

"Quit shoving me!" Upal said to Preet.

"Shhhh" muttered Preet as he reached in and easily moved his pal out of the way. Sticking his head in the window, he mouthed "I love this story".

Upal tried to force his way back under the gargantuan boy's arm. "Come on, let me in."

A choir of "Shhhhh" greeted them from inside the house.

The Old Lady had already stopped her story mid sentence and speaking to all the children in the room said, "My little orphans, it's time to go and play outside."

"No, please finish the story." they begged.

"Another time, possibly." As the words left her lips, her smile faded for a brief moment and Preet was sure he saw her eyes well up. "I have something to discuss with Lashra's

48

brother and his friends. Go on, outside with you my little nippers." Her smile returned.

Friends? Upal thought to himself.

Chapter 8 Saudj

Upal turned to see who was standing over his shoulder. It was Saudj, Upal's nemesis. He was about two inches taller and a year older. They shared the same physique and that's where the similarities ended. Saudj had a head full of curly blonde hair and dark brown eyes. He was an only child.

His father was a maker, seller and drinker of Glumvyn, a poisonous beverage with a high alcohol content. He was a mean drunk. Saudj had felt the back of his hand on many occasions.

Like his father, Saudj had very little patience and at times could be utterly brutal. He enjoyed picking on the weakest people he could find. He reasoned in his mind that he was helping them, by toughening them up and preparing them for the real world.

He had bullied and tortured Upal for the first couple of years after Upal's family had been forced into the West Gate. In time Upal stood his ground and there was a delicate and unspoken truce between them. Deep inside, Upal feared him. He'd witnessed his cruelty often and knew that if pushed hard enough, Saudj was capable of anything.

Saudj, Preet and Lashra had known each other all their lives and yes Preet was bullied by Saudj too, but now that he'd grown so big, Saudj was taking no chances.

"When did *he* become our friend?" he whispered to Preet.

"Don't be an ass Oop." came Preet's reply.

"It's the only thing he can be. Isn't that why you call him Poop?" came Saudj's response.

Upal quickly turned around, and Preet put his giant torso between them.

A maternal voice was heard calling from inside the house, it was Lashra. "Come now children, we mustn't fight."

"Come in." said The Old Lady.

An excited Upal instinctively dove in through the window. He'd forgotten about his lack of a rope but was quickly reminded when the waist of his pants caught the window sill and stopped him in mid flight.

He abruptly landed halfway through the window. He was bent over the edge and almost fell out of his pants and into the room. There he was dangling, his naked bum in the air. Luckily his quick reflexes got him off the windowsill and outside before anyone was the wiser. Upal pulled his pants up and decided to use the door.

Preet was about to make his entrance when his afro caught the top of the entrance. His head jerked back and he stumbled backwards. "Ah! Darn it! Everytime?" he said bitterly. "Do I have to do that everytime? My neck is killing me." he said as he bent over and made his way into the house all the while rubbing his neck.

"One day buddy, one day." Upal noted.

Saudj quickly made his way toward Lashra and sat on the floor beside her. Like all the other boys, he was not unaffected by her beauty and charm.

Upal wasn't sure if anyone had seen his misfortune but he assumed since no was making fun of him, he was probably safe.

Lashra noticed that he was holding his pants up with one hand. She reached into her hallowed bag and procured, as if by magic, a piece of rope. She tossed it in his direction, "Catch." she called out. "You wouldn't want to be caught with your pants down again would you?" She winked at him.

"How did you know?" asked Preet.

Upal's face was all shades of red. He quietly tied his pants up, then made his way to the floor facing Lashra.

Preet could only shake his head in disapproval of both boys. He sat in front of the two, to keep an eye on them.

The Old Lady made her way to her old worn and battered up cookstove. She handed each child a cup then grabbed a pot of hot tea. Slowly her celebrated beverage was poured into their cups. Not a word was spoken as she finished her round.

She gently put down her kettle on a short overtaxed wooden stool that stood next to her chair. Gracefully dropping her enormous body down, she sat and stared into her tea for a long thought-out moment. Her face had a somber and serious look to it.

She took a deep breath, exhaled and said, "I have something important to tell you." The children looked at each other in wonderment and surprise.

"My time is at hand." she said softly. "And yours has just begun."

Chapter 9 The Prophecy

Seeing the worried look on the woman's face, Lashra's eyes moistened. She didn't know what was going on but she knew enough to know it wasn't going to be good. She began to babble out all kinds of questions.

"I don't understand. What are you trying to say? You said you could live a thousand years. You can't leave us, we need you. Why are you doing this?" She knew what the woman was about to pronounce was going to be poignant and lamentable, but she couldn't stop herself.

"Don't say another word. This is foolishness." She got up, desperate and confused. She threw herself onto the woman, her arms wrapping around her giant neck and she began to sob.

Lashra was ready to contest anything and everything The Old Lady was about to say. But deep inside she knew that nothing would change the words about to be spoken.

"I love you so much." she whispered sorrowfully in her ear. Her tears had already saturated the old woman's garb. She did not want to deprive herself of the moment, so she held onto her, thinking perhaps, if she just held on long enough, nothing would change.

The Old Lady was patting her hair, "Lashra my darling, my student, my child, my friend." she murmured affectionately. "We must all accept what is to come. We must drink from the cup we are about to receive." As she spoke the words, she guided the young girl back to the floor. Lashra sat quietly at her feet, tears still streaming down her face. The Old Lady rested her hand on the child's shoulder and continued.

"Everyone has a beginning and an end; I am no different. When our light is extinguished all that remains are the lessons we learned and passed on. The love we have accepted and the love we have given. Let all the memories that you leave behind be good ones. Let them be your shining light, the sparkle no one can extinguish." She slowly sipped her tea, giving her a moment to think of her next words.

"It is not the number of years we spend here on Eternal that truly counts. It is the impact that our time here has on others. Therefore, do not mourn for me when I say that my time is at hand. Instead, rejoice in knowing that I have loved you with all my heart, until my last breath." As she spoke the words, she took in a deep breath and sighed.

Lashra laid her head on the woman's lap as she continued to speak. "I have outlived..." she started counting on her fingers and muttering names. "Seven husbands." she said with a weak smile.

"I have had a long and prosperous life. I have seen many things. I tell you the truth, my heart has been longing and dreaming and waiting for this day to reveal itself." As she spoke the words her eyes lit up. "When my ancestors wrote The Scrolls of Tralatitious, they did not know when the time of the end would be. Every one of my descendants had longed to see what I see now. Every generation of our people dreamed of this day. How wonderful it is for this generation to be the one to witness all that is about to take place. How blessed I am that your identity has been unveiled to me. I am the last pure blood of my tribe, therefore, I had faith that you would arrive in my lifetime."

"When you first came to me I did not recognize you. No, not one of you. However, last night I had a prophetic dream and you were at last revealed to me. I know that today I am experiencing the beginning of the end of this age and you shall bring forth a new age and a new world."

The children sat listening, but were exceedingly confused. "You have been chosen and are fortunate to be the ones who will fulfill the vision given by the Prophet Of Peace. In his own time, he could not find *The One* who could bear the weight of the armor. He knew that one day peace and salvation would return to our world. He prophesied that the armor would be restored."

Saudj stood up and gestured toward the woman. "Quit speaking in riddles, Old Lady. Just come out and tell us what you mean." he said impatiently and brusquely.

Preet speaking for the rest asked, "Why should we be chosen to find The One? We're just a pack of ignorant kids who don't even understand what you are saying."

"You are so wrong my little Preet." she said with a smile. "You are all gifted with skills and talents that will see you through the commission you have been designated for."

Upal was now pacing the room, "Who is this person? The One who should bear the armor? How do we find him? Why can't you go and tell him he's *The One*?" His voice was distressed and anxious.

"It could be a she." muttered Lashra.

"Really? That's your big concern here? His use of pronouns? Really?" Saudj said, raising his voice. He was visibly shaken and irritated.

The Old Lady slowly got up from her chair and walked to Saudj. She took his face in both of her hands, "My time is nearing its end. Your time is just beginning." She tried to guide him back to the floor, motioning him to sit next to his friends, but he would have none of it.

She returned to her place and sat down before she continued. "During the day of Liberation, Mater the leader of my people said that three must die, that all may live. He sent out Paladin, Protag and Patron with the armor and they disappeared into the Rubicon. Now *I* say, *you* also must enter the Rubicon. This time one must die, that all may live."

Saudj was highly agitated and interrupted her, "I have a question. Do you mean to say that you actually think we believe all those old tales and stories you tell? We're not stupid little children."

Upal glared at Saudj, "Maybe you should shut your mouth and give The Old Lady the respect she deserves."

"And maybe, you should be careful how you speak to me, Upal. This foolish escapade she's sending you on will be much more difficult with only two fools going." Saudj spoke with a wickedness that took them all off guard.

The Old Lady leaned forward and looked deep into Saudj's eyes. "Do not let your anger betray you." she whispered. "Your time is fast approaching." Her words only confused him more, adding to his uncertainty.

He began to make his way toward the door. He stopped abruptly, looked back and left with these words hanging in the air: "Nothing ever changes. Your great-grand-parents, your grand-parents, they all talked about *The One* returning in their time. Your parents taught you to believe it would be within this generation. For thousands of years people have claimed and preached that The One's arrival was imminent. Now, this old lady says she's dying and in her desperation to fulfill some groundless prophecy, she's willing to send you to the Rubicon." Saudj could only shake his head in disbelief.

"She would have you die, or worse, have you tortured and eaten alive by wild beasts. No one ever returns!" his voice kept rising. "That's the truth we know. Wake up to the reality of her folly. If you choose to listen to this craziness and go, you will die! That is the only thing you can be certain of. You know the only true statement of Eternal? The Rubicon Forest, from where no one ever returns. That's it, that's all. That is the only thing we're sure of."

He put his hand on the door latch and threw it open. He took one step out the door and turned around. "Our walls have been standing for thousands of years waiting for the day that Demorg would invade and return to his rightful place. Yet he has not even scratched the surface of our precious wall. The only true invasion is the one these old fools have put into your minds and hearts. Generation after generation of simpletons. They have been controlling your people for thousands of years, poisoning you with lies and deceit. They have trapped and jailed you like slaves. They talk of love and peace, but their true objective is slavery. Slavery of the body, slavery of the mind, slavery of the soul. Yes, your soul, your mind, your body. Not mine. They sing you songs of comfort but nourish your minds with fears and phobias."

He took a step backward fully exiting The Old Lady's domain. "Leave with me now while you still have your lives and some of your sanity. Come with me that you might be free of all this. Come with me and live."

They sat and watched as Saudj became enraged to the point of madness. He raised his fist then pointed to the woman in the chair. Filled with bitterness and enmity he shouted. "You alone are responsible for their deaths, Old Witch!"

The Old Lady looked at the three sitting in front of her. "You are all free to choose your destinies. I will not judge you nor will I love you any less."

Saudj walked out the door, stopped for a moment, turned and put his head through the window. "Lashra, I'll miss you the most." He walked away, then quickly returned. "Actually, you're the only one I'm going to miss." Then, he left again.

As he walked down the dusty road his anger and resentment toward The Old Lady continued to boil up inside him. "That crazy old hag is sending them to their deaths. Blind, all of them inebriated by her poisonous words. Oh Lashra, you're so smart why can't you see through her lies?" His mumblings and grumblings continued as he walked heading nowhere in particular.

The kids were caught staring at the window in a long awkward silence. After a few moments, Upal tried to break the silence. "He's gone mad."

"Whatever it is that we must do, we'll do it." Lashra said with confidence.

"I know for one that if Saudj would have been involved, he would have been a stumbling block to us all." Upal chimed in.

"We all have our role to play Upal. Don't be so quick to judge." The Old Lady's mood was now more dark and somber and she appeared fatigued. "I am tired. Come back tomorrow, then you will know all you need to know."

Lashra was still sitting by the Old Lady's chair. "I'll stay here with you for the night. You shouldn't be alone."

"Go, my children. I must meditate and get some rest. Please come back tomorrow." As she spoke her words, she placed her hands in her lap and closed her eyes.

Chapter 10 Mrs. Nibbledent's

The three teens reluctantly got up and left the The Old Lady's home. Preet took hold of his sister's hand and pulled her close. He wrapped his arm around her shoulder and comforted her in silence as they walked.

Without a word spoken or so much as a look exchanged, they all had the same idea. They were going to find Saudj and straighten him out, but their efforts were lackadaisical. They were more concerned about The Old Lady and her mysterious message. Little if anything was said as they traveled throughout their neighbourhood.

Their unintentional wandering somehow led them to Mrs. Nibbledent's. Standing at the entrance of the home they looked to the sky. The sun had called it a day hours ago. The moon was in its third or fourth day of waxing gibbous and tonight it shone as bright as two moons.

Suddenly the night sky was blasted with hundreds, nay, thousands of shooting stars breaking through the blackness of deep space at a rate of forty or fifty per second and as quickly as it started it was over.

The three stood there in utter silence with mouths gaping, stunned, breathless and bewildered.

Lashra looked down and noticed she was holding both their hands. She squeezed them both tightly and whispered to them, "The Tratalitious says... *Tears of fire burned up the sky, when the Prophet Of Peace went out to die."*

She let go of their hands and grabbed hold of their shirts. "The Old Lady. Something's happened to The Old Lady."

Upal took hold of her hands, "She's fine, Lashra... We'll be seeing her in a few hours."

Preet added, "If she knew she was going to die tonight, she wouldn't have told us to come back later. Let's make our way home and get a couple of hours of rest."

"I think we should all stay together tonight, then we can head over to The Old Lady's house at sunrise." she said, still worried about the woman's solitude.

Preet had stayed at Upal's a few times over the past year, but never had Lashra ever even considered doing so. Even if she had, Preet would not have allowed it.

"We should go home." Preet repeated. "We'll come get Oop as soon as we see daylight."

Upal was bummed by Preet's insistence that she not stay the night. So, as was often the case he spoke up. "Lashra's right Preet, we should just stay together tonight. The sun will be up in a few hours and I don't think it would be a good idea for me to be alone right now."

He moved closer to Preet and whispered, "You know, The Old Lady saying she's dying, Saudj going mad and there's the whole fire crying star thing we just witnessed." He tapped his temple, "I'm pretty frenzied up in here. Me alone? In this condition? That's gonna do some damage." He smiled curiously hoping his argument was winning Preet over.

"Really?" Preet said, with lighthearted disdain. His eyebrows raised with skepticism and head shaking, he agreed to stay even though he had reservations.

Slowly and with purpose Upal opened the door. They quietly made their way into Mrs. Nibbledent's house, where she was found asleep at the table, grasping her glass of wine.

"Wow, she must have had a hard day." Upal said sarcastically. "I can't ever remember her leaving behind a half empty glass of wine, let alone one that's half full." He chuckled at his own remarks.

Lashra, who had never been in the house before, bumped into a small stool next to the stairs and knocked over an unlit candlestick. The noise it made partially woke the owner of the house. They all stopped moving and waited. She looked up to see her glass still half full.

"What's this?" she garbled out. They stood in silence, not moving, hoping she hadn't seen them. "What? Is that you my precious?" She lifted her head just high enough to drink the last of her wine. Her head fell back onto the table and instantly snoring was heard.

"That's better," said Upal, smiling.

The three friends made their way up to Upal's cell, exhausted from the day's events. Lashra threw herself on the bed of hay, the boys fell to the floor and before any of them could comment on anything that had happened on their whirlwind of a day... they fell asleep.

Chapter 11 Saudj Returns

Saudj spent his night walking and stewing, drifting and fretting, wandering and seething. The agony and stress of the situation was crushing him. He thought mostly about Lashra and how he could insulate her from The Old Lady's insane ways.

"I have to save her. She's blind to what's going on. They all are." he said uproariously to no one. "How can I be the only one that sees things clearly? She's been manipulating them all these years. All of Eternal is under her spell."

He was growing more delusional with every step, his brain was swirling with thoughts and images of what would happen if he didn't do something, anything. Saudj abruptly stopped as he unknowingly found himself at the entrance of The Old Lady's abode.

He placed his palm on the wooden door and slowly ran his fingers down the entrance door. "This is a sign." he whispered ever so quietly.

"Ouch!" He ripped his hand away from the door. He examined his finger and carefully pulled out a small sliver of wood. Upon exiting the wound one drop of blood was released. His eyes followed its long journey to the ground. The blood landed in the sand producing an outward explosion, forming a small crater.

He put his finger in his mouth and sucked on the tiny yet nagging wound. Carefully and quietly he stepped to the side and looked through her window. The door to the children's bedroom was closed. The deceitful, lying dragon was fast asleep in her chair, grasping her beloved scrolls.

He slowly and quietly breathed out, "The Scrolls of Tralatitious. If only they could be destroyed, then the lies would end."

The wood stove had been left unattended and only a few red embers could be seen. The candle by her chair was flickering and darting with its last few breaths of life.

"That candle will be dead in a minute" he said in a hauntingly low drawl.

He glowered at her, his jaw clenched, his teeth grinding and whispering to himself he muttered "She's going to send them to their deaths. Lashra believes everything this old hag says. She'll be gone forever if I don't do something about it. They'll all be gone."

He heard a dark and sinister voice echo in the back of his mind. "Only you can save Eternal, Saudj. Be the savior they need."

"But how?" he questioned himself. "What can I do?"

"You must rid the world of those scrolls." The despondent voice was becoming less recognizable. "No one should ever be deluded by her fables again. Destroy the scrolls of Tralatitious and you erase the lies of history. You can bring forth a new world, a new future."

"She'll wake up if I try to take them." he countered the voice. "Then what will I do?"

The articulations of his twisted mind were becoming more desperate. "Stop the lies." Saudj's heart was pounding hard and fast as the voice grew more frantic. "The truth belongs to you." His breathing was quick and shallow; the agent grew more determined. "Do not let this moment pass." He felt faint and confused and the propagandist's declarations magnified. "Slaughter the Wolf, destroy the Dragon."

The dizziness was intoxicating. "I can't kill her?" he said.

"*One* must die, that all may live." The thought echoed through Saudj's mind as he recalled the words spoken the previous afternoon.

"She was begging for you to help her fulfill the prophecy." He pressed his eyes tightly closed and put his palms against his ears in an attempt to block out the voice demanding the unimaginable and grotesque request.

His attempt to silence the voice failed. "Let her false prophecies be self-fulfilling; she will live and die by her own words."

The exchange of controversies in his mind were beginning to take a toll on him, weakening and eroding what little will he had left.

"Your time is fast approaching, let her revelations be your guide."

At that point, the voice took a comforting and tranquil air. "Help her Saudj. She needs you to help fulfill her dying wish. She knew she was going mad. You are her last hope."

Exhausted and terrified he mouthed, "I will not murder."

Sympathetically the voice replied, "Suffer her to live, but get the scrolls."

Chapter 12 One Dark Night

He scanned his surroundings to see if anyone was in the streets. He was alone. Of course he was alone, it was the dead of night. It felt hot and muggy, his skin was clammy and damp. There was not even the slightest breath of air to refresh him. It was a deathly, eerily still evening.

The moon seemed to shine with the brightness of an afternoon sun. He stood alone and motionless, pressed against the wall by the window of her abode, hopelessly trying to cover himself in darkness. The silence was deafening. He looked around again. Nothing, no one. Not even one stumbling Glumvyn-soaked vagrant could be seen or heard.

Noiselessly he snaked his way over the window sill and secretly he crept in, inch by inch. Slithering and stealing his way down to the hard timeworn floor. Painstakingly rising to his feet he stepped aside so as not to cast a shadow through the hole in the wall.

I don't have much time, the sun will be up in a few hours, I have to hurry. He thought to himself. I can't wake her, I mustn't wake her.

He was eight maybe nine steps away. His head was spinning and his vision was constricted. He tried to focus out of his tunnel vision. She seemed to be a mile away. His vision felt thick, somehow massive and heavy. He found it unsettling.

The distance seemed insurmountable. He counted the steps anxiously. One, he took his first step and *crack*, his knee made a sound that must have been heard throughout all of Eternal. He stopped and held his breath, the woman twitched, the candle's light flickered, then vanished. Saudj went blind. His head was pounding with the hammering rhythm of his blasting heart. The high pitched notes of silence were ear-piercing.

A small sense of relief came when his eyes readjusted to the dark room. He continued, two, he tried to focus on the scrolls in the woman's hands. Three, with each step he tried to embolden and calm himself. Four, I will save Eternal. Five. He softly and deliberately lowered his foot. Si…, his sixth step came into contact with something unusual. He stopped mid-landing, it was merely a cup that was left behind earlier by one of those dim-witted kids, probably Upal. He stepped to the side, avoiding it. Seven, he was distressingly close to the sleeping Longevite. Slowly, carefully, quietly he continued. Eight, even closer. Nine, his trembling hand reached out for the scrolls. They were within reach.

The drumming in his chest progressed into an excruciating and uncontrollable pain. He watched her face as his quivering fingers reached out and touched the edge of the scrolls, her hands clenched, her eyes opened.

He looked down at his hand and discovered he was holding a large rock. It was heavy, oval and smooth; he could scarcely wrap his hand around it. Startled by her presence and without thought, he swung his arm and it came to a sudden and jarring stop.

The rock's pounding strike made contact with her head, violently driving it against the back of her seat. The force fractured The Old Lady's skull, a warm, wet deluge of blood from her injury splattered and sprayed his face; the madness of the situation was quickly unseating any sanity that remained in him.

The woman attempted to lift and straighten her head, he bludgeoned her again. Blood spewed out and covered his face. His mouth seemed to be filled with it. He gagged and spit the contents at her.

She found the power to turn her head and their eyes made contact. The Old Lady found the strength to reach and grab hold of his garment. She pulled him in close and with her free hand gently touched his face and garbled out of her blood dripping lips, "I forgive you."

Her words propelled him into an uncontrollable and unmanageable rage. Over and over he pounded her with the stone. Time slowed to a near halt. Everything moved in slow motion. The room was suddenly bright as day. His vision, crisp and clear. At that very moment he was able to ponder the dull, blunt sounds of the uncontrolled whipping and pounding. It was softer and more hushed than he would have imagined.

Her heavy body tipped to one side and slid awkwardly to the floor. He watched her as she lay on the ground, blood pooling around her head. His blood stained hands reached down and grabbed hold of the scrolls. His feet were drenched in her marrow. In a flash of lucidity he realized he was standing in a quagmire of blood. He stood high above and looked down on her.

"I will not murder." he said to her.

Chapter 13 Run Saudj

His mind was a corkscrew of images, sounds and memories, past, present and future. All of it a crazy, crooked, twisted, tortuous winding helical of phantasms that could not be controlled. He was running toward the city gate. This portal would lead him to his freedom.

The main gate would soon be open. He knew enough to get out before anyone found out what he'd done. He struggled to unlock and push open the eye of the needle.

This little door seemed to help justify his earlier actions as it persuaded him even more of the peoples' shortsighted, irrelevant, futile, simpleminded ways. "Aahhh!" He let out an involuntary scream of frustration.

The small door had been built for *safety* reasons; the leaders imagined that if Demorg's army ever attacked at night there was no way for his troops to flood the city through the small entrance. The main gate was open from sunrise to sunset, a tradition that went back thousands of years.

The large doors gave everyone access to go in and out of the city during the day. Citizens of the West Gate used this time to trade wares, herbs and trinkets with the Romas (a tribe of gypsies who made the outside wall their domain). At night you could only leave the city through the eye of the needle. It was sometimes used by the Patrol to rid themselves of the *unwanted*. It was better for the Patrol that housebreakers, pinchers and purloiners be cast out for the night, lest they get in the way of the Patrol's pestiferous ways.

He lifted the large bar that kept the door securely locked. He pushed the cumbersome door open. He made his way out and ran a short distance and fell to his knees, exhausted.

A thousand questions swirled in his mind. What have I done? I saved my friends. What have I done? I killed The Old Lady? What's going to happen to me? They won't understand. They'll banish me. I don't know what to do. What do I do? They'll banish me. I have to hide. They won't know it's me. Why would they think it's me? It was a painful mind-bending process, a constant reenactment of the night's events.

He prostrated himself, stretched out with his face on the ground. He covered his head with his hands trying to stop the unyielding playback of the unimaginable. I have to hide somewhere, but where?

Saudj raised his head from the soil. His eyes met the horizon. The spectacle was transcendent. He gazed in wonderment. Hundreds, nay, thousands of shooting stars showered the Rubicon. The heavens had sent him a sign. The Rubicon, no one will come look for me there.

He scrambled and fought his way to his feet and ran and ran and ran. It was imperative that he make it.

Exhausted, depleted, confused, alone and desperate, he stood at the dreaded entrance. He peered into its tunnel-like structure and closed his eyes.

"There he is! Bring him to me!" The Patrolman shouted. "There's no use fighting it boy. You know you're guilty and you know your punishment."

"You can walk in or we can throw you in. One thing is sure, boy. You will never return. No one ever returns."

Chapter 14 Enter The Rubicon

Saudj opened his eyes and shook himself out of his trance. He was alone. Had he imagined the whole night? He gazed at his blood stained hands and sighed in disbelief.

He looked deep into the Rubicon's entrance. What was he thinking? He tried hard to see through to the other end of the tunnel, but it was too deep and dark.

The first blush of morning light was making itself known. The breaking of day brought with it a warm breeze that worked diligently at drying the long grass that the night had filled with dew. He cast his eyes over the land that separated him from the city. What a beautiful day, he thought to himself.

He turned back to face the dreaded entrance. "No!" he said to himself. "I can't go in there." Turning away from the exit he proceeded to walk the edge of the forest. The Rubicon's boundaries were framed with a throng of beautiful pink flowers that bloomed on the poisonous and thorned filled Euphorbia shrub. Its barbs were razor sharp and a simple scratch was said to be enough to take a life (and quickly).

The shrubbed flat lands soon turned into a jagged and almost unmanageable rock formation. Slowly and meticulously he made his way up and down and side to side. One misstep and he would find himself pierced through by a sharp-spear like rock.

Barely a few feet into the treacherous terrain he stopped dead in his tracks. His eyes caught a pile of dried up bones that had been picked clean. All the stories he'd heard as a child, the same ones he'd repeated to scare the kids he knew, flashed through his mind.

"There are some who try to run from the Patrol when being brought out to the Rubicon. Their escape is short lived.

Run, the Patrolmen shout as they prepare their javelins and arrows. But they never shoot, they simply watch as the fugitives attempt to make their way through the jagged rocks. It's never long before they slip and are skewered. Their destiny and yours if you ever try to escape the Patrol, is to die a slow death. Left out on the rocks to be slowly eaten alive by the condors, vultures and crows."

Lucky for Saudj, he wasn't being chased by the Patrol. But he was tired and thirsty. He continued carefully for a while. He could see flat desert sand just up ahead. With painstaking vigilance, he saw his way through. He flopped onto the barren no-man's-land, closed his eyes and rested.

He lay still for a few moments. He opened his eyes and could see nothing but an unending desert landscape to one side and the Rubicon on the other. Nowhere to hide. That's all that kept running through his head. Nowhere to hide. It was lingering over him with every breath, every heartbeat, every thought. It was a morass that was covering every inch of his being. A sinking, suffocating, strangling, squeezing sensation that was paralyzing and slowly swallowing him up.

He made his way to his feet and walked it's boundaries until a few hours before sunset. The day was spent longing and yearning to find a way out of his unspeakable situation.

Saudj had been without sleep, water and food for too long, and the effects were taking its toll on him.

"Bring me the Scrolls." He looked around and could see no one.

He stopped and heard the haunting voice again, a voice that could have been mistaken for the breeze whooshing and murmuring through the trees and shrubs.

"Saudj." the woods whispered. Yes, it was coming from the woods.

"Deliverance." The sound was almost indistinguishable from the air.

"Solace." The sound became an anesthetic, casually lessening his awareness.

Saudj stood staring at the Rubicon. He was in a dispiriting state of mind as he responded in a melancholy voice. "If I enter I will die."

The wind echoed a comforting, "You will live."

Unknowingly he inched his way forward. "No one ever returns."

"I am Rubicon." the trees rustled.

Unwittingly he budged forward. "I will never return."

The wind insisted, "Come to me."

Unknowingly he moved closer. "I need to rest."

In one breath the sky grew dark and the sun vanished. A long booming, roaring, rolling sound of thunder was heard. An ear-splitting crack followed. Saudj looked up to see a tree falling. It smashed down at his feet opening the Rubicon.

A sudden intense gale pushed him closer. The cold wind pierced his ears with the ringing sound, "Come to me my son, I will give you the Rubicon and the whole world."

He climbed onto the slaughtered tree and made his way into the forest. At the last moment he realized what he had done and turned to make his escape. It was too late. Thorns had already covered the sprawling tree.

Over tired and run ragged, Saudj fell to the forest floor. His eyes closed and he was comforted by a gentle breeze that caressed his face and hushed gently in his ear, "My son."

And with those final words he passed out knowing he was truly in his father's house.

Chapter 15 Sunrise

Upal was staring out his window. It was the beginning of a new day. He smiled and was filled with a sense of happiness he hadn't felt in years. The last time he could recall feeling like this was when he was eight. It was a day etched in his mind, a simple day spent at the watering hole. His mom had come to watch him play and swim and as usual she'd brought sandwiches and apple cake. That delicious apple cake, with her not-too-sweet icing on top. It was a simple memory, but one that stuck with him.

"This is going to be a wonderful day." he murmured as he turned to face the not-so-appalling bed of hay where Lashra lay. Yup, a wonderful day he thought to himself.

Preet was lying in a mangled and uncomfortable position, three quarters of his torso on the floor and the remainder spread out across Lashra's bed. She was still asleep, covered by a thin patchwork that didn't do much to cover her or keep her warm.

He observed her quietly and longingly, daydreaming of laying down next to her. The two of them being all toasty and warm. He would gently kiss the back of her neck and stroke her hair all the while trying not to wake her. Loving her, caring for her and being loved in return, all the while knowing how undeserving of that love he was; this thought alone sparked his passion and admiration for her.

"Oh – My – World! Stop looking at my sister like that you sicko!" Preet's eyes were still closed as he shouted the words, then cringed when he realized he might have woken Mrs. Nibbledent.

Upal was shaken out of his daydream. Embarrassed and confused he blurted out, "What? What? What are you talking about?" He turned his gaze back to the outside. "I can see light. Wake her up and let's get going."

Yawningly she admitted "I've been up for a while now." She stretched and spread herself out and playfully kicked the remainder of Preet's body off the bed.

Upal could feel Lashra staring at him and even though he felt somewhat embarrassed, he took pleasure in imagining that she might be smiling at him and the situation. She wasn't.

"Let's get going." Upal threw the words outside.

"You know he's always staring at you right? Preet said to his sister.

"Shut up Preet." she said.

"Ya Preet, shut up." Upal repeated, "Let's go." He was eager to leave and change the subject.

They made their way down the stairs. When they reached the bottom they could see that Mrs. Nibbledent had not moved one wit. Her hand was still grasping her empty glass and a puddle of pinkish drool could be seen on the table. They made their way toward the exit and Lashra once again knocked the stool over; this time none of them cared about waking her up.

The sky had scarcely been lit by the time they hit the streets. Taking a hurried pace they made their way to The Old Lady's house. The thoroughfares and alleyways were quiet. No one could be seen buying or selling. No kids out playing and running a muck. Just a couple of stray rats, running from a stray cat and a few snoring sots tucked away in corners seeking shelter from the world and possibly their wives.

Upal thought this morning's peace and quiet seemed unusual, maybe even out of place, but really he wasn't sure. He rarely if ever got up at this time of day. He was thinking about doing it more often, maybe everytime Lashra spent the night. Why would he bother sleeping when he could be spending time with her?

Their pace had been a quick one and as they approached The Old Lady's home, they noticed the door was half open. They ran. They had a notion that something was wrong. Preet's giant legs took him past the other two and just before he reached the door he fell to the ground at the entrance of the house. Upal quickly arrived and ran on top of him followed closely by Lashra.

Their hearts instantly sank when they came upon The Old Lady's giant body laying on the floor in a pool of blood.

Chapter 16 Why?

Confused and unable… maybe unwilling to register the horror, they stood there trying to reject what they were witnessing. A dead and still hemorrhaging victim.

A sudden and unyielding wrath filled Lashra, "Ahhhh! Why?! Why? Why?" She ran to the woman's side. Falling to her knees she begged, "Preet! Upal! Help me turn her over! She's drowning in blood."

With great force they rolled her over and Lashra gently lifted the maton's head and placed it on her lap. Lashra's tears flooded The Old Lady's blood covered face. As they ran down her crimson colored cheeks, Lashra used her hair to wipe and clean her blood stained face.

She tried to force herself to regain composure by taking deep breaths and quietly repeating a mantra "Breathe, calm, breathe, calm." she needed to regain her senses in order to think clearly.

Lashra was having a difficult time reclaiming her senses. The events were moving so fast, yet everything was so clear. The room seemed to be spinning at a dizzying rate but in the same moment, time was moving in slow motion.

The Old Lady slowly opened her eyes and gave a slight groan.

"She's still alive!" the girl said as she wiped her eyes and used her sleeve to wipe slime from her nose.

The aged woman was weary and anaemic. She did her best to speak but could only manage a raspy whisper. "You must listen. Her eyes closed and Lashra bent her ear closer to her. "I don't have much time left, my child."

Lashra pleaded, "No, you'll be fine. I'll clean you up and bandage your wounds. I'll do all the work, I'll take care of the children, the garden, the house; you'll rest, you'll rest, you'll get better."

The Old Lady continued. "The scrolls, the Armor. Three…" she choked then coughed up blood. "Gather the Armor." She closed her eyes for a moment to rest and gather her strength, "Restore peace."

Lashra began frantically quizzing the dying woman. "You said three. Three what? How do we restore peace? Where is the Armor? Stay with us, you need to tell us more, we don't know anything."

The two boys were paralyzed. The unfolding scene left them helpless, powerless and impotent. They watched as Lashra tried to shake the injured woman awake.

She was weeping and blubbering, her sobs made it impossible to speak clearly, but the woman understood every word, "You need to tell us more. Please, please, please.Tell me who did this to you?"

The Old Lady used the last of her strength and reached her arm up to touch Lashra's face. She gently pulled her down even closer and gurgled her words out through a thick red liquid that was filling her mouth and throat, "My pocket, scrolls, Saudj, Rubicon. Three arrive. The Forest of Eternals awaits you." With those final words she closed her eyes. Her hand fell from Lashra's face to the floor.

Through her tears she cried out to the old woman, shaking and pleading, "No. I don't understand. How you could be asking us to do this. Why?"

Preet was filled with disbelief, confusion and sadness. He took one step toward the woman and his knees gave out. He dropped down next to the lifeless body and leaned into her. He wrapped his arms around her and laid his head on her chest. "Thank you for loving me." he said, weeping.

Upal put his hand on Lashra's shoulder. "What's going on? What are we going to do?" he muttered. He tried to shake himself out of his stupor. He wanted to think. He wanted to be strong. He needed to be strong for Lashra and Preet. "This is all too much to bear."

The sound of a creaking door made all three turn.

Chapter 17 The Children

The creaking sound came from the children's room. Lashra's maternal instincts kicked in. "Upal" she said, grabbing his arm. "Keep the children in their room." She looked down at The Old Lady and back at him. Her lips quivered as she said, "I need to cover her."

Lashra and Preet grabbed the blood splattered blanket from her chair and covered the slain body. Lashra made her way to the kid's bedroom door, she did her best to quickly wipe her tears and snot filled nose. She gently knocked. Upal opened the door and with his help they quickly led the kids outside. Preet did his best to shield the children on their way past the body.

Once outside, she set Timmy the Beautiful on his bike and told him to be back for his afternoon snack. She gripped the oldest of the children and pulled her to the side (she must have been about ten or eleven).

"You need to find a Patrolman and tell him there's been a murder." Lashra was gripping the girl's shoulders and looking her square in the eyes. "You need to tell him that The Old Lady has been murdered by Saudj."

The child was crying. Lashra was trying hard to control the quiver in her voice as she told the young girl, "You must also tell him that we have gone to the Rubicon to find him."

Lashra could see by the look on the poor child's face that she was completely lost and confused. Lashra took her in her arms and hugged her tightly. She put her hands on both her shoulders and held her firmly.

"There is no time to waste. Can you do this for me? Can you?" The child nodded. "Go!" Lashra commanded, "Go!"

Lashra walked over to the other children and took them into her arms. "You have a very important task ahead of you." she said bravely. "You must *not* go into the house or let anyone in until the Patrolman arrives." She nodded her head and gave the children a weak smile. "You have the biggest responsibility, I believe in you. Do this for me. Remember no one must enter the house." She reached into her bag and gave each child a small candy. "She hugged them again and made her way to Upal and Preet.

She grabbed them by the hand. "We need to go."

With urgency they ran out of the city toward the Rubicon. A short distance away from the city they stopped and turned to face the only home they'd ever known. The feeling of loss was abundant and it came with a heavy heart and a sense of uneasiness.

Lashra stepped away from the two boys and glared at the west. "I hear the forest calling me." she spoke with a soft voice.

"It's calling the three of us." said Upal.

She stared at him with such intensity, that Upal felt as if she was reading his soul. "Is it?"

Chapter 18 Ray

"Unkindness, conspiracy... that's what they call you." Crawford was bored and desperate for conversation. "Hey Ray, don't you think that's a little mean? Why do you think they call you that?"

The sandy brown haired stripling questioned his black bird. *Caw, Caw* his pet responded. "Ah, don't take it personally buddy, I've been called worse."

He sat on the ground petting Ray, who was not only his best friend but his best raven, well, his only raven. Ray was a majestic and ravishing black bird that stood twenty six inches tall and had a wing span just short of four feet. He was a powerful and sinister looking creature. If he was ordered to attack (as he had been in the past), Ray could easily frighten off any would-be aggressor.

Ray was as clever and crafty as he was big, which made sense since ravens are one of the most intelligent animals in the world, something Crawford often pointed out to the girls he met, in an effort to keep their attention.

"He prefers to be called handsome." he'd interject when the girls would comment on Ray's beauty.

"He gets that from me, by the way." he would say while attempting a smoldering look (which sometimes worked).

"He knows over a hundred words. He's almost as intelligent as I am." Crawford would say with a smug smile.

If he found a girl pretty enough (and he often did), he'd lean in and secretly whisper, "Why Ray here... he can easily tell the difference between silver, gold, diamonds, rubies; he's a master at finding... *exquisite treasures*." then he'd unabashedly chirp, "That's why he made his way to you." It was often enough to make a girl blush. Of course it didn't hurt that he was a tall, good looking lad who came from a wealthy family.

But at the end of the day, it was always Crawford and Ray. Their friendship went way back to a time when Crawford was about seven or eight years old. He was walking home from school on his customary route when he happened to hear something squawking and yelping in an alley. Entering the backstreet to investigate the sound, he spotted a little black bird, limping and protecting his wing.

"Oh, look at you, what are you doing here? What happened?" He carefully picked up the bird, tucked him in his jacket and made his way home. Sneaking up the stairs to his room he said to the bird, "Father won't mind. He's rarely home. But try to stay quiet in any case."

Crawford was thankful to the housemaid who brought them both food, water and bandages. Without her help the child would probably have killed the bird with love. After about six weeks of nursing, the raven was looking pretty good. The day had arrived; Ray was ready to return to the sky.

Crawford so badly wanted to keep Ray as his pet, but even at his tender age, he knew something about being locked up and caged. "I wish I could fly out of here with you Ray. I won't hold you back. Fly, be free."

Caw, caw, caw the sound of his voice echoed against the nearby houses as he flew high into the night sky. The housemaid held the boy as he sniffled and whimpered. Once the bird was out of sight, she layed Crawford down in his bed, tucked him in and silently patted his head while he cried himself to sleep.

At sunrise the very next day he was awakened by the sound of gurgling and croaking. Ray had returned. He jumped out of bed with wonderment and delight. He ran to his window and grabbed hold of his friend. Henceforth, they were inseparable.

Chapter 19 Nuts

Crawford was willingly and happily being pelted and showered with a variety of nuts and berries falling from the sky. He looked up at the hundreds of crows circling above his head. The murder of crows and the conspiracy of ravens stayed busy swooping, gliding and circling, up, down and around the boy.

Crawford used a couple of rocks to break the hard shells surrounding the delicious fruit, "One for you, two for me." he would say to the birds.

With Ray's encouragement the birds quickly found the human practical, and the human enjoyed the company.

It did come as a bit of a surprise how easily the birds trusted him and how that trust was rewarded with berries, mushrooms and other treats that seemed to magically appear from the Rubicon.

He remarked to himself more than a few times how they appeared to have no difficulties going in and out of the ghastly forest. "Ray," he said leaning back on a large flat rock, "it seems to me that not *everything* gets trapped in that place."

The notorious saying, *from where no one ever returns*, tumbled through his mind and a chill ran down his spine. He reached out to pet the bird and commented, "Apparently that doesn't apply to you or them, does it buddy? Maybe it's because even the Rubicon fears murder, unkindness and conspiracies." A sense of uneasiness came over him after speaking those words out loud and he tried to shake it off by looking the other way and eating more nuts and berries.

The sun was now at its hottest point and bit by bit the sizzling heat was baking Crawford. He crawled back to his makeshift canopy. It would be a little easier to rest and cool down in the shade provided by the broken branches and shrubs. He lay there staring longingly in the direction of the city.

Peering through the cracks and crevasses of his makeshift shelter he thought about returning home. It's not all bad, he thought to himself. He stretched out trying to find a comfortable position, "I may have to rethink my life's goals, buddy." he said quietly to the raven who'd jammed himself next to the chap. "Well, if nothing else," he rolled over onto his stomach and reached out for a handful of nuts, "at least I... I mean, we have food."

Crawford found it hard to get comfortable on the rocky soil. He rolled over onto his back and stared up at the blue sky. I miss my bed. I *miss* the housemaid, he smiled coyly to himself.

"You know Ray," he said in a reflective manner, "being alone isn't all it's cracked up to be."

It was hard for him to imagine that just a few weeks ago he was at home enjoying a peaceful and untroubled life. Well, maybe not untroubled. Over the years Crawford had taught Ray numerous tricks and stunts, many of which got them (but mostly him) into trouble.

Crawford's stunts had come to their natural culmination. The result?

His home was a shrub. He was sleeping outside. He was dependent on his raven for food. And as if that's not enough, all of it was happening an hour's walk away from the Rubicon.

Chapter 20 And We're Walking

They'd been running for almost twenty minutes. Upal was trying to keep up to Lashra. Her words… "Is it?" What did she mean? He thought. She's just shaken, sad and angry.

Lashra hadn't slowed down since she started running. She glanced back and saw Upal about a minute behind her. As for Preet? She stopped and waited for Upal to catch up. Upal was happy to stop and catch his breath.

Grunting and wheezing and hacking, he squeaked out, "You must be the fastest person in all of Eternal. How did I not know you could run like that?"

"You have no idea." she murmured.

"Sorry I couldn't hear you over my grunting and wheezing and hacking."

"Where's Preet?" she said.

"He could be hours behind us. Maybe days." he smiled.

They waited and waited. Then, Lashra waited and waited. Upal sat and rested on the sand.

"I think I see him." Upal thought he heard the sound of irritability in her voice.

"Seeing a whole new Lashra today." He smiled again.

She was filled with emotion. "Not everything is funny all the time, Upal."

Upal was ashamed of himself. How could he turn so cold so quickly. "Sorry."

Preet could see that Lashra and Upal were waiting for him. "Oh, this is so good. They're not shrinking anymore… Oh, this is great. They're getting bigger."

He was tired and breathless. He waved his large arms in the air to show he'd seen them. Then fell flat on the ground. "They can wait a minute more."

"I think he fell again." quipped Upal.

Lashra looked at him.

Upal looked back. "What? That's funny… come on that's funny."

Lashra started walking toward Preet. "Let's go and get him."

Upal caught up to Lashra. "It's funny 'cause he's always falling down."

Chapter 21 Crawford Must Go

It seemed Crawford had a bad habit, a thing, a quirk, a... *weakness*. He was bored. Life was dull. Why should he deny himself a little pleasure? A little joy. A little... *adventure?* A mostly-harmless-and-no-one-ever-gets-seriously-hurt, kind of adventure.

"These aged, rusty, senile shopkeepers are behind the times. How can they appreciate my... resourcefulness?" he'd often quip.

The problem was that Crawford's father was an important man. He was a councillor in the South Gate. Not just any councillor, he was *the* Councillor, that is, the one in charge of advising and instructing the Leader of the South Gate. Second in charge, as it were. He was also a prominent business owner. He spent much time traveling, making deals and negotiating terms with various businesses throughout all the gates.

Unfortunately for Crawford, his father didn't see things his way. His long record of stealing trinkets, semi precious loot, vandalism, and one time maybe unintentionally and definitely not on purpose, setting the local market on fire, was not helping his father's reputation. All of this and more, had finally caught up with him. He did protest, saying that *officially* he hadn't done any of those things; it was Ray.

However, after years of being defrauded by the young swindler, the vendors had had enough of his little enterprise. Not only was he tormenting shopkeepers in the South Gate, he had taken it upon himself to pluck wares and create havoc in all the gates, omitting only the West Gate. After all, what could they possibly have that was of any value?

The merchants endlessly complained to the councillors of their respected gates. Be that as it may, the prominence and influence of his father was too much to overcome and the verdict of guilty was rendered powerless.

Because of this, the merchants devised their own solution. A unionized group confronted Crawford's father and issued an edict; the boy and his notorious crow had to go.

The union's steward ranted and complained to Crawford's father, "You've sat idle for years and have done nothing to remedy this situation."

"He burned down half my shop!" interjected a vendor.

The Steward continued, "We've been more than patient with you and the boy. We've petitioned, we've pleaded, we've tried to appeal to your sense of justice and nothing."

"Tell him," The vendor sandwiched in again nervously, "he leaves us no choice."

The Steward raised his hand to silence the agitated vendor, "You leave us no choice but to..." he paused a moment and thought carefully about his next words. "...warn you about the harm your boy is inflicting upon *your reputation*. One might even say jeopardizing it."

The Councillor's jaw was clenched in anger, not only toward these men standing before him, but for his son who had been given clemency once too often. "Are you threatening me?" He knew they were.

The vendor prompted the Steward, "Tell him he leaves us no choice."

The leader brought his finger to his lips and shushed his companion once more. "My friend is right. You leave us no choice." He continued nervously but firmly, "We have all agreed that if a solution is not found by the end of the week, all of the shopkeepers, South, North and East will vote unanimously to have you removed from the council and if that fails, we vow that we will discontinue doing business with you. Good luck making a living with only the West Gate to deal with."

"What do you want from me?" came the father's reply. "Would you have me forsake my son?"

"Send him away." they said in harmony.

"Where should I send him?"

"Send him to the Rubicon for all we care." the man said.

One shopkeeper shouted from the back of the room, "Or worse, send him to the West Gate!" and the entire room broke into laughter.

The councillor fully understood the shopkeepers' position and their frustrations with his son. "I will speak with my son."

The Steward raised his voice. "You need to do more than speak with him." He was growing impatient with the Councillor. "You've been talking for years and nothing has changed." His courage was building. He slammed his fist on the table. "Action is what is required here."

The group of men turned around and walked out of the room. The Steward turned to remind the Councillor one last time. "By week's end."

That night Crawford's father took him aside and layed out his only option. "I can no longer protect you or myself from the merchants. My business, my reputation, my standing in the South Gate and across Eternal for that matter, all of it, collateral damage due to your years of turmoil and mayhem."

Crawford opened his mouth to interject, but was cut off by his father's screams. "It's as if you take pleasure in destroying everything I have worked so hard to create!" He lowered his voice and was almost cathartic when he told him he had been left with no option but to send him away.

Crawford was taken aback by his father's words and the seriousness and finality of his decision. He begged his father, "I'll stop, I'll be good."

Words he had spoken many times before. Sure, he'd be good for a week maybe two, but then it would start all over again. His father was too familiar with his son's double talk. This time his words were ironclad.

"Your old and worn out promises are no longer good here. You will relocate yourself to the West Gate or live with the Romas. Don't try hiding out in any other Gate."

He warned his son that the merchants had made it clear that the Patrol would be on the lookout for him.

"The West Gate is your only true hope of staying out of the Rubicon. I've had the housemaid prepare your clothes, some food and a few dollars. It will be enough to keep you for a few months, if you don't gamble it away."

Chapter 22 Alone

Crawford was astute and shrewd. Surely someone as clever as he was could come up with a plan that would have him *forgiven* or at the very least excused. With any luck he could conceive of a scheme that would have his father absolve him of his past sins and allow him to return home.

"We'll be back in business in a few days." he said to Ray.

Despite all his shrewdness, it was two weeks later and he was but a short distance from the bewitched gateway. In fact, he was no closer to achieving his aspirations than he was the day he left.

As of this very day he still had not figured out a way to safely stay in the city or find a way into his father's heart.

"Well, at least your friends are keeping me from starving." He paused to eat a few berries. "The nights are still manageable. But we have to figure something out before winter hits." he said half jokingly.

His nights were mostly sleepless with a lot of tossing and turning. The days were long, hot and boring. He was re-thinking his life's decisions and what it would mean to go back home and beg for forgiveness.

"Looks like danger." Ray croaked.

The bird caught Crawford's attention. "It's the Patrol. They've come looking for me."

Crawford layed low and whispered to his friend, "Ray, look over there, is that the Patrol? Why are they looking for me?" He squinted to improve his view. " Maybe they're bringing a criminal out to the Rubicon."

That's how it worked. If you were found guilty of a Rubiconian crime, two to seven patrol men (depending on how dangerous you were) would lead you to the tunnel that led into the unknown world. You would be told to enter it or forced to enter it. Most thought it better to go into the Rubicon with all their senses and limbs intact. It would surely give them a better chance at survival.

Crawford forced his eyes, trying hard to make out the figures more clearly. "This criminal must be marginally dangerous since there are only two patrolmen with him." He said to Ray.

Crawford decided to lay low and stay out of sight. No need to take any unnecessary risks. He would hate for the patrol to think he had been condemned to the Rubicon, yet somehow managed to avoid entrance. If he was spotted they'd surely recognize him as the son of the Councillor and throw him in without question. He began feeling anxious.

As they got closer he realized none of them were wearing Patrol uniforms. A little closer and he thought they looked like three teenagers not much younger or older than he was. "Hey Ray... is that a girl with them?" he whispered.

"Beautiful girl" croaked Ray.

"Shhhh, not now Ray."

Crawford had taught his raven a few choice words and phrases that he could use to start a dalliance with a Miss Right or at least Miss Right-now. He found the raven to be a great ice-breaker and a wingman.

"They're either in the same situation I'm in or they're crazy. I wonder if I should take a chance and talk to them? It's surely better than being alone."

His raven squeaked out. "Looks like danger."

"Shut up, you're gonna get us killed. "But, maybe you're right my feathered friend, maybe I should avoid contact."

He stayed still and quiet in his little makeshift shelter. The teenagers finally came clearly into sight. The three walked by without even a glance his way. He couldn't make out what the two boys were talking about, but wow! Was she ever beautiful.

"What are they doing this far out of the city?" he breathed.

"Beautiful girl" came Ray's response.

Preet stopped dead in his tracks and listened inquisitively. "Did you guys hear that?"

Upal and Lashra stopped and glanced back at Preet.

"I didn't hear anything."

"Me neither."

Preet looked around. "It sounded like, pretty girl."

Upal exploded with a loud guffaw. "Dude," he shook his head in a pitiful and hapless manner. "Your obsession with everybody obsessing over Lashra…" He closed his eyes and swayed his head back and forth slowly. "You gotta bring that down a notch. It's getting a little… uh, *eccentric*."

Lashra turned to Upal in surprise, "Wow, Upal, good effort with a new word. But, not the best. I would've used…" She was also growing tired of Preet's overprotection. "…strange, bizarre, idiosyncratic…"

An annoyed Preet responded, "Ya, ya, I get it. You're both really funny, but I know what I heard."

Upal condescendingly added, "You're right Preet, even the bushes and shrubs are trying to charm your sister. Let's go, we need to make up time."

Crawford couldn't quite make out what they were talking about. Then it hit him.

"Of course Ray!" Crawford finally saw the situation clearly. "She's being kidnapped. That giant monster and his miniscule comrade have abducted her. That's the only logical explanation."

He turned so he could see the three. "I have a plan, Ray. I need you to dive-bomb the giant, and don't stop. While you do that. I'll take care of the dwarf. We'll save that poor girl if it's the last thing we do... But just to be clear... It won't be the last thing we do."

"Go!" He sent the raven off on his task. Suddenly Crawford had a change of mind and decided to stay in position to rethink the second part of his plan.

"Maybe, I'll wait here a little to see how this goes. I don't want to be too hasty." he muttered to himself.

Ray's huge body came down and attacked Preet. "Ahhhh! What's going on?" He tried to duck and dodge the bird. Panic-stricken he shouted, "Help me, that crow is demented. He's trying to kill me."

Without thinking Lashra picked up a large stick from the side of the trail and started batting at the bird.

Preet continued to scream and wave his arms frantically. "It's the curse of the Rubicon, Demorg's demons are attacking us!" Frenzied and delirious he cried out, "Go after Upal, he's bite-sized!"

Upon hearing Preet's comment, Upal chose to watch instead of coming to his friend's rescue. This gave him time to question why the bird was not attacking him or Lashra.

She on the other hand was busy in her rescue efforts.

Whack, the stick missed the bird and hit the ground. "Get away!" The raven dodged.

Thwack, another miss. "Leave him alone!" Ray weaved.

Swat, "Stop it!" He avoided the large stick.

Lashra made another attempt. *Whack! T*his time she made contact. Her branch hit the raven. "Gotcha!" The raven crashed to the ground. "He's not moving."

"Good!" shouted Preet.

Lashra ran to the bird and immediately started caring for him.

"What about me?" cried Preet.

Crawford left his nest yelling and waving his arms. "Hey! What's wrong with you? What are you doing? Leave my bird alone!" he growled at Lashra. "Are you crazy hitting him like that?"

Startled and confused by the sudden appearance of, well, *anyone* out there, she moved away from the raven. "What?"

Crawford was losing it. "What's wrong with you? We're trying to save you from the giant and his sidekick."

"These are my friends, you imbecile!" she said angrily.

Upal looked around as if there must be someone else with them he didn't know about. He elbowed Preet, "Did he just call *me your* sidekick?"

He quickly verbalized his irritation to the stranger. "Hey! If anything he's *my* sidekick."

Crawford ignored them while he examined his friend. He gently set Ray on his shoulder, then began to question the trio. "What the heck are you doing out here? No one ventures out this far. Unless..." he paused dramatically. "Unless they're criminals."

"Really?" said Upal as he stepped toward him and looked him square in the eye. "What kind of criminal are you?"

"The innocent kind of course." He threw an arrogant smile in Lashra's direction.

Lashra ignored his smugness. She stepped in between the two and separated them. "Hold on boys. Let's all calm down and start over."

"Start over what?" Crawford was visibly annoyed. "I tried to save you and for that you tried to kill my best friend."

"Ya, well your best friend tried to kill me, so I think we're even." Preet added.

"Stop. Everybody." Lashra just wanted to get back to their prime objective. "Maybe you should go back to your hiding place and let us get back to making our way to the Rubicon."

"On purpose?" he interjected.

"Yes, on purpose." She realized how ridiculous the situation must have looked to an outsider. "A boy named Saudj murdered The Old Lady this morning and stole some of the Scrolls of Tralatitious." She could feel herself welling up.

She took a deep controlled breath and continued. "We believe he made his way into the forest. I'm going in to find him, retrieve the scrolls and find the Armor of Peace."

"Oh, is that all?" He sarcastically waved his hand toward the Rubicon. "Please don't let me stop you."

"Like you could stop us." Upal said with a strong sense of loathing.

"The Old Lady's been murdered?" Crawford had suddenly registered some of her words. He sighed, "I saw her once, when I was about five years old. I remember she came to our house and spoke with my father. She said something that seemed to upset him, then she was gone. Everything else I know about her are the stories that travel through the gates. That's so sad." He paused for a moment and tried to grasp the situation.

"I don't get it." He reluctantly continued. "If her murderer went into the Rubicon, then he's pronounced judgement against himself already. Why go after him?"

"I just told you." Lashra continued. "We need to retrieve the scrolls and find The Armor. The Old Lady told us it was our destiny to do so."

"Your destiny? To go into the Rubicon?" he said, obviously questioning her sanity. "You don't actually believe in the Scrolls of Tralatitious? I mean I'm sure they're physically real, but… what I mean is some people believe the stories in them, but they're mostly uneducated or they're zealots and scammers."

Upal spoke up, "We are the chosen ones. We must fulfill the prophecy."

Lashra pulled out the scroll The Old Lady had tucked away in her pocket. "She left us with this final message."

As I lay down and send you out, to do the things untried,
The forest greets you and protects, 'til deeper you abide.
The one who fell, seeks his revenge, your plans he will curtail.
The armor sought will be revived, but not with friendship frail.

*****

Evil is rising and darkness is growing
The blood he desires is no longer flowing
The sword he is raising to quench his thirst
The one he feeds, let him be cursed.

Enter the forest to change the story
One heart is darkened by their own glory
When it is darkest a light shines through
Peace will return like the morning dew.

Crawford looked at the three in absolute disbelief. "Hey Ray do you believe this?" he sarcastically questioned the raven sitting on his shoulder. "We were prophesied to do this. Enter the forest, story, glory. Have another brew, I'm missing a screw."

He backed away, turned and started making his way back to his shelter. He looked back, "That's my prophecy." He laughed uncomfortably.

"Come on Ray let's go into the Rubicon and DIE! Are you guys kidding me? That scroll is meaningless, you could come up with a thousand renderings for that thing." he said as he continued walking.

Lashra was filled with all kinds of feelings and emotions and maybe she was just looking for a reason to explode and release some of her tension. She ran to Crawford, grabbed his shirt and spun him around and let him have it.

"You don't know anything. We've been sent on a mission by The Old Lady, a fact you can't grasp or even begin to understand."

He tried to turn away, but she held him in place. "We've known The Old Lady all our lives. I spent all my days with her, she taught me everything she knew." Lashra was getting emotional and her anger boiled up.

"She told us the night before she was viciously murdered that our lives were about to change in monumental ways!" She was crying and yelling at Crawford. "I held her in my arms while she died! I heard her final words."

Preet moved in and took her into his arms.

She was sobbing, "I held her while she died. She's dead Preet, she's dead. Gone forever. Why did he do it?"

Preet was overwhelmed. Tears were streaming down his face. "I don't know. I don't know anything anymore."

Lashra pulled herself away from Preet, wiped her eyes and took a deep breath. "We need to get moving. We need to enter the Rubicon before dark."

Crawford was moved by her words and tears, but tried not to show it. "Ok, well, have fun."

Lashra began to walk toward the forest by herself.

"What are you doing out here anyways?" Upal asked the boy.

"Just hanging out." was his response.

"The words of a coward." Upal remarked. "It's more likely that you're hiding out." He turned and walked away.

Preet and Upal picked up their pace and the threesome was restored. Crawford watched for a moment and then decided to follow from a distance. He wanted to see with his own eyes if anyone could actually be so unhinged as to enter the Rubicon willingly.

When the three were a few feet away from the entrance, he shouted, "So, you're actually going to go into the Rubicon?"

"Yes we are, coward." said Upal.

"It's pronounced Crawford, by the way." he shouted back. "But I'll let it slide this time, because you don't seem to be too right in the head."

Upal had a slight quiver in voice, "Whatever Crow-boy." He was feeling anxious about the whole situation. Were they actually going to do this?

She took a few steps forward, leaving the boys behind. "We've already lost so much time and sunlight. We need to get in before dark." Lashra was trying to sound brave, but inside she was also questioning the validity of her decision.

Crawford was standing only a few feet behind them. "If it's daylight you're worried about, I wouldn't worry too much." he said. "Rumour has it that light does not penetrate the Rubicon and I think you guys are in the dark on just about everything right now."

With small short steps they made their way down the tunnel and closer to the unspeakable point of no return. The sound of the birds, the wind, the whole of the outside world sounded muffled.

They paused but a few inches away from the threshold. All the stories and myths were swirling around in their heads.

I can just reach out and touch it, thought Lashra. She slowly reached her hand out. She wondered how close she

99

could get before… Startled, she jumped back. Ray had flown and landed between her and the Rubicon. Flapping and beating his wings he squawked and cawed his warnings.

"Hey, Ray, come back here!" The raven ignored the call. He stayed close to the girl, trying to scare her back. Her heart was pounding. She was second guessing her decision to have come this close. "Bird?" she asked. "Are you saying we shouldn't go in?"

The boys stepped forward to join her side. They stood looking and peering into the place from where no one ever returns.

Preet and Upal reached out and took hold of Lashra's hands.

"We go in together?" she said.

The two replied, "Together."

All at once the sky grew dark and the sun vanished, all five turned back to see the opening of the tunnel entrance.

Preet nervously squeezed Lashra's hand, "Is that a good sign or a bad sign?"

"I'm not sure." As she spoke the words, an endless resounding blast of thunder bellowed its admonishment; Lashra leaned heavily forward and pulled the two boys in with her, while secretly hoping that they would hold her back.

The final sound they heard from the outside world was the roaring voice that seemed to echo from the thunder. A warning. The warning. "No one ever returns!" The words penetrated and cut through them as they pierced the chasm of the known to the unimaginable.

Crawford watched as the strangers vanished before his eyes. He shouted over the sound of the roaring rumble, "No one ever returns!"

Silence. "Where did they go?" he asked Ray.

"Looks like danger. Pretty girl. Looks like danger." was the raven's response. The bird moved closer to the entrance trying to entice his friend.

Crawford's heart was pounding, aching with fear. "I can't." He fell to his knees. "I can't Ray."

And so the raven chased after them, leaving Crawford behind.

Chapter 24 Into The Rubicon

Lashra closed her eyes as she stepped into the Rubicon. She held Preet's and Upal's hands tightly. An indescribable energy surrounded her as she left everything she knew behind.

She kept her eyes closed and stood silently still, holding tightly to her friends' hands. The sounds of singing and chirping filled the air. A distant pecking sound echoed through the woods.

Lashra slowly opened her eyes, but nothing seemed to register except soft low waves of the murmuring wind rustling through the branches and leaves.

She closed her eyes again for a moment and focused on an ambient sound. She was sure she could hear the sound of flowing water all around her. Then other sounds filled her senses, tweet, tweet, peck, peck, caw, caw, shhhh whispered the wind. It was amazing.

She took in a deep breath and her senses were filled with the smell of mint and lavender. She opened her eyes once more; this time her sight was filled with lush green foliage topped with an endless array of purple petals.

The sun shone through the trees. A short distance away she could see a path of light. It was filled with every shade of green imaginable. A bird, two birds in the distance. Butterflies and small insects fluttered to and fro. The sun's light was dancing like fire on one long strand of a spee's web that floated on the air high above the ground.

Another flying creature, swooped gracefully down then ascended back up again. Darkness and light, shadows and highlights. The depths and layers, everything was magnificent. She stood frozen and hypnotized by the majestic beauty.

She stayed silent and thought about the dreams and stories of what the Rubicon would be. It was not so.

She looked to one side and took in the scent of the damp earth and moss. Her eye caught the bright orange color of a large Pendulous Pudding Mushroom that had nestled into the limb of a tree. It made her smile.

Lashra's attention turned to the mesmerizing song of a Cerulean Crooner that was sitting on a rock a few feet away; a tiny bird covered with every shade of blue imaginable.

Turning in another direction she was instantly absorbed by the freshness of a pine covered path and the enticing smell of life producing trees. It was as if she could smell the aromas of the color green.

The wind's movement was an orchestra of sound that filled the air. She wondered how all these acoustics had not been audible a few inches outside the forest.

Then it struck her. She turned to see the outside world, it was gone. The Eternal she knew had somehow vanished. It was as if the Rubicon had enveloped her and taken her away from everyone and everything.

Her eyes closed as she paused for a moment to absorb the whirlwind of emotions. It was too much to bear. Tears began to well up and in an instant she was weeping uncontrollably.

Preet said nothing; he reached out and put his arms around her and pulled her in close. She took in a deep breath. In a strange kind of way, she felt at peace, like she belonged. As though her whole life was meant for this moment.

"I never could have imagined beauty like this. I was expecting death and destruction." she whispered. "I don't understand." she continued. "How could everyone have been so wrong?"

She moved away from Preet and cautiously proceeded deeper into the woods. Upal and Preet followed close behind. Upal was about to suggest trying to leave, when all of a sudden... *Caw! Caw!* The sound of the raven jolted them and made them jump.

They all looked up to see a raven on a branch above their heads.

Preet shook his fist at the raven. "Are you Crowboy's foul bird?" he demanded.

And as if to answer Preet's question, the bird called out "Pretty Girl". He dived down barely missing Preet's big hair. Preet jumped back in fear and tumbled to the ground as Ray set himself down at Lashra's feet.

"I guess that answers your question." said Upal.

Preet was peeved at the bird's attempt at attacking him again. "Lash, shew him away. We don't need him attacking us again." He gave the bird a dirty look. "He's been enough trouble already, and if there's one thing we don't need it's more trouble."

They were startled by an unnatural cracking sound coming from the trees behind them. They turned only to see trees.

Chapter 25 Apologize

Crawford poked his head out from behind a large tree. "Of course he's my fowl bird. What other kind of bird could he be?"

Lashra chuckled to herself. Preet and Upal gave her a look.

"What?" she questioned their look. "That could be funny."

"Really?" Preet interjected. "Why wasn't it funny when I said it a few seconds ago?"

"Delivery." replied Crawford.

Lashra chuckled again. "Ok, that *was* funny."

Upal let out a disgruntled sigh. "Did you not just hear Preet say we didn't need any more trouble? What are you doing here?" He took a few steps forward placing himself squarely in Crawford's path.

Crawford gestured to Lashra. "Somebody's got to protect the lady."

Upal shoved him hard enough to make him take a step backward. "I'm here to protect the lady!" he pointed to himself. "I mean Lashra."

"Hello? I'm right here." she said as she waived her arms in the air. "Am I invisible?"

She walked up to Crawford, looked him square in the eyes and punched him in the stomach, knocking the wind out of him. "Still think I'm the one who needs protecting?"

Upal watched in dismay. "Why is she flirting with that jerk?" he mumbled under his breath.

"I am so sick of everyone..." she raised her fingers up making quote signs "... trying to protect me." She shook her fist in the air, then pointed to the ground in anger. "You can all stay right here and leave me alone. I don't need anyone to protect me from anything." Her face was as red as her hair and the wrath she displayed was real. "If I need protection from anything or anyone it's from you three."

Upal and Crawford took a step backward in fear.

Preet moved closer to his sister. "Don't group me in with those two." he said.

"What? You're worse than Upal!" she yelled at him.

"Ya, worse that me." echoed Upal pointing at himself. Then he turned his finger onto Preet. "How exactly is he worse than me?"

Preet was in shock. "What? Who? How? Oh please tell me how am I worse than Oop?" he exclaimed.

"He's waiting…" Upal muttered with apprehension.

Her ire boiled over onto her brother. "I don't need you to be constantly looking over my shoulder Preet. I don't need your consent and/or your constant protection from every imaginary thing your brain comes up with. I can make my own decisions and protect myself."

"I don't do that?" he said defensively.

"Really? If a boy even looks at me, you get upset and start puffing out your chest."

"That's true man," said Upal nodding in agreement with Lashra. "Wait, what boys?"

"Shut it Upal you're no better." she growled.

Preet tried to shift some of Lashra's wrath in Upal's direction. "Ya Upal, shut it, you're no better." he repeated.

"Ahhh!" she lamented.

"You're my little sister, it's my job."

"Really Preet, it's your job to protect me from everything?" She took a step toward Crawford who instinctively jumped back a little. She grasped his face in her two hands and laid a long and gargantuan kiss right on his lips.

"There you go Preet, protect me from that."

Crawford stood there motionless, in what could only be described as, a state of shock. The awkward smile that covered his face disappeared suddenly when he noticed smoke coming from Preet's ears.

"Uh, I didn't do anything you know. I was just standing there, uh, here, then her lips, her soft lips..." The thought lulled him into a joyful revery, but quickly ended when Preet instinctively took a step toward his soon to be victim.

Crawford pleaded with Lashra, "Tell your giant, it's not my fault. I didn't do anything."

Meanwhile lost in the background, Upal gaped at the situation. Confused, stunned, appalled, horrified, shocked, confused, jealous, depressed and once again confused.

"Why would she kiss the new guy?" he mouthed quietly.

Lashra made her way to Upal and grabbed hold of him. She took hold of his face. Upal smiled as he closed his eyes. Just as she was about to plant a kiss on him...

Preet cried out. "Stop it! I get it, I get it."

Upal opened his eyes. "No!" A look of shock covered his face. "I mean, no... look at him he doesn't get it."

Lashra let go of Upal and turned toward Preet.

Upal was disappointed to say the least and reached out and grabbed Lashra's arm. She turned and glared at the hand that had a hold of her. She made reprimanding eye contact with its owner. Upal gently released his squeeze on her arm, and with an apologetic tone said, "He doesn't get it." He lifted his shoulders in a pitiful way. "You need to teach him a lesson."

"Nice try." she said as she made her way to Preet's side.

Upal glared at Crawford.

Preet conceded to his sister, "Sorry Lash, I didn't realize I was so possessive."

He looked over at his friend, and quickly recognized that Upal was less than happy with the lip-locking tragedy he had just witnessed.

He reached over and shook his friend. "Oop, tell her you're sorry."

"I'm sorry? *I'm* sorry?" he uttered out.

Lashra turned to Crawford and raised her eyebrows.

"I'm sorry that I'm living in a bush next to the Rubicon. I'm sorry I followed Ray into the Rubicon. I'm sorry I tried to help you earlier. I am sorry I ever made contact with you." He was raising his voice uncontrollably. "And I never thought I'd say this to a beautiful girl." Crawford stepped backward as Preet took a step closer to him. "But I'm sorry you kissed me." He raised his hands and shook his head.

Lashra nodded her head forgivingly. "Apology accepted." she said to Crawford demurely.

He reached out his forearm and called his bird. The raven landed on his arm. "Look what you got us into, you stupid bird."

"Looks like trouble." Ray answered.

Lashra composed herself and assumed responsibility for their situation. "Ok, now that we all agree with me, we can set this matter aside. We have more pressing things to do." She looked around. "Which way should we go?"

"This way." she heard the three call out. When she turned around she could see they were all pointing in a different direction.

Listen, we're going to need some kind of shelter for the night and if we hope to survive for any length of time here we'll need to find that water."

She looked around. Where to go? She thought to herself. She searched for clues that might guide her. She soon realized she had no idea what to do or where to go.

The boys were still traumatized by her recent outburst and individually decided not to question anything she said, at least for the rest of the day.

"Crawford, can Ray find water? Anything really, a river, a stream, a lake?"

"Are you kidding? If I tell him to pick up gold, he doesn't pick up silver." he said proudly.

Upal nudged Preet, "What is this guy talking about?"

Crawford continued, "He's probably the smartest one here. Ray, go find us some water."

The bird left his arm and headed up over the forest. He began to circle and then started heading in a direction they argued might be North. I hope you're right buddy, thought Crawford.

"Ok, well, let's go." he added, trying to sound confident.

Their pace was quite slow. Every sound or breaking twig made them all nervously stop and listen. Who knew what kind of dark dreadful creatures lurked behind every tree.

Preet felt somewhat vulnerable. He figured his size made him a target for any kind of hell that might be hiding in these haunted woods. His stature did nothing to quench his sense of fear.

Lashra led the pack followed by Crawford then Upal. Preet trailed in the back. He began to feel slightly nauseous, then a little dizzy. A chill went through his whole body, then came the sweats.

Being at the back of the line no one noticed his discomfort. His heart started to race and he felt himself getting increasingly woozy. All of a sudden he could not take in a deep breath and he started panting. He fell over onto a branch and his weight snapped it from the tree.

They all turned to see what had caused the sound. Lashra saw her brother struggling for air. She turned and made her way past Crawford and Upal and went to his side.

"What's wrong Preet?"

He tried but he couldn't make a sound.

Chapter 26 Panic

Preet was kneeling heavily against a tree. He gripped his chest with his trembling hands. His heart rate had accelerated to the point where he imagined it would soon explode. Feelings of derealization filled him. He was rapidly losing control of his senses.

Lashra could see he was struggling for air. She moved in closer and held his head against her chest, patting him on the head trying to calm him.

"I can't breathe. I feel like I'm choking. I need to get out of here, I can't stay here…. I'm gonna die… I can't breathe. I'm gonna die."

"It's ok," she said gently. "We'll be fine as long as we're together." She held him tightly and did her best to keep herself calm.

"I don't think I can do this." Tears were rolling down his face. "I don't want to die."

She brought her body down to match his and looked into his eyes. "I can't do this without you Preet" she whispered, "Who's going to protect me from Upal?" She gave him a quirky smile. "We can do anything if we're together, you know that."

Crawford stared at the two. He was baffled and disheartened. "We're ten feet into this thing and the giant is having a panic attack? Are you kidding me? What's gonna happen if we come face to face with something other than trees?"

"His name is *Preet. Crawford.*"

He looked to the sky and raised his hands and cried out "Ray! What did you get me into?"

Upal chimed in. "You can leave anytime you want Crowboy. We don't need you."

"Whatever, I'm better off alone, then with a bunch of wuds." he said. He turned and walked in the opposite direction, hoping it was toward the exit out of this bewitched timberland.

Lashra paid no means to Crawford. Her only focus was to help bring Preet back down. It seemed to be working.

Only a few feet away and Crawford was already regretting his words and his actions. In truth he was not sure where he was going. He took several steps into some soft shrubs and long grass. "The exit is just over here." he told himself.

He turned to look back and was surprised by how quickly the others had disappeared from view. Finding himself alone, everything seemed to become much more quiet. The crackling leaves and broken branches beneath his feet resonated throughout his body.

Strangely the outside world had been swallowed up by trees and poisonous shrubs. In some mystical way he had traveled much deeper into the forest than the few minutes he had walked.

"What's going on, what kind of trickery is this?" he questioned out loud.

The ground cover was becoming impenetrable. With sweat pouring down his brow, he made great efforts to conquer the vegitation. Clawing and climbing his way through and over brushwood and thicket. Within a few minutes he found himself toiling and plodding a dense almost unimaginable growth.

He thought he saw light from the outside world. A spark of hope filled him. At that moment, from out of nowhere a root jumped up to trip him. He fell face first onto the ground landing at the base of the tree that tripped him.

He tried to work his way up, however his feet were tangled in vines that covered the forest floor around the tree. He pulled and worked one leg free and as he devoted himself to freeing his other leg, he came face to face with a horrifying sight.

He was strongly rattled and was thrown back with fear. His one leg still stuck in the vines he shook and pulled with all his might to free it. Regardless of his efforts he stayed stuck and his eyes remained glued to the nightmare before him.

He tried to call for help, although nothing came out. He continued his fight with the woods, only to become more entangled in a wiry brush. It was as if it was trying to hold him down. The harder he tried to free himself the more difficult it became. His eyes were locked onto a stranger's eyes.

A face at the base of the tree, in the tree. A mask frozen in time, crying, calling out for help. A visage filled with distress, suffering and torment. "It's me. That's *my* face!" he cried out.

He tried to move. His hands were now being gripped by the vines. Horror-struck and scared to death, he attempted another call for help.

"Somebody help me! Help! I'm sorry, don't leave me! Help me!"

Could anyone even hear him? Had they already made their way without him? He was quickly losing strength and energy, his heart was pounding a thousand beats a second, his chest could no longer expand to take in a deep breath, he could no longer gather enough air or strength to yell for help.

The trees were moving closer and leaning down toward him. The floor of the forest was gripping him tightly. They would over take him at any moment. It was so real, but it couldn't be. He must be in his bed having a nightmare. Then again what if it was, what if this was to be his fate?

Crawford could see nothing but a trapped soul, locked in the tree. In a near state of madness he heard the voice of the underbrush crinkling into his ear. "No one ever returns."

There was no way out, the feeling of hopelessness engulfed him. He tried one last time to yell for help, but not a sound could he make.

Exasperated, he closed his eyes so as not to witness the final calamity that would soon overtake him.

He surrendered himself to the woods as one final thought passed through his mind. I'm alone.

Chapter 27 All For One

"You're not alone." Crawford thought he heard a voice say.

He opened his eyes to see Preet standing above him. His large hand wrapped itself in Crawford's shirt. He grunted loudly as he pulled Crawford's haggard body from the brush. He stood him erect. Preet looked into his eyes, reached around and wrapped his giant arm around Crawford's shoulder and pulled him tightly into a monstrously affectionate hug and in a calm and gentle way he comforted him.

"It's ok. I'm right here with you."

Crawford bowed his head in shame and relief. He thanked the boy by name.

"Are we done here girls?" Upal shook his head in disbelief.

They congregated together and Lashra spoke up. She insisted that if they were going to weather these storms and the calamities that were sure to arise, they had to work as one. She emphasized that if any of them should have a moment of weakness, the others needed to rise up to the occasion and be strong.

She looked each one in the eye and in a motherly tone said, "We're all going to falter at some point. The Old Lady used to say, "The bonds of friendship can be broken by the point of a finger."

"I pray that in my time of weakness," she placed her hand onto her heart, "that you will do for me, what I am prepared to do for you."

She reached her arms out and they settled into a tight ring, arms around one another.

Upal spoke at a volume that was almost inaudible, "We need each other whether we like it or not. Our alliance needs to be real and unbreakable."

"Unbreakable." they repeated.

Lashra once again took the lead and started walking back leading them west. Crawford followed as Upal and Preet walked the back of the line together. Preet, speaking loud enough to make sure Crawford heard his words, quipped, "Hey Oop, I hope I didn't look as foolish as Crowboy did when I was having my panic attack?"

Crawford turned to look at Preet who had a big smile on his face. "It could have happened to anyone, big guy." He smiled back and turned around. The smile left his face immediately. What did I get myself into? he thought to himself.

They continued on their walk, occasionally looking up to see if Ray was still guiding them. He would disappear and return about every fifteen minutes.

"There he is." Crawford stated, "We must be getting close."

"What makes you say that?" asked Lashra.

"He hasn't left; he's just circling us now."

"Of course. I should have noticed that." Lashra quietly noted to herself.

"I wonder how much farther we have to go?" she queried audibly.

Crawford stopped for a moment and pointed to the sky. "You see the way he's circling? He makes ten circles then flies straight, he then returns and does another ten. Every circle represents 10 minutes of time. So he's saying we've got about 100 minutes before we reach our destination." He was so proud of himself. "It's a fact that ravens much like crows fly instinctively towards water." He nodded in agreement with himself.

"Wow!" Preet remarked, "You can tell all that just by watching him fly? That's pretty cool."

"Wait a second…" interjected Lashra, "Crows instinctively fly for land not water. You just made all that up didn't you?"

"Maybe." chuckled Crawford.

Lashra wasn't sure if she was amused or not. "Ha, ha. So, as I was saying, I wonder how far he's taking us."

Sunlight was fading fast and they all felt a sense of urgency to find a place to stop for the night. They spent long moments walking in silence, each praying and hoping that Ray wasn't leading them down the wrong path. But what choice did they really have? The day was quickly coming to an end and none of them wanted to spend the night in the middle of this thickly wooded forest, surrounded by who knows what, and not being able to see, *who knows what.* Not that they *wanted* to see, who knows what.

Lashra suddenly realized she was hungry and was wondering why no one had complained yet.

"I wonder if there's anything to eat in here?" cried Preet from the back field.

She smiled to herself. She was just about to say something when she looked down and saw a cluster of mushrooms. "Hey guys, look at this."

Preet ran up and looked at where she was pointing, "This is awesome! They look just like Spems."

"What are Spems?" Crawford asked.

Preet gave him a strange look. "Where have you been your whole life? Spems are a delicious treat. The Old Lady handed these out all the time." He was so excited at the prospect of food. "I love these things."

Lashra bent down to pick one up; she took a closer look, "Yup, they sure are." she said enthusiastically. "She grew these S.P.E.M.S. in her garden all year round." She took a bite and smiled, "Oh my, they never tasted this good."

The three all reached down and started picking, eating and harvesting. Crawford stood by and watched.

Lashra reached out to Crawford and held one for him to take. "You seriously have never eaten a Spem? Try it."

He took it... looked at it... and carefully placed it in his mouth. His grimace soon turned to joy. "These things are delicious." he smiled.

They used their shirts as baskets and filled them up. There were hundreds of them. Preet took one and was about to put it in his mouth when, "Hey Lash, take a look at this one it has a small Spee on it. Oh, it looks like it's pooping into the spem. Oh well, that one's no good." He threw it over his shoulder and reached down for more.

Lashra broke into an uncontrollable giggle. "Have you never been in The Old Lady's garden before? Those are Spee-shrooms. That's what they do. They find these Burnt-Umber mushrooms," she picked one and held it up close to his face for him to see, "then they poop in them. When the mushroom is full, the universe appears on it." (They said this because tiny yellow dots would appear on the S.P.E.M.s and with the burnt-umber color as a background they looked like little stars.) "That's how you know they're ripe and ready to eat."

Preet was starting to worry that she might be telling the truth. "You're making that up. How do you know that?"

"Preet, they're called S.P.E.M.s. It stands for Spee Poop Edible Mushrooms. What did you think it stood for?"

"I don't know? Special People Eat Mushrooms?"

"Ya, you're special all right." quipped Upal.

"What did you think I did every day at that house? I read all the books, helped her in the garden, I learned everything I could. All you, Upal and Saudj ever did was play and eat. So ya, that creamy filling you love so much?" She continued with a massive grin on her face.

"No way?!" Preet started to gag. "I'm gonna puke."

Upal reached into Preet's stash, "Hey, if you're not going to eat them I will."

"Keep your hands to yourself, these are mine."

"It's Spee poop." Upal said disgustedly.

"If it tastes good, I'll just eat it and won't ask anymore questions about anything." Preet replied with a sour look. "Hey Lash, they are safe to eat right?

"Of course they are." she said as she put one in her mouth.

"Ok then, let's eat up." Upal attempted to grab a few more from Preet's supply and was shoved away. "You don't want to eat Spee poop do you Preet?"

"I'm hungry." he said disappointedly. "I'll eat just about anything right now."

They carried what they could and continued to walk. Suddenly Crawford realized Ray had disappeared. Crawford looked around and tried to listen for his call.

"Quiet for a second! Ray's gone." He craned his neck forward, "Listen. I can hear something."

Chapter 28 Good Night

"It's water! He did it!" shouted Lashra. They followed the sound. There he was, that wonderful, magical raven, drinking from a stream. "Good boy Ray."

"Ya! Good boy Ray!" they all shouted and cheered. They made their way to the water and started guzzling, slurping and lapping as much of the miracle liquid as they could take in. It was like they had never tasted water before.

"This is so good, we couldn't have done this without you Crawford." Lashra noted.

Upal was annoyed by Lashra's apparent gushing. "The bird did all the work you know. We should be thanking the bird."

"You're so right Upal." She walked over to the bird, who happened to be standing next to Crawford. She bowed down next to him and pet the bird. "Good boy Ray. He's such a good boy isn't he, Crawford?"

"Yes he is." Crawford agreed with a sly smile.

"That's not what I meant." mumbled Upal.

Filled with water and having rested a few minutes, Lashra got up and started collecting branches, shrubs and any dry kindling she could find. "We should try and start a fire to keep warm and have light overnight. We'll need some twine and a bendable peace of wood to create a bow drill."

"What *don't* you know how to do?" Upal flattered her, trying to shift her attention.

Preet sighed heavily and shook his head disapprovingly.

After thirty minutes of hard work, she was able to exclaim, "We have fire!"

They all praised her skills and joined into the building of the fire by adding branches and twigs, little by little so they wouldn't put it out, as they were so gratefully told multiple times by the fire starter.

Within a few hours they were exhausted to the point of sleep. They laid on the ground searching the stars.

"Looks like it should be a full moon in the next day or two." she said casually.

For a moment she almost felt like they were all just camping. Friends out for a few days of relaxation under the stars. Somehow, the Rubicon didn't seem that dangerous. Of course she wasn't about to take any liberties. As they climbed deeper into the night Lashra suggested taking turns keeping guard.

"We should change every two hours, that way we all get some sleep."

They drew straws to see who would go first, Upal drew the short straw. "I'll wake you up in about two hours, he said to Preet. "Better get some shut eye, it'll come quick."

"What are we going to do tomorrow?" Upal questioned out loud.

"Where do we start looking?" Lashra asked.

"Do you even know what you're looking for?" asked Crawford.

"Are we only going to be eating Spems from now on?" Preet was hungry again.

"Ray's pretty good at finding nuts and berries." Crawford answered him.

"I wonder if Saudj actually did come in here by himself." asked Upal.

Crawford observed his surroundings and thought about the Scrolls of Tralatitious. Could they be real? I mean, he knew they were real, but were they true? Well, he was in here now and it seemed pretty real to him at this moment.

What about this crazy bunch of kids? Were they willing to lose their lives *in case* the scrolls were true? It didn't make sense. Although he had to admit that he really didn't really know much if anything about the scrolls. He thought about his school lessons on the subject.

"I probably should have listened." he muttered out.

"Did you say something?" asked Preet.

"Oh, I was just thinking about the scrolls and how I should've listened more attentively when I was being taught about them." Crawford continued to stare at the night sky. "You guys were lucky to know and learn things from The Old Lady. I know almost nothing about the Scrolls of Tralatitious." he said disappointedly.

Lashra didn't take her eyes off the stars. "You're not the only one. Those two dum-dums never listened either. Most people think they're just fables. Sure there are a lot of symbolistic tales in the scrolls, but I don't think it's all allegory. Look at Saudj and his family. They seemed to believe that the scrolls were used to enslave people."

Crawford was lying a few feet away from Preet and gave him a nudge with his foot. "Hey Preet, what do you know about the scrolls?"

"Uh? Plenty…" He rolled over away from Crawford. "But uh… ask Lashra, she knows everything." He whispered, "Just know that once she starts she doesn't stop." He rolled over pretending to fall into a deep sleep.

Crawford asked Lashra to tell him what she knew. And, she did. She went on and on and on.

"…As time went on, the stories surrounding Demorg's departure grew. Some said that he and his people found their way through the forest. On arrival, he enslaved all those who were not from the Sword Tribe and made them build a tower, his tower. When it was done Demorg had all the slaves killed. He and his clan feasted on their bodies for seven years."

Crawford was slowly starting to fade. "Then what happened?" he yawned. Boy, Preet wasn't kidding, he thought to himself.

121

Excited that she'd found someone who was interested, she continued. "He then began to wipe out his own clan. Slowly and meticulously killing everyone and absorbing their life force. It was whispered that the tower was surrounded by a moat filled with the blood of his victims and that it fed all kinds of wild grotesque animals and insects."

Lashra stopped for a moment and yawned, "Crawford, are you still listening?"

He was almost asleep and wasn't really listening. "Insects." he murmured.

Her eyes were getting heavy, but always one to maximize an opportunity to share her knowledge, she continued. "So, from that day forward, anyone who broke the law and was found guilty of an unforgivable crime was banished to the Rubicon Forest."

Tired, she rolled over and made herself more comfortable. "If you were unlucky enough to be relegated to the Rubicon, it was believed that its magic would lead you to Demorg's tower, where he would without a doubt devour you, absorb your life force and add your blood to the deep wide trench that surrounded the walls of his dreaded black tower." She closed her eyes and stopped for a moment.

"He's sleeping." said Upal. "He's been out for a while."

"Oh? Well..." She was nodding off. "...I was talking... to all of you. Maybe *you* learned something tonight?" she said as she fell asleep.

"I learned something all right." He looked up from his resting place and could see that all three were now sound alseep.

Chapter 29 Exhausted

Saudj flew back and slammed against the wall. His face was burning and pounding.

"Husband!" Saudj's mother cried out. "The boy's only five years old." His mother came to his rescue.

"The boy needs to learn." He was drunk. "And I'll be the one to teach him good."

Saudj had dropped a small bottle of Glumvyn on his way up from the storage room and his father's discontentment was swift and clear. "That's four weeks of hard work in that bottle!" he yelled at his wife.

"He fell on the stairs. He's got such little legs and he works hard for you." She defended her son.

"Fine!" he cried out. "*You* take the rest of his beating and let him be a coward." She bowed her head submissively.

Saudj watched as his mother took two hard slaps to the face. His punishment.

He jumped awake from his nightmare. It was still dark. How long had he been sleeping? He picked himself up off the ground. He was cold and shivering. He walked to the nearest tree, sat tightly against it and clutched his knees, in hopes of warming up.

His mind drifted back to his nightmare.

His father was a mean unforgiving man, angry at the world. Husband, as his wife called him, was a proud member of the sword tribe. His family's heritage could be traced back for generations in the westgate and he made sure everyone knew it.

He was feared by his neighbours and trusted by no one. He made his money making and selling his Glumvyn to the poorest and loneliest. Saudj was responsible for being the runner. That is, running up and down from the storage room with bottles of the toxic liquid.

For some reason he remembered one lonely, homeless man in particular. He was one of the many people who made their way around the city collecting apple cores and peelings and would bring them to his father.

"What do you have there old man?" his father grabbed the bag of scraps from the man.

He looked inside and dropped it on the scale… "Looks like it's just under two pounds." He'd usually grunt the numbers disapprovingly.

The pitiful old man looked up, "Well that's ten pounds for the week master, I'll take my bottle."

"Saudj, go fetch me a small bottle."

Saudj remembered running down the stairs and grabbing a small bottle of Glumvyn. He was always careful not to slip and fall on the damp stairs. He handed it to his father who gave it to the old man.

That one little bottle would make the old man's day. Glumvyn was a sour apple wine his father made. It was easy, it was cheap and had an alcohol content that was high enough to start a fire. The potent formula had put many homeless men to sleep for the night. It was also used for cooking, cleaning and even as a cure for many ails.

"Boy!" the sound of his father screaming echoed through the forest; Saudj jumped awake once more. He sat alone staring into the darkness and waited for the sun to rise.

Saudj started walking at first light. Where was he going? What was he doing? He didn't have an answer to either question. So he walked and walked and as the sun faded he found himself a small hole in a tree where he tucked himself in and away for the night.

The young girl found a patrolman. He was a well known figure around the neighbourhood. He himself had been placed in the care of The Old Lady as a child. This honest, caring man was now on his way to The Old Lady's house.

"The Old Lady's been murdered?" said the Patrolman. He didn't believe it. He couldn't believe it. "How is that possible? Why would any living soul want to harm the woman who loved everyone as if they were her own? She survived over eight hundred years, and this is her end?"

The Patrolman was frantic. "Who is this Saudj? His punishment will be so severe that it will be remembered for as long as *she* was alive." He spoke with a passion that was uncommon to see in a patrolman.

He looked down at the child who was pulling his arm to speed him up. The man was surprised by the calmness shown by the child. She was delivering horrific news with hardly an emotion to show for it.

Of course... he explained to himself, the child was in a deep state of shock. "What will we do without her?" He spoke the words under his breath.

The Old Lady's abode was surrounded by dozens and dozens of people. The children of the house did their best to keep people from getting too close.

They arrived at the home. He gasped. She hadn't been discovered for an hour yet and it seemed the entirety of the West Gate was making its way to her house. Rumours were already circulating that councillors from the other gates were well aware of the situation and were on their way to confirm the unimaginable.

No one had dared to enter her house. Citizens circled and surrounded the area. It was a dense assortment of every kind of person. Some in the multitude were wailing and crying out. The Patrolman had never witnessed such a scene. His heart was heavy; he could not recall a time he'd been more saddened or shaken.

The young girl and the Patrolman fought their way through the crowd. He stood at the entrance door trying to prepare himself for what he was about to see. "Stay here." he told the children. He opened the door and entered the home. "What the…" He could not find the words to finish his dreaded thought.

He pulled the blood soaked blanket off the giant corps and wept.

Chapter 31 Sweety-Pie

Having the last watch allowed Lashra to have a long and unbroken sleep during the night. By the time her watch ended she was wide awake and was glad to see the sunrise. The forest's understory started filling with long shadows and color was slowly returning to the enchanted woods.

Lashra casually rose from her wooden seat. She made her way around the perimeter of the camp collecting bits of fuel for the fire. Kneeling before the fire she warmed herself. She watched the three boys sleep and wondered what this day would bring. She was about to find out.

She got up and walked around nudging the boys with her foot. "Wake up, wake up, wake up you lazy boys." she sang.

Upal rolled over onto his back and placed his arm over his eyes to block the light from the morning sun. "Shut up." he tried unsuccessfully to garble out of his still sleeping lips. His arm blocked out just enough light to let him fall back asleep.

Preet slowly opened his eyes. For one brief moment he'd forgotten all about the events of the last couple of days. "What? What's going on?" he asked himself drowsily.

"Uhhh, we're actually here?" he squeaked out of a yawn.

He stretched his arms out and sluggishly made his way to his feet. He embarked on a voyage that took him around and around the fire pit. "Yaaawn." Still half asleep he stretched his arms out and purposefully thwacked the back of his sister's head while making his rounds.

"Hey!" she squealed as she shoved him out of the way.

"Oh, sorry. I didn't see you there." He smiled to himself.

He shook and jiggled his king-sized trunks, "Come on legs, wake up."

Crawford had not heard a thing. His second wake up call came in the form of a raven pecking at his head.

"Stop it." He tried to wave the bird away.

"Stop it." Another wave.

"Stop it." he uttered, as he failed a third consecutive time to halt the bird's jabbings.

"S-T-O-P I said!" This only encouraged another peck.

"Ray." He paused for dramatic effect. "One more time and I'm having you for breakfast."

His comment made Lashra smile. She gave the bird an appreciative thumbs up.

"Good boy Ray." she giggled.

"I'll help you eat that black bird for breakfast." Preet voiced half jokingly.

Ray turned and cawed angrily at Preet. He took flight and charged the juggernaut, coming down toward his head.

"Are you crazy?" Preet shouted, flaring his arms in all directions.

The ebony devil made a second raid at the terrified boy. Preet recoiled and leaped out of the way, tripping over the rocks that surrounded the fire pit falling onto the last smoldering remains of the fire.

He quickly rolled out of the firepit and alarmingly launched into an effort of brushing embers from his smoking clothes.

"I swear Ray," he said under his breath. "Come at me one more time and I *will* eat you!" he bleated discreetly and somewhat cautiously as he finished dusting off his pants. "Foul bird."

"Looks like danger." Ray gurgled out from a branch above Preet's head. He spread out his wings and came down for another close landing. This time it was a peaceful descent next to Lashra. "Pretty Girl." he whistled.

"You are so cute." she replied as she bent down to pet him.

Preet cussed him out. "Don't trust him Lash."

Lashra simply smiled. Thanks to the bird's buffoonery, at least Preet was fully awake, she thought to herself.

Preet made his way to Upal and sat on a log next to his *trustworthy* friend. He stared at him in amazement.

"There is no way he slept through all that." he stated.

"Oop?" he fired out. "Yup, still sleeping."

He moved closer to Upal. "I know what will get him up." He leaned down slowly and with his best Lashra impression, whispered into his friend's ear. "Wake up sweetie pie, it's morning time." He gave him a gentle kiss on the cheek.

Upal's face instinctively smiled as his semi-dreamland fantasies played out in his mind. He could see Lashra next to him, speaking softly and lovingly. He slowly opened his eyes only to come face to face with Preet. His whole body jerked, he shoved Preet away and jumped to his feet.

"What's wrong with you?" exclaimed Upal.

Preet laughed uncontrollably, "I knew you'd like my kisses." he said trying his best to give him a smoldering look.

Upal was flustered. "What's wrong with your face?" he exclaimed. "Are you having a stroke?" Preet's wake up call had whipped him into a small frenzy. "You should never mess with a man when he's sleeping."

Preet was in stitches, "I was just helping Lash out, she was too busy to do it herself." He was still cracking up from his little joke.

Still agitated, Upal growled, "You could have been *severely* hurt pulling a stunt like that." He was trying his best to regain some sense of composure.

Crawford snickered, "Oh yeah, killer instincts there sweetie pie." he said as he poked the fire.

Preet added, "I had no choice. She's been trying to wake you for hours."

Upal looked to the sky, "Hours? The sun is barely up."

He turned his attention to Lashra and Crawford, "What happened to one for all and all for one? I need to be able to trust you guys."

Upal was flailing his arms around still feeling defensive. "No more stupid pranks or else I'll have my revenge when you guys fall asleep."

In a sinister voice he uttered, "Oh, it'll be just as funny. Oh yes, *just*, as funny."

Lashra attempted to ease his mind. "Upal, take a deep breath. The boys have only been up a few minutes and for what it's worth, I think it's kind of sweet that you believe I'd actually kiss you."

"Whatever." he said in a lackadaisical fashion. "You could do worse." he continued as he gave a passing glance at Crawford.

She playfully smiled at him, "You really think so? *Sweetie Pie.*"

"Ok, ha-ha-ha, we've all had our fun. You do realize however that I am now seriously traumatized by this whole thing. Who knows if I'll ever sleep or trust any of you ever again." he said with a dispelling groan.

"I'm sure you'll get over it, Upal." She winked at him, "After all you're a big boy."

"Not really though." Crawford muttered under his breath.

Upal stood close to the fire in saturnine silence.

Preet and Crawford spent time drying their dew-filled clothes while Preet went on about the boredom of the previous night's watch.

Lashra debated with herself about what course of action should be taken. Upal pouted in silence. Preet continued to rant about his night and Crawford seemed to be lost deep in thought.

"Well?" Lashra questioned them. "What should we do?"

"What should we do about what?" Upal sulked.

Befuddled, she exclaimed, "About what? About anything. About everything, about this... this... this whole situation we find ourselves in." Her voice rose in volume. "What *other about* could I possibly be talking about?" She massaged her temples in frustration.

Preet looked over at Upal, who was still moping. He turned his attention to Crawford who was daydreaming. "Hey, Crowboy?" he gently elbowed him, "Are you pouting too? 'Cause I think Upal's already got that one locked in."

Crawford was still lost. Preet reached over again. This time he gave him a little shove, "Wake up!"

"What? Sorry..." he said and immediately returned to his daydream.

Lashra walked up to him and put her hand on his shoulder asking sympathetically. "Are you ok Crawford?"

He sighed heavily. "I don't know."

"Do you want to talk about it?" she asked supportively.

"I was just remembering an uncanny dream I had last night. I forgot it until just a minute ago." His face was pale and his eyes distant as he uttered in a disquieting tone, "Now it's haunting me."

Chapter 32 Crawford's Dream

Lashra was instantly curious by Crawford's air of mysteriousness. "Please tell us." Her eyes grew at the idea of hearing a strange and veiled nightmare. "Well, let's have it. I'm sure we could all use a little weirdness to start our day." She half laughed and smiled at Upal.

"I remember so little of it. It's just a feeling, a fog."

"Try." she encouraged him.

"I was walking through the forest collecting firewood and I could hear these birds chirping. No. They were singing. No that's not it either. Maybe they were plucking?"

Upal was quickly getting annoyed, "Making sounds. We get it." He waved his hand as if to encourage him forward. "Please, move on."

"You're right, short person." Crawford mockingly nodded. "They were making sounds." Crawford's eyes turned to the sky as if he was searching deep within his mind to remember. "It was like a lyre harp. You know, the kind played by the Romas in the marketplace of the Crossroads."

"Crossroads? Music? Harps?" Upal grimaced. "Where are you from?"

Preet commented, "Doesn't sound like *our* part of the West Gate.

"Yes, that's right." Lashra said sarcastically. "This rich Westender, has nothing better to do then to die in a forbidden forest with three dystopian kids from the bad part of the Gate."

The three burst out laughing.

Crawford grimaced and laughed uncomfortably trying to mask his anxiety. He quickly continued his story to avoid the subject of his home. "Anyhow... it sounded like they were calling my name. It was mesmerizing and I couldn't stop myself from walking toward it. I kept moving forward, collecting branches and twigs as I went along." He stopped speaking for an instant, as if he'd just remembered something. "That's right." he said to himself. "All of a sudden I was in a clear patch and there was this old witch sitting on a throne made of stone. Behind her was a long path of gold, it seemed to be endless, only stopping at the horizon."

He closed his eyes, trying hard to remember. "She sat in her chair kneading dough. She looked up and saw me staring at her. She froze me with her gaze. She pointed to an old wood stove with a tea kettle on it.

"Come, sit with me; we'll have tea." she said. "She pointed to her stove and spoke to me in rhyme."

"My children left to gather wood,
but now I fear they've gone for good.
My fire now is sure to die,
unless on you I can rely."

Crawford continued, "She went on talking in rhymes, she asked me if she could purchase the pile of wood I'd collected, but then goes on to tell me she has no money, even though I can clearly see that there's an endless stream of gold behind her. So I asked her, and this is where it gets weird,"

Preet nudged Upal and whispered, "So none of this was weird before this point in the story?"

"I started talking in rhymes."

"If not a purchase with gold of pleasure,
You pay me how, if not with treasure?"

Crawford raised his hands and shook his head nonchalantly. "Blah blah blah, she tells me that she has a much more precious gift that she's willing to exchange for the wood. I

133

ask what it is, she tells me it's a poem, I say, "A poem?" she says not just any poem, this one is a map to an ancient treasure. Blah blah blah, I gave her the firewood and then I woke up."

"Wait a minute" Upal chimed in. "You're going to take a poem instead of insisting on the gold? What's wrong with you?"

"It was a dream and I... anyways, I said yes... BECAUSE I like helping little old ladies in distress. Is that ok with you, Upal?"

"That was truly gracious of you Crawford." Lashra said as she poked Upal. "Don't you think that's gracious of him Sweetie Pie?"

Upal grunted his displeasure.

"That's it." said Crawford.

"No, no, go on, we're sorry. We won't interrupt you anymore." she asserted.

"No, I mean, that's it. That's the whole dream."

"She never told you the poem?" interjected Preet.

Crawford stood there for a moment looking around, up and down, side to side, searching his mind, trying to remember. "Oh ya... she did tell me." His eyes widened. "She asked me to put the wood in the stove. When I was done, I closed the door and she gently patted me on the head with her staff. She sang the poem to me and the next thing I know Ray is pecking at my head."

"Do you remember the poem?" asked Lashra.

"Hmm." He thought for a moment. "I think I do?" He recited the words.

"Lore and vision are guides for your duty.
Anguish will grip you with sunlight's beauty.
Safely guided through the golden path,
Hunting widows, you'll escape their wrath.
Retrieve from the rock what is incomplete,
Altruism bestows you death's defeat."

"What does altruism mean?" asked Preet.

Lashra and Crawford responded in unison. "It means putting others before yourself."

Upon hearing their chorus, Upal rolled his eyes.

Lashra finished her sentence. "Or being selfless." She paused in thought for a moment. "Hmmm? There is something familiar about that poem. I just can't put my finger on it."

Upal stared at her in disbelief and a smattering of incredulity as he haphazardly blasted out a "You're kidding right?"

She was surprised by his outburst and confused by his demeanor.

Upal returned her glance with a suspicious and disbelieving glare. "Really? Something familiar? Like you didn't notice that the first letter of every sentence spells your name?"

Upal turned his attention to Crawford. "When did you find time to sleep?"

"What?" Crawford was confused.

"I can only imagine it took you all night to come up with that load of gewgaw."

With his most sarcastic Crowboy impression he pressed on. "I had a dream, an old witch on a throne. I need some attention, someone throw me a bone. I make up stuff while I'm up keeping guard, 'cause my name is Crowboy, I'm a dim-witted..."

"UPAL!" Lashra cried out, "Don't you *dare* finish that sentence."

"What?" he paused. "I was going to say," he paused again, "ahh, dim-witted dumb-dumb."

Displeased, he aired his grievances. "I don't think you really appreciate what's going on here." He made his way to Lashra and placed his hand on her shoulder. "We don't have time for this gewgaw."

Lashra gently removed Upals' hand from her shoulder. "Ok..." she started.

"Buggeration!" Crawford exclaimed. "You're right. It does spell Lashra."

Preet needed clarification and questioned Crawford, "I have two questions. One. It took you that long to get there? Two. You didn't make all that stuff up?"

A look of excitement covered his face. Preet excitedly pointed at Crawford. "Oh, oh, oh... oh dude... It's a message from The Old Lady." He grabbed Crawford by the shoulders shaking him briskly. "The Old Lady is the witch in your dream. She's trying to help by sending us a...a..."

"A delusion?" Upal chimed in capriciously.

"No, the other thing." Preet said.

Lashra stood in silent astonishment. Was it possible that Crawford had actually received a vision from the great beyond? Why Crawford? He wasn't part of their inner circle. He hadn't even met The Old Lady. He'd only seen her once as a toddler.

Be that as it may, what if The Old Lady really was sending them messages? If so, what were they supposed to do with it? How could they decipher the communication? What did all this mean? If The Old Lady was trying to correspond with the kids, wouldn't she have given them clues to solving this riddle? What did all this mean?

"Do you remember anything else about the dream?" Lashra asked him.

He shook his head. "No." He thought for a second. "That's everything."

She thought out loud and paced the area. "There's got to be more to it. You're forgetting something. If this dream of yours is a message…"

Preet interjected, "What do you mean if?" He raised his hands and looked at her in disbelief, "She's literally spelling out your name."

"*Lore and visions are guides to your duty?*" Lashra had memorized the poem having only heard it the one time.

"Well, Crawford's dream must be the vision." She continued talking out loud to no one and everyone. "What's the duty?" murmured Lashra as she continued meandering around the camp. "Find the armor and find The One." she answered her own question.

Upal begrudgingly spoke up. "I'm not saying that I'm buying into this dream thing… but, *Retrieving from rock what is incomplete,*" that could be referring to the armor. After all, it has multiple pieces and each one is in a different location." He couldn't admit it outright, but his gut was telling him that the dream was probably real.

"What else could we be retrieving? Unfortunately, the whole *rock* thing has me confused. Hmmm. I hate to admit it, but this dream might actually be a real something."

Upal bounced his shoulder off Preet. "I think this place might be making me smarter. Is that possible?"

"Sorry Oop, no magic's that powerful." Preet said as he slapped his short friend on the back.

"Hey guys, I think we're forgetting the most important verse." Crawford seemed a little uneasy. "*Altruism bestows you, death's defeat*? What the heck does that mean? According to this we have to figure out a way to defeat DEATH? Maybe we should focus on that part of the riddle."

Upal interrupted Crawford before he could finish his thought. "I really think we need to focus on getting a move on. We're not gonna find anything standing around here." he said.

"But where?" queried Crawford.

Lashra gave the area the once-over. "If this secret message is truly from The Old Lady, I'm sure she'd expect us to continue with our mission."

Upal turned to Crawford, "What was the first couple of lines again?"

Crawford thought for a second. "*Lore and vision are guides to your duty. Anguish will grip you with sunlight's beauty*."

"I think we figured out that our duty is to find the armor, but what does "*Anguish will grip you with sunlight's beauty* mean?" asked Upal.

"I don't know." Preet uttered. "But it doesn't sound good."

Lashra kicked sand into the fire pit. "I never thought I'd say this, but Upal may be right, perhaps we should just start moving.

She put her hand on Crawford's shoulder and moved him to the front of the pack. "I think you should take the lead. After all, it was your vision and I think you may have forgotten some of it. Maybe you'll see something, anything that looks remotely familiar. Something will trigger your memory."

Crawford looked around at his environment. Nothing came across as being familiar. No, not one thing. He decided to go with his gut. "In my dream I was in the forest carrying firewood. I think we should go this way." He pointed into the thickly wooded forest. He sent his bird to go look for food as they pushed and fought their way through the greenery.

"I sure hope he gets a poem dream about me." said Preet. "Why does Lashra get everything?"

"You know I can hear you right?" shouted Crawford from the front.

They laughed.

The grass was long and filled with condensation, the warmth of the sun's beams had limited access to the floor due to the full and lush canopy overhead. Within just a few minutes of walking their shoes were sodden, their pants dank and their shirts clammy and smothering. The ever rising temperature was only made worse by the humidity. It didn't take long for them to start complaining about the mugginess and crying out for the sun's rays to take it all away.

"My kingdom for dryness!" cried out Crawford.

"His kingdom." Upal muttered to himself, "Who does this guy think he is?"

Then, as if by magic the late morning sun appeared through a few thinning spots in the canopy. In a short time they found themselves wandering through a giant open field, where the bright sun vanquished any and all traces of moisture. Therefore they had nothing to complain about, except for the excruciating dry heat.

The last few spems disappeared as quickly as the moisture. Preet's complaints of hunger returned just as swiftly.

Crawford kept an eye on the sky, hoping by some miracle that Ray would bring them some kind of food or lead them to a patch of edible goods.

Every once in a while Lashra would stop to study flowers and shrubs to see if they were edible. Sometimes she'd stop just to satisfy her curiosity. The drawings in the botany books she'd read during her time with The Old Lady had nothing on the real thing. She'd seen and read about many of these plants but never thought she'd experience touching and smelling so many of them.

They walked quietly for a while. A few more hours passed and they found themselves back in the thick bushes of the forest. Slowly plodding through.

Crawford was desperate to break the silence. "Tell me more about the scrolls Lashra. Last thing I remember you saying was that Demorg eats everyone who comes in here."

"Well that's what people thought happened. Since no one ever returns, no one really knows." Lashra was happy to talk to anyone who would listen to the stories. So, she went on, and on.

"With Demorg gone, struggles and conflicts between the remaining three armored tribes began. Beria, the leader of the Shield Tribe, went mad trying to gain power and Kingship. He believed that he was *The One, The Shepherd*, that could protect the people from the coming onslaught that would surely be ushered in by Demorg. His words and actions began to worry and strain relationships with other tribes. His demands to be the sole possessor of the remaining pieces of armor were worrying. One night on the way home from a briefing, he was assassinated."

"Bravo of the Casques, believed it was his duty to resolve and administer judgment against Beria and the precarious situation he was creating. When the Shield tribe discovered Bravo's involvement in the murder of their leader, an insurrection ensued. Those who supported Beria, planned to assassinate Bravo in an act of retribution in an operation they called the *Rebellion of Sagacity*. Their success created a series of vendettas."

"As these battles were occuring between the Casques and the Shields, there were also struggles for leadership within each of those tribes. Multiple splinter groups began to form. For three and a half years there were battles both within and between them. A time known as *The Cabal*."

Lashra tapped Crawford on the shoulder. "You are paying attention right?"

"Ya Crowboy, there will be a test." Preet chimed in.

"Sagacity. Cabal. Got it." Crawford nodded.

Lashra was happy to continue. "The Cabal was a period of murders, suicides, assassinations and massacres. As quickly as a faction was formed it would fall. Discord and distrust were rampant amongst all."

"For all their fighting and disagreements, the leaderless Casques and Shields were united on one matter; the belief that Purdah of the Breast Plate Tribe could not be trusted. Her constant contact with both sides began to be worrisome. It was understood by both the Shields and the Casques that it would be prudent to remove Purdah from her position permanently, lest she join forces with one side and give them the advantage."

"Hearsay and rumours were spread throughout the two rudderless tribes. Confabulation took hold of the masses. Every type of paranoia and hysteria was put on display, and it became natural for them to behave in these manners."

"*She's preparing to take control of us!*" they cried out from the windows.

"In the gin mill they would whisper, *she's plotting to hold all the pieces of the armor. She will be invincible if she's not stopped.*"

"On city streets they cried, *Purdah will kill us all!*"

"An agreement was reached by the two distrustful groups during a covert merger. They agreed that on the morning of her 75th Jubilee, she would be purged."

"Hold on!" Crawford interrupted her. "It looks like another open field just ahead."

"Thank goodness." cried Preet. "I have more branches and leaves sticking out of my hair than most of these trees. Hey Lash? Can you help clean me up?"

Crawford picked up his pace and left the others behind. He stopped in his tracks when he arrived at its entrance. His eyes bulged out at the sight of what was in the field. His jaw dropped, as he took in the scene. His heart raced and the feeling of panic rose within him.

"This can't be good." he said to himself.

Chapter 34 The Orchard Of Souls

"What's going on up there?" shouted Preet from the back. "Did you guys find food? Are you eating right now?"

Upal passed by Lashra to get a look. He caught up to Crawford who was motionless. He gazed past the entrance into the field; it was an ominous orchard-like setting. Only this one was not filled with trees containing fruit.

"I've seen this before." Crawford said, thinking he was speaking to Lashra.

"In your dream?" questioned Upal.

He was surprised to see Upal next to him. "Yes and no. Remember yesterday when I tried to leave the Rubicon? I saw something very similar. It was enough to make me scream and freak out."

"*Anguish will grip you with sunlight's beauty.*" he quoted his dream, unaware he was even speaking.

"Move out of the way, I want to see." Upal squeezed his way past Crawford to get a better look. As he did he tripped and tumbled almost landing into the troubling plantation. He slowly looked up and his curious facial expression soon turned grave. His eyes and brain struggled to assimilate what he was seeing. "This is wrong… so very wrong."

Lashra reached the two, and when she peered into the open field she was instantly taken back to The Old Lady's house. She could hear her voice as clear as a bell.

"There is rumoured to be a place they call, *The Orchard of Souls.*" Lashra remembered how The Old Lady's description of this place affected her. The words alone had the power to torment her soul, freeze her blood and cause her hair to stand on end.

A chill went up her spine, as she heard the woman's gravely voice narrate what her eyes were seeing.

"Hundreds, maybe thousands of trees. Each tree's roots weaved in such a fashion as to create a chain that winds itself around a giant stone. A stone that is used to hold its victim in place."

"Pray child that your eyes never have to fall upon this orchard filled with nightmarish individuals who wrap themselves in thorn bushes. Their long slender branches laced with prickles and barbs."

All four were mesmerized by the creaturesque beings. Their heads were covered with light greenish-brown moss-filled dreadlocks that swayed in the breeze. Each one was uniquely ornamented with a sublimely radiant arrangement of large colorful blossoms. Yellow golden flowers that twisted and curled. Others were filled with explosive spurs and outlined with a sharp blood red contour. Still others had round glowing moon-like colored flora that wrapped their necks like a choker.

There was an endless multitude of petals and polychromatic blossoms that encircled the sorrowful prisoners. The calm cool breeze that made its way through the grave, gave them the appearance of being adorned with long flowing garments.

Lashra stood gazing at the sardonic tableau. A beautiful orchard filled with tortured souls. Their screams of agony were surely caused by the giant thorn spike piercing their thorax and exiting out of their backs.

Every life, every being, every soul, bent over backwards, arms reaching out to the sky, crying out for mercy to the heavens above, tormented and cursed forever.

She was fixated on the scene. She wondered if these trees were really living people at one time? Was that even possible? She knew one thing; simply looking into it filled her with a sense of foreboding. She was sure that entrance into the orchard would bring death.

"Do you think this is the *sunlight's beauty* we're looking for?" Upal whispered to Crowboy.

"I hope not." Lashra responded.

Preet was eyeing the ground hoping to find something to eat; his eye caught a movement just inside the orchard.

"Oop! Your leg. Get out of there!"

Chapter 35 Trapped

Upal happened to have stepped into the Orchard of Souls. The vines that covered its floor were making their way around his foot. Hearing Preet's cry, he instinctively tried to lift his leg. It was too late. A blood curdling feeling filled him.

Feeling his foot rise, the vines spontaneously clutched onto him and climbed his calf in an effort to stop him from fleeing. He pulled harder. He was shocked. The vines tightened their grip on his leg. A look of terror covered his face. Crawford instinctively reached out and grabbed hold of his arms.

"Pull!" Upal's plea was filled with spine-chilling fear.

Crawford pulled, using all his strength. He cried out, "Preet! Help me!"

Preet lunged in and the two teens did their best to pull Upal out. The harder they pulled, the more the vines worked at imprisoning him.

Lashra dropped to the ground and launched herself into a pecking frenzy. She picked up a rock and attacked the flourishing creeping plant with precision. She banged and smashed at the vines trying to cut them or at least make them loosen their grip.

Terror-stricken and about to become fully hysterical, Upal continued to cry out. "Pull harder! Harder!"

Preet and Crawford pulled their hardest. Ray joined Lashra in a continuous attack on the stalks. After a frenzied battle, the three boys flew backward onto the ground piling up on top of each other. Upal was free.

They broke into awkward laughter as they released their joy and relief of escape.

"That was insane." Upal said as he rolled over and sat up against a tree. "Thanks. I thought I was going to become one of those things."

Upal kept his eyes on the orchard. "I vote we go around."

"You think so?" the rest said unanimously.

They sat taking a long hard look at the orchard. It was immense. They deliberated on the subject for over an hour, concluding in the end that it could take days to walk around the orchard, if they could even manage the task at all.

They moved back a few more feet to sit in the shade of the trees and to be farther away from the bedeviled gateway.

"Anguish will grip you, with sunlight's beauty." Crawford said.

"Ya so?" Upal retorted.

A light went on in Lashra's mind. She looked over to Crawford who gave her a knowing nod.

"Anguish will grip you with daylight's beauty." she repeated Crawford's words. "Well, if those trees don't look anguished, I don't know what does and they're being gripped by those beautiful thorny vines that almost got you Upal." She stopped for a moment, trying to take in her own words. "I think if we try to cross at night, we may be ok. I'm hoping that the grip is only in the daytime." She didn't seem very convinced about what she was saying.

"That's what I was thinking too," said Crawford.

A green-eyed Upal mumbled under his breath, "That's what I was thinking too."

With a trembling voice Preet questioned the decision, "Oh, great, not only are we going to walk into a nightmare, we're going to do it at night?"

They spent the rest of the day sitting around waiting until nightfall. Not much was said most of the day. Preet might have mentioned his hunger once or twice and wondered where Ray and his hopeful bounty of food could be. Other than that...

147

they rested in the coolness of the shade and were caressed by the breeze making its way across the open field.

At one point or another they'd all fallen asleep.

"Looks like maybe another hour or so before it's dark." Lashra commented.

Crawford nudged Lashra. "Hey, were they successful?"

The expression on her face was that of confusion.

He explained. "At purging Purdah? You said the leaders were in agreement, *she will be purged.*"

That was enough encouragement for her to continue the story and so she went on and on.

"True to their words, Purdah was ambushed on the way to her jubilee. All of her entourage was killed. Her body was found slashed in two. The tribes were so deep in their misgivings they believed (falsely of course), that by slicing her body in half, her followers would believe that Demorg was somehow responsible for her death. Of course Purdah's tribe did not even consider this."

"All three tribes were now without leaders. Panic was followed by hysteria, which soon led to lawlessness. Leaders rose and fell by the week and sometimes the hour. Eventually this led to chaos, disorder and anarchy. All three armored tribes were at war. Their efforts to build truces between one another, to try and gain an advantage in their power and position, fell apart before the ink could dry."

"The feuds brought with them famine and an immeasurable amount of gore. Blood flowing from the city at its most wicked period of combat was said to be waste high. This contaminated the water supply and made it undrinkable. By the end, the food supply was almost non existent and most went days without eating. It became so bad that people were eating clay to stop the pain of hunger."

"The smell of death that came with the decomposing bodies was atrocious. The dead bodies were mounting and streets were overflowing. Left with no choice, the living dumped

148

corpses and those who were effectively dead, over the city walls. Many of the carcasses were bloated from the long warm days and when the bodies were moved they often forced out gasses and human waste. Some had laid in the streets so long that their bodies were split and they were filled with pests."

"There were so many bodies that it seemed there were more slain than alive. In the dark of night when the fighting slowed, you could hear the moaning and whimpering of those not fully deceased. It seemed to many that the sound of battle during the day was easier to bear. After three and a half months of combat, and extinguishing thirty percent of the population, an armistice created by the Longevity Tribe was subscribed to by all."

"A pestilence soon followed as a result of the interment. Four more years of slow, painful and feverish death followed. Another forty percent of the population was lost. The survivors had no other option but to help each other out. It wasn't enough not to be at war. If they didn't ban together soon, not one soul would be left alive."

"During the war, the Longevity tribe was a neutral party. However, neutrality was not an option during the time of the plague. They were hit the hardest. When the blight finally ended, only twelve could be accounted for."

"The night of the last death from the plague, all twelve members of the Longevity tribe received the same prophetic dream."

"I hate to interrupt all your talking Lash... but I think it may be time to go?" (Preet didn't really hate interrupting her.)

Lashra stood up and took in a deep breath. "Well, at least we'll have the moon to light our way." As she spoke a thick patch of clouds rolled in to darken an already dark night.

"Great." they said in unison.

"I'll go in first." Upal said, trying his best to garner up the courage to actually follow through with his offer. I really have to think before I speak, he thought to himself.

149

Lashra spoke up quickly. "No. We should all go together."

Upal made his way to the entrance. "We can't *all* go in together, not this time anyhow. The Old Lady needs us to finish this and we can't do that if we're all frozen in time. If I walk straight ahead it should only take about twenty minutes to cross the field. I'll yell for you to come when I'm safely on the other side."

"What if you don't make it?" Preet accidentally uttered.

They all turned to face him and if he could've seen their faces in the dark, he would surely have died that instant.

"*Well*," Upal groaned out. "I guess you guys will have to figure another way around."

"Lashra," Upal took her hand, "If I don't make it, I want you to find someone else." He was trying to let her know his feelings, but even at a time like this he was too afraid to let his guard down and chose instead to jape. He did it mostly to stave off the fear of what he was about to do.

She gave him a quirky half smile and quietly told him, "I don't think it will be that difficult." Then her tone became serious. She put her hand on his shoulder, "Are you sure you want to do this alone?"

Upal was having a hard time breathing. "No." he said.

He turned and stepped in.

Chapter 36 The Other Side

He placed his foot on the ground and waited two seconds. Then he attempted to raise it off the ground. He was successful. "So far so good." he whispered back.

Upal's pace was slow at first. Everytime he was able to raise his foot freely and take another step his heart lightened.

Preet shouted lightly, "Are you ok?"

"I'm good." he responded.

The night was dark, still and silent. As he moved deeper into the Orchard of Souls he began hearing long-drawn-out sounds. They were low and inarticulate. He was sure it was the sounds of tortured souls and internal suffering. It made his skin vibrate.

The trees are moaning, the trees are making those sounds, he thought. His mind flashed back to a childhood nursery rhyme.

Full moon, full moon, makes you groan.
You're trapped there with thousands, yet you're all alone.
No one can save you from the full moon night;
The Rubicon has you and it's holding tight.

Full moon, full moon, your wide awake,
Living your nightmare with no chance of escape.
No one can save you from the full moon night;
The Rubicon has you and it's holding tight.

The childhood poem gave him the willies. He picked up his pace. He did everything he could to not get too close to any of the tortured trees. Less than a minute in and he was already second guessing his choice to go first.

"Are you still ok Oop?" he heard Preet call out.

Upal stopped, looked back and could no longer see his friends.

"Oop?" he heard his friend cry out again.

"Yes, I'm fine. Can someone please shut him up?" Upal didn't mean what he said. He was actually grateful to be hearing something other than moans and groans.

Without warning something touched his leg. He pulled up quickly. He was still free. He wasn't taking any more chances. In an instant he found himself running. He did his best to keep his feet off the ground, as much as humanly possible.

After *much less* than twenty minutes, he found he'd made it through. He was fully charged. He noted that his heart was racing faster and pounding harder than the first time he met Lashra (and that was saying something).

Taking no chances, he walked a little farther into the woods looking for a safe zone. Looking back he started laughing and jumping with joy. He fist-pumped the air and gave himself a few high fives.

"Way to go Upal, you did it!" he shouted.

He yelled across the valley and they responded with a loud and encouraging yelp.

Chapter 37 Luciferins

Before long they had all gathered safely on the other side. Then as if to mock them, the clouds thinned out and the moon returned to light the night. They shook their heads in disbelief.

As they moved away from the plagued orchard and deeper into the woods, it suddenly began flickering. Tiny dancing sparkles were appearing here and there. The farther they traveled into the woods, the closer they got to the twinkling star-like objects. It seemed as though the lights were getting bigger, burning brighter and increasing in numbers.

Lashra was leading the way. "Look at all those blinking lights." she whispered. "I need to get closer."

"Uh, no Lash, you don't *need* to get closer." Preet said as he grabbed her sleeve to slow her down.

She stopped. "Oh my." she mouthed silently.

She gazed at a long line of bright fluorescent yellow and purple flowers that were lighting up the area as bright as day. As she moved in closer she realized it wasn't the flowers that were glowing, it was the insects inside them. She carefully guided the troop down an open path. As they made their way through, the insects would glow with an intense brilliance and as they passed them, the lights would die down to a faint haze.

"Luciferin Apoidea" she whispered to Preet. "These insects only feed and pollinate at night." Lashra lit up almost as bright as a Luciferin as she continued educating her brother and anyone else who would listen. "When they sense any kind of danger, they light up. That's how they warn the others."

Preet was feeling quite nervous. "I've got an idea. How about you get us out of here, then you can share the copious amounts of knowledge you have on these things."

She looked at her brother and smiled. "First of all, *copious*? Way to use that word. Secondly, we'll be perfectly safe as long as we leave them alone and don't give them reason to attack us."

"Attack us?" Crawford whispered from the back.

Hearing those words, Preet tried to shield himself behind his sister.

"Stay calm." she said. "You'll probably survive one sting, but never two. The first sting is a warning that comes with a mild venom. It's the second sting you really need to worry about. That one comes with a toxic poison."

She looked over at Upal and Preet and repeated the particulars.

"Ya, ya, one bite good two bites bad, we get it Lashra, you're smart and you'll outlive us all." Upal quipped as he waved his hand in a disconcerting manner. He too was distracted and astounded by the massive species.

She paused once more to absorb the marvel she was witnessing. "This bright light shines from such a cute and delicate, yet dangerous insect. I just want to take one in my arms and squeeze it." she whispered.

Each one was about the size of Lashra's hand. They had beautiful translucent oversized wings. Their fluffy, furry bodies were constantly changing from crimson to gold to a fluorescent green. Four black hairy legs were outlined with bright green razor sharp lines. They had two large black eyes on each side of their head and four tiny eyes at the top. She spotted one whose legs were filled with pollen to take back to its hive.

They continued their journey away from the notorious orchard, their path being constantly lit up by the Luciferins. Even though they were surrounded by a swarm of large hazardous insects, somehow it gave them a sense of safety. She decided it would be safer to camp in an area *sans* deadly giant light-up bees. So, they kept walking.

Crawford had been uneasy ever since Ray had left his side earlier in the day. He rarely slept a night without him. He worried the bird might have been captured or killed by some wild animal. "I hope Ray's ok out there on his own." he said in an apprehensive and fatherly tone.

Preet reassured him while he looked around almost expecting the raven to attack at any moment. "I wouldn't worry about him."

They stopped in an open patch. The moon was high above their heads.

"I think we should stop here for the night." Lashra said.

Still unnerved by the day's and night's events they sat back to back in a small circle. The sun would be making its appearance shortly and it couldn't happen soon enough for Preet.

Crawford was still worrying about Ray's situation. "I'll stay awake for the first watch. I can't sleep right now."

"I think this place is trying to starve me to death." Preet said in the middle of a yawn.

"Tomorrow is the third day." said Lashra.

They silently nodded to themselves. They all knew that Lashra's reference to the third day meant it would be a day of mourning in the city. The day of The Old Lady's funeral. No one said another word.

Soon everyone but Crawford was sleeping. A half hour into his duty, alertness failed him and he too was fast asleep. The crack of dawn brought with it a soft glowing orange light and the patter of crackling twigs. Floating on the morning breeze were the echoes of approaching croaks, gurgles and shrills.

It seemed nothing could wake them from their lifeless coma.

Chapter 38 The Third Day

It was daybreak on the third day. The gentle morning light calmly bathed the sea of people standing quietly, shoulder to shoulder.

The Old Lady's requiem was about to begin. It was common knowledge that anyone who could attend her funeral would. For the first time in more than a thousand years, Eternal held its farewell outside the city walls of the West Gate. The crowd was so large that it seemed to flow into the Rubicon.

The Leader of the South Gate stood on top of the West Gate's wall, next to its entrance. As he looked over the scene, he struggled to grasp the number of mourners. Did Eternal truly have this many citizens? he questioned himself. He began to speak; his voice echoed down the valley and over the crowd.

"Is there anyone alive who was not in one way or another impacted, influenced or inspired, by The Old Lady?" He bowed his head in silence as the words lingered in the air.

"You could have been two hundred years old, and to her..." the auritor took a deep breath and looked to the sky, trying unsuccessfully to compose himself.

He choked out his words "... and to her, you were but an infant." His lips quivered and he paused again.

"There is not a soul dead or alive, not one, who in the last eight hundred years did not want *and need*, to know her." The eulogist was speaking from the heart and the crowd held on to his every word.

"Everyone... As parents, we made a commitment to our children before they were even born that in their lifetime they should be blessed by the presence of this woman. Not only our children, but their children's children."

He went on to exalt and honor her life for over an hour.

A second leader took the stage and continued the dirge.

"She was charming, mysterious and mythical. She was more than just her years, more than her stories, more than her patience, more than anything we could ever fathom. She was a combination of all the love and goodness that, in our deepest hearts, we desire to be. She was all that we dreamed her to be. She was a healer, a teacher, a peacemaker; she was... *our* Keeper."

Another Leader rose to the stage. "She's been gone for only three days and in that time, a thousand years has passed us by. Our world has lost a shining star, but let me assure all of you who stand here with me today, that her light will shimmer and sparkle for an eternity. We will tell her story to our children and they will tell it to their children. Yes, it will be an everlasting, imperishable story for all ages. She will live forever and the brightness that was her life will shine; it will never be diminished."

With those words the lamenting crowd broke into applause and cheers.

The leader of the West Gate was the last to speak. "As we leave here today, may we go in peace. If you can, live as she would have lived, love as she would have loved."

Each of the Gates' Leaders had given their parting words and tributes in remembrance of The Old Lady. A decision was reached the previous night by all the Gates' Leaders and Councillors, that the day of her departure would be considered an annual holiday.

Every year, on the *Day of The Old Lady*, all the doors to all the gates would remain open from sunrise to sunset and travel to the Crossroads by all the gates would be encouraged. It would be a day of kind words, sharing of drinks and food. It would be a celebration of her life, the sharing of stories, a day of love, laughter and cheer. On that day no one would be a stranger.

He dismissed the crowd with these words. "We will be a symbol of her light, she will shine through us. We will honor her memory with the same compassion she showed the world."

Chapter 39 Timmy

As the people made their way back to their respective Gates, some chose to travel outside the city walls, while others *risked* passage through the West Gate. No one living there could ever recall seeing so many people in their part of the city.

Meanwhile... Timmy and the four children had spent the previous days alone at The Old Lady's house. A few of the West Gate councillors debated what to do with them. They took care not to dishonor The Old Lady's memory.

An agreement was reached by the council. They realized the children had been through unimaginable grief and enough heartache to last a lifetime. They consented to keeping the five together, if it was at all possible.

They charged a patrolman (who had once been in the care of The Old Lady) with the duty of stopping by the house frequently to monitor the children.

Timmy had spent the last two days asking everyone he met if they had seen Lashra. He'd grown attached to her over the years. She was as much a staple in his life as The Old Lady.

The ten year old would tell him over and over, "Lashra went to the Rubicon with Preet and Upal to find Saudj."

"Timmy should go to find Lashra" he would answer.

"No, Timmy can't find Lashra." she said sadly. "Lashra is gone forever."

"Timmy will find Lashra." he said with a smile.

On the day of the funeral the crowds filled the streets. Timmy was unfazed by the amount of people. He did as he always did. He left the house, got on his trike and made his way around the West Gate and continued to question everyone he made contact with.

The kids spent the day doing their daily tasks out of habit. They still were not able to fully grasp the recent events. Everyt ime they looked at The Old Lady's empty chair, they simply imagined her working in the garden or out doing one of her daily chores. The world they lived in was a hard one and they weren't new to the concept of death. If it were not for the fact that The Old Lady was an everlasting fixture in their world, maybe then they could have registered their loss, but their minds simply rejected the notion of a world without her. And so they went about their daily lives doing what was expected of them.

"Where's Timmy?" asked the ten year old.

"I don't see his trike. He must be out questioning everyone about the whereabouts of Lashra." one of the four said casually.

"He'll be back for his noon time snack, he never forgets that." said a third.

It was high noon and Timmy hadn't returned. By two o'clock the kids began to worry. The eldest of the children began to ponder Timmy's obsession about finding Lashra.

"Timmy's not back for his snack? That never happens." she stated as a fact.

"He's been yammering about Lashra nonstop over the last two days. NO!?" she yelled out.

"He wouldn't have?" Panic filled her voice. "Oh my!" Do you think Timmy's heading to the Rubicon to find her?"

Chapter 40 Lashra Gone

The young girl threw the door open and headed toward the main gate with three bodies trying to catch up to her. As they made their way through the crowded streets they asked anyone and everyone if they had seen Timmy. No one had.

When they arrived at the gate, the ten year old told the youngest to find the Patrolman, tell him that Timmy had headed to the Rubicon and that she had gone after him. The three ran toward the forest as fast as their feet could take them. The adrenaline coursing through their body made it almost impossible to control their feet. They made it in record time.

The ten year old cried out, "Look, it's Timmy's trike!" It was at the edge of the path leading to the entrance.

Apprehensive, the kids moved closer. Filled with unspeakable fear, they guardedly made their way down the long path.

"There he is." the eldest quietly pointed into the deep.

Timmy was standing at the very edge; his feet were only inches away from the entrance. He was yelling into the woods. The children stopped a fair ways away. They didn't want to unwittingly startle him into the Rubicon.

The ten year old whispered, "I think he's calling out for Lashra."

Carefully they continued their approach. The ten year old was right. She could just make out what he was saying.

"Lashra! Lashra, Timmy will come find you."

Even with his slowness of mind, Timmy understood the dangers of the Rubicon.

The children gently pushed forward, inching their way in closer and closer to the young man.

The ten year old gently called out his name. "Timmy? Timmy?"

He turned his head to see them. "Timmy will find Lashra." he said.

"Lashra is gone Timmy." The child took on a motherly tone. "Timmy should bring his trike home and have snacks."

"Timmy needs to find Lashra."

He reached into his pocket, took out his locket and kissed it. He safely put it back into his pocket. He looked back once again. The children carefully moved in closer.

"Timmy will find Lashra." As he spoke the words and without looking he took one small step forward and vanished forever into the unknown world from where no one ever returns.

"Noooooooooooooo! Timmy! Timmy!" they called out as they ran to the spot he had just recently occupied. They stopped, their noses bordering the edge of the forbidden zone.

The Old Lady's warning permeated their minds. "No, not even your little finger should enter the Rubicon, lest you be pulled in and disappear forever."

"How can he be gone already? He just stepped in." the kids asked themselves as they observed the woods with amazement, reverence and fear.

"I have to go in after him." said the ten year old. "When the Patrolman arrives you must tell him that I've gone in to bring Timmy home."

The two remaining children were crying. "You can't leave us."

With reservation she said, "I must."

She raised her hand anxiously moving it forward, guiding it in a most delicate fashion. All of her attention was focused on the tips of her fingers as they approached the unsearchable, the unexplained, the undiscovered. How long would it be before she was pulled into the hidden universe that would take her far away from her world? A scream of terror ran through her mind as she was brutally propelled away.

"Are you crazy?" a voice yelled at her. "What are you doing you foolish child?"

In an attempt to save her life, the Patrolman had grabbed her shirt and flung her backwards a great distance. He quickly realized that she was as frightened by the situation as he was.

He ran to her, knelt down and held her. "You know the danger that lies in the Rubicon." he said softly.

"Timmy went in." she sobbed.

"Nothing can be done now my child. You know that, don't you?"

He looked back with sadness and wondered what kind of monstrosities resided within the woods. He picked up the child, dusted her off and gathered the others.

"Come on, I'll take you all home."

The ten year old uttered, "We no longer have a home."

The Patrolman camouflaged his sadness with a frail simper as he did his best to sound reassuring and comforting. "Yes you do. I've found someone who is willing to take the four of you and Timmy." He paused briefly realizing what he'd just said. "You'll have to help me break the news to your new Keeper."

The Patrolman had no children of his own, and with all the calamities that had befallen the West Gate in the last few days, he wasn't sure he'd be able to ever manage the responsibilities of safeguarding the lives and emotions of such tender creatures. There is so much tragedy for these deprived children, he thought to himself.

The youngest of the children pulled on his jacket sleeve and asked, "Who is this Keeper that we are going to stay with?"

"This old lady told me that her last child had sadly departed her dwelling and that nothing would please her more than taking the lot of you into her home."

The little girl pulled on his sleeve once more and smiled at him, "Who is this Keeper?"

He smiled at the little girl and gently said, "Her name? It's Mrs. Nibbledent."

The little girl smiled. She grabbed hold of his hand and said. "That sounds like such a friendly name. She must be so lovely."

Chapter 41 The Witch

Preet forced his eyes open. He thought he felt something bounce off his hair. "What was that?" he grumbled.

He darted his eyes back and forth but saw nothing suspicious. He was sure he felt something that time. Oh, there it was again. Suddenly the sound of squawks and screeches were heard. He looked up but the brightness of the sky blinded his tired eyes. Once again, something small like a pebble hit him, then another, then another; all of a sudden everyone was being pelted by rocks falling from the sky.

Preet's vision adjusted to light and he looked up. The sky was filled with crows. He looked to the ground and realized that in fact they weren't being pelted with rocks, it was nuts falling from the sky.

Crawford heard the familiar caws of his friend and cheered him on. "Ray! Way to go buddy!"

Ray had returned with hundreds of crows and ravens, all carrying a variety of nuts that they used to bombard the kids with. After a few minutes the birds were all gone and Ray circled the sky and cawed thanking the flock with whom he had roosted the night before. He came down and was greeted by a cheerful crowd and a very relieved Crawford.

The kids got up and gathered the nuts. They sat around with rocks in hand and smashed open their breakfast from the sky. They gorged themselves until they were full and satisfied.

After breakfast they did their best to gather every morsel. With full bellies and the successful crossing of the Orchard of Souls, their spirits were lifted and they resumed their walk and wondered what was awaiting them around the next tree.

Crawford once again led the group. Lashra stayed close to Crawford continually asking him if anything seemed reminiscent.

"How about now?" she'd say.

"No" he'd respond.

"How about now?" and so on and so on.

Getting tired of the same question, he raised his hand in an effort to stop her from asking again and interjected, "I'll tell you when I see something familiar. In the meantime, why don't you tell me about the Longevites' prophetic dream." He figured that would keep her occupied for a while, and, truthfully, he was enjoying the stories.

Preet and Upal took that as their cue to fall back and talk about anything else. They'd heard the stories plenty of times before. They knew Lashra could tell a good story, but nothing compared to hearing it from The Old Lady.

Lashra smiled as she continued from where she left off. "Oh yes, the dream. Well... the next morning the twelve gathered together and summoned the newly elected leaders of the three tribes. They instructed them to unite all the people and bade them to gather at the city gates on the first day of the week. It was mandated that all who were able, must attend."

Lashra was having difficulty narrating and keeping up with Crawford's pace. She raised her voice, "On the first day of the week the populace had gathered to hear from the Longevites. They stood motionless and soundless. An unprecedented calm filled the air like a sea of tranquility."

"Does it actually say *like a sea of tranquility* in the scrolls?" Crawford needled.

"Do you want to hear the story or not?" she responded, slightly out of breath. "The twelve stood great distances apart on top of the walls of the western part of the city. They spoke as one and the people were amazed."

"*I was standing in the darkness. It was a lightless and dreaded night.*"

"The people were astounded at the thundering sounds of their proclamations."

"*The smell of bursted bowels and decay was in the air. The sounds of lamenting, of moaning and of wails surrounded us. As the sun slowly started rising, I could see that I was standing in a circle with the others, facing three beautiful and hearty trees. A chestnut, an olive and a plum tree. Outside of our circle I could see thousands upon thousands of our dead and withering brothers and sisters. The cries of torment lingered and my soul was filled with distress and anguish. Why have you betrayed us? They groaned. Is death and destruction our reward? The dead and decayed rose from their graves and pointed to the trees in our circle.*"

"Oooooh... scary stuff." Preet crooned from behind.

"Go easy on him Lashra. You're going to give him nightmares." Upal chipped in.

Preet and Upal could be heard giggling in the background.

She ignored their childish comments and continued., "*I turned to see that the trees were infested with palmerworm. I watched as the trees were being eaten. What might we do, that you may rest in peace? we trumpeted.*"

"The Longevites' voices were filled with misery and remorse. The crowd was silent. No one understood the meaning of the vision. The Longevites continued."

"*The dead laid hands on three of us. Unearth the trees.* they susurrated. *We did as we were told. Each person was commanded to carry their tree away to the Rubicon forest. They were told to hold the tree and to not bury its roots in the ground. They obliged the three to sit with it and mourn its passing for the remainder of their lives.*" The twelve paused, bowed their heads and wept."

"Many people were moved to tears. *What does this mean? they whispered to one another.*"

167

"The meaning of our dream will not be hidden from you! they shouted. *This is the meaning...."*

"Hey Crowboy!" Crawford's attention turned from Lashra's history lesson to the voice calling him.

"Can you send Ray out for more food?" shouted Preet.

"I was talking Preet." Lashra sent back.

"Surprise." retorted Preet. "How about it Crowboy?"

"Well, first of all, my name is Crawford not Crowboy." he finally let them know.

"That's just a smooth appellation they gave you." said Lashra.

"It's not a smooth anything." Upal wholly disagreed with Lashra.

"Kids." Crawford mumbled. "Ask him yourself Preet." he responded.

He looked up at the bird that was sitting on his shoulder. "Ray go sit on the giant." The bird took off and headed toward Preet who immediately panicked. He yelled and waved his arms around. "This isn't funny Crowboy."

"Just calm down and let him land on your arm or shoulder." said Crawford.

Preet took a deep breath and stopped flailing. The raven landed on his large shoulder. Soon Ray was pecking at the boy's immense hairdo.

Nervously Preet asked, "Hey Oop, what's he doing?"

"I think he's eating."

"Hmm... that actually feels kinda good." Preet's eyes closed a little. "A little to the left Ray."

" Hey Crowboy, what do I say to him if I want him to find food?"

"Go find food?" he responded.

"That makes sense," said Preet. "Go find some food Ray." The bird took off and landed a few feet behind Preet. Ray began foraging under a large leafed tree and brought him back a cluster of tiny, dark purple berries.

"Hey!" Preet shouted to everyone, "Those trees have berries."

He walked over to where Ray had gotten the berries. He lifted the large leaf and found hundreds of clusters of the beautiful (and as it turned out) delicious berries. Almost every leaf he turned had a cluster hidden under it.

How did I not see that? thought Lashra.

"Hey Lash?" Preet cried out. "How did you not see that?"

Her face turned red and she threw her arms up in the air. "I was giving a history lesson. Sorry. *I* can focus. And it may surprise you to know that this is my first time here too. Big brother." She turned away frustrated more at herself than her brother."

Why is she so hard on herself? thought Crawford.

Preet on the other hand, did not hear a word she said after "I was". His head was already under the leaves in search of more berries.

The rest of the troop joined him. They feasted on berries until they could eat no more. Their hands and faces were covered in the purple dye of the sweet pulp.

"That's some ugly tattoos you got going on your face Oop." he said pointing.

He looked over at his sister and Crawford who had not fared much better. He wondered what he looked like.

Preet loaded his pockets with berries. Filling them as much as he could.

"What are you doing?" questioned Upal.

"Duh? Loading up for later on." he replied.

Upal shook his head as he watched his friend filling his pockets with the juicy berries.

"What?" Preet asked him as he continued to stuff his pockets.

"Nothing."

Crawford was once again leading the way. They continued trekking, working and fighting their way through sometimes almost impenetrable brush. Within a short period of time Preet understood Upal's dismay and his pocket filling blunder. The berries in Preet's pockets had turned to juice and it trickled down his legs and left him quite sticky.

Not letting all this sweetness go unnoticed, were the nats surrounding his legs. All of his complaining fell on deaf ears.

"Why didn't anybody stop me? Ray, why didn't you say something? I thought we had something."

They walked, climbed and fought their way through all kinds of wild mazes throughout the day, only resting here and there so as not to get completely exhausted from the day's heat.

To pass the time, Crawford questioned them about what life was like knowing The Old Lady.

Lashra and Preet told him that they didn't know life without her. Their earliest memories all involved her. "I've been reading books from her library since I can remember." Lashra mentioned.

Upal, on the other hand, had only known her for a few years. Ever since he became friends with the twins. But he'd collected a few choice stories in his short time with her.

They agreed to start looking for a suitable site to rest for the night.

After a short moment of silence, Lashra returned to *educating* Crawford on the history of Eternal.

"What was the last thing I told you Crawford?"

"About what?" he joked.

"The story."

"I'm kidding." he said. "Let's see… people, tears. What does this mean? And the meaning of the dream is..." he finished.

"Oh?" She was pleasantly surprised. "You were listening."

"I heard everything."

She continued. "Yes, well." She cleared her throat. *"The meaning of our dream will not be hidden from you. They shouted. This is the meaning… the vision tells us that our shame has been exposed. Not one of us is worthy of the armor. Therefore it must be taken and concealed in the Rubicon. But know this. Like a tree that was once thought dead, a branch will grow from its root and from this branch a giant tree shall rise from the forest and cast its shadow over all the people of Eternal. On that day we shall be refreshed by its shade and comforted from the burning sun."*

"Yet, there will come a time when your children will be delivered to the forest and many calamities will come to fall upon them. After a time they shall conquer and suppress the beast that tortures them. On that day the Armor of Peace will be once again reunited and peace shall be restored."

The crowd was silent. Their thoughts turned to themselves and they began to whisper *"Who will go? Who will bear this tragedy that befalls the whole world? Who will give up another brother or sister?"*

"The Longevites knew their hearts and spoke up. *We understand your fears. We will not ask any of you to sacrifice a life. Three of us were anointed in our dream. They will die, so that you may live."*

"Three remained silent, as their names were pronounced. *Paladin, Patron and Protag will make their way tonight."*

That evening everyone bade them farewell. Hands were laid on the chosen as they made their way out of the city gate. Not a word was spoken. Only the somber sound of tears and mourning could be heard as they made their way toward the Rubicon Forest. When they entered, each went in their predetermined direction. North, South and West.

Paladin with the Shield, Patron carried the Helmet and Protag the breastplate. They were never to be seen again." "After they had vanished into the Rubi…"

Crawford raised his hand and hushed Lashra with an almost inaudible volume. "Shhh. I see something moving."

"Did you just shh me?" She felt slightly disrespected. "When did you stop listening?"

"Shhhhhhhhh!" he forcefully repeated.

"That's funny." Upal shook his head in a drolly disagreeable fashion as he watched the event unfold.

"What?" Lashra queried Upal.

Upal hadn't realized he'd spoken out loud. "I said, uhm... that's not funny."

He turned his attention to Crowboy. "Why would you disrespect Lashra like that Crowboy?"

"Shhhh." Crawford begged.

"I'm hungry." cried Preet from the back.

In frustration Crawford yelled out. "Can everyone, please, just shhhhhhh!" He emphasized it with all his might.

"Look, out there." he whispered. "I thought I saw something move."

He'd gotten Lashra's attention. "Where?" she spoke quietly.

Crawford's eyes locked with another's, just past the bushes. A chill ran through his spine.

"She saw me." he stated despondently.

"Who?" whispered Lashra.

"The witch."

Chapter 42 Angry Widows

They peered quietly into the foliage trying to see what Crawford saw. All at once, they saw her, an old decrepit hunchback. Her hands braced each side of her majestic chair. Her emerald bug-eyed gaze had the power to see through any soul that might dare come this close.

All four were frozen in time. She didn't move. Had she even seen them? Crawford freed himself from her hypnotizing gaze and broke into an ill-timed laugh.

"It's a rock." he said light-heartedly. "It's just a rock formation."

He's right Lashra thought. She moved in for a closer look. She studied every crack and crevice and all its beauty and mystery.

The top of her head held a tremendous dark purple flower. It looked like a bell; it was rounded and it sat on her head like a crown. At the base of the petals was a large wide band, the color of gold. It looked like the sun setting in the horizon, with streaks of silver shining upwards back through the purple petals. On either side of the band grew two large burgundy orchids. She watched as each orchid was being occupied with a hummingbird.

Her eyes traveled to the woman's cape, which upon closer inspection looked more like enormous wings. The first layer was made up of small faint, wispy feathery petals the color of lavender. She could make out dozens of layers, each one larger than the next while their color grew more transparent. She leaned in and her senses were filled with a delicate floral scent.

Behind her throne was a river of golden flowers. They hovered a few feet above the ground. Hanging down from the branches above, sitting only inches away from each golden flower was a red and white bloom. Each bloom was decorated with a blue tear-drop-like dot.

She moved in closer yet. She was amazed by the beauty and details of what could only be a natural formation, or was it? Either way, she marvelled at the majesty of it all.

Lashra stepped back and stared deeply into her emerald eyes. A smile of discovery appeared on her face.

"She's not a witch." she said. "She's a queen."

Crawford approached the witch. "Safely guided through the golden path," he said.

"I remember something. After she finished her poem, she turned and pointed to the path of gold. *Follow the path of gold to your reward.* she said to me."

"This must be the path we need to follow to find a piece of the armor. Come on, let's go!" he shouted excitedly.

"Wait." Lashra said.

She was searching her mind. "I've got it." she exclaimed.

"The flowers above the path, they looked familiar. I've seen those flowers before. Let me think."

She scratched her head, closed her eyes and combed through the books in The Old Lady's library. "I've got it." she said excitedly. "They're called Veuve-en-Colère."

Upal did his best to repeat what he heard. "vuvencollar?"

Lashra corrected him. "Veuve-en-Colère. Loosely translated it means angry widow."

"Ok." Upal replied. "And what are the golden flowers called?"

"Oddly enough, they're called Golden Flowers." she said shrugging her shoulders.

"From what I remember," she paused, "these *Angry Widows* are poisonous."

She picked up a few scraps off the forest floor and threw them onto the golden flowers. A drop of liquid from the Veuve-en-Colère fell onto the scraps of leaves causing them to smoke and dissolve, quickly turning them into a liquid that was absorbed post haste by the Golden Flowers.

"These highly acidic drops fall from the petals." She pointed to the small amount of liquid about to drop from another flower. "They feed the Golden Flowers below. If they get on your clothes they'll eat through them and if they get on your skin," she paused for a moment to make sure Preet and Upal were paying attention.

"Go on, we're listening." Preet said slightly annoyed.

Lashra tilted her head and hesitated.

"I was listening. You said that we can eat through them." She shook her head in disbelief.

"I'm kidding Lash." He shook his head. "Acid bad, acid bad, I get it."

Annoyed with her brother's lack of seriousness, her voice took on a stricter tone. "*If*... a drop lands on your skin, you'll get a burning rash that spreads rapidly. It's so severe and angry that it will drive you insane before you have the time to die from its effect." She hoped to scare the boys straight.

Preet bumped Upal and smiled. "So you're saying we shouldn't make any rash moves." He smiled again.

Upal looked up at him in dismay. "You'll have to do much better than that."

Frustrated Lashra laid the hard facts out. "This rash works its way through your entire body eating you from the outside and by the time it's done you're just a pile of edible liquid. Then, the golden flowers absorb your mindless, unlistening, irresponsible dead bodies.

Upal patted Crawford on the back. "I'm sure you're going to want to take the lead this time, *right*?" he said smiling and nodding.

"Come on Crowboy, take a run at it?" He pushed Crowboy toward the poisonous path.

Crawford stumbled over a root. He fell to the ground and slid almost a full body length underneath the golden petals.

Just as Crawford was about to get up Lashra shouted. "Stop! Don't move!"

A drop of acid fell onto the leaf above his head. They all stood still, hearts racing. The drop slowly rolled down the golden leaf. They held their breaths. The drop was almost at the edge of the leaf. If it fell onto Crawford? What would they do? At the last second the drop was absorbed and he was safe.

Preet grabbed him by the legs and dragged him out.

Furious, Crawford started toward Upal.

Lashra was irate. "Stop these antics now! We don't have time for this. Upal you need to watch what you're doing. You could've killed him."

"Sorry." he said to Crowboy. "I just nudged you. I didn't realize you were so delicate."

Crawford wasn't sure that was actually an apology.

"Yes!" Preet said to Crowboy, sensing his dismay. "That's an apology."

Lashra walked closer to the golden path. "Someone has to try and make it through. I think Crawford's right. This is the way to the armor." she said. "I'll go first."

"Slow down a little bit." Crawford turned his attention away from Upal and interjected immediately. "We're not going to just let you run through there."

"We still have some light, we should go now." she persisted.

Crawford walked away and sat down in the middle of the opening. "We should camp here tonight and think about what lies ahead of us. We can't even see beyond the path. I for one would like to make plans for tomorrow, one that keeps us all alive. You're not going." he stated firmly. "We're all staying right here." Crawford cleared a spot on the ground and stretched out.

Unwillingly and with regret Upal spoke up, "I hate to say it Lashra, I mean I really do hate to say it. But I agree with Crowboy."

"Me too." said Preet.

The vote was three to one, the decision was made to rest for the remainder of what little daylight was left. It was decided that it would be best to think things through with a clear and rested mind. They could make their move at the first sign of light if need be.

Chapter 43 The Spee-Eyeder

They settled in and lit a fire. It was Crawford's turn to go pick branches and shrubs to help keep the fire going for the rest of the night.

Lashra sat on a small stool sized rock that happened to be under an umbrella shaped tree. It was just high enough not be set on fire and low enough to keep some of the heat down and around her. She looked up and discovered bluish moss like plants hanging from some of the branches. She climbed onto her seat and grabbed a handful. She placed a small amount on her tongue, it was bitter.

"What are you eating there Lash?" questioned Preet.

"I'm pretty sure this blue moss is edible." She thought about it a little more. "There's something about it?" She hesitated before going on. "Oh, yes, you have to cook it slightly first before you eat it."

She reached over and grabbed the stick she was using to stoke the fire. Putting a little moss on it, she placed it over the fire, just high enough to dry the moss out. After a few seconds she removed it from the fire and took the blue stuff off the end of the stick and ate some while Preet and Upal waited for her reaction.

"Mmmm… it tastes like candy." she said smiling and putting more in her mouth.

That was enough for Preet and Upal. They both jumped to their feet and ran to the tree. "There's hardly any!" they complained.

"It grows in the shade." she said.

Preet and Upal stared at her in confusion.

"The other side of the tree." She shook her head and laughed.

The boys made their way around the tree and collected the candy. They headed back to the fire with an arm full of blue moss and a stick.

Lashra entertained herself simply by watching Upal and Preet trying to figure out how long to cook the moss. They put some on a branch just long enough to dry it out, but the excitement was a little too much for them. Every time they tried to pull the sticks off the fire they dropped the candy moss into the flames.

Lashra used her motherly inflection to caution the boys. "Take your time or you'll never eat."

"Success! Oh yeah, this is the perfect amount of time. Oh, that's good." Upal said with a smile. "Who knew moss could taste so good?

"Let me try that." said Preet, as he reached over and snatched Upal's branch and ate the rest of what he had on it. "You're right, that was the perfect amount of cooking time. Make me some more."

"Hey! Come on. Cook your own candy."

While the boys were busy arguing, Lashra spent some time looking up at the shapes, sizes and colors of the leaves. She loved watching the flickering jumping shadows created by the fire. The leaves looked to be dancing.

She spotted a little Spee making its way down a silken fibre it was slowly weaving. "You're such a tiny little one, but I see you coming."

"Wait… I know you…" Before she could finish her sentence the spee fell from its lattice and landed in her eye.

"Ahh!" she exclaimed, "A spee fell in my eye."

"Just blink it out." commented Preet, who was more focused on Upal's moss than his sister's problem.

"I can't," she said in an eerily calm yet spooked voice.

"I've seen this spee in the book of spees." she said panting and trying unsuccessfully to stay calm.

"This is a Spee-Eyeder. One small bite and I will be paralized."

Her words got the boys' attention.

"The paralysis makes its way to your heart and within two hours you're dead." she continued as she held her eye open with her fingers.

She looked up toward the bright light of the full moon. "I'm afraid. I don't know what to do."

Chapter 44 The Rescue

Upal scratched his head, "Let me think," he said nervously. "What if we wash it out with water or something?"

"I'm afraid guys... I don't want to die like this." she sounded unnerved.

"What about the water idea?" repeated Preet.

Perturbed, she shouted, "We don't have water!" She did her best not to cry. "I know if they feel threatened they'll bite."

"It's kind of ironic eh Preet?" It was staggering how quickly Upal could be distracted. "I mean it's a Spee-Eyeder and it's in her eye." he quipped.

"You idiot!" Lashra lashed out. "It's called a Spee-Eyeder because it looks for eyes to lay its eggs in. The first bite is to paralyze then it lays its larva into the eye."

She continued berating him. "The larva takes less than an hour to eat your eye, *while you're still alive*." She was beginning to hyperventilate and gulp for air. "Are you happy you know everything about them? Think of something before I die."

Crawford was making his way back with an armful of fuel. As he walked in from behind Upal and Preet he could see Lashra with her head back and her finger holding her eyelid open. Saying nothing, he put down the pile he was carrying next to Lashra, leaned over her and could see the tiny spee in her eye and without question he blew a puff of air in her eye.

Upal and Preet jumped up and shouted at the same time. "Are you crazy?! She's got a Spee-Eyeder in her eye!"

Lashra was laughing hysterically. "It's out, it's out. I'm ok, I'm going to live."

She jumped up, hugged Crawford and covered his face with kisses.

"Thank you, thank you, thank you." She laughed merrily as she danced circles around the fire. She made her way to Preet and gave him a big kiss on the forehead. She reached Upal and held her hand up excitedly waiting for him to clap it. He didn't. So she simply grabbed his hand and helped him.

She made her way back to Crawford. "I'm going to live. Thank you." She grabbed his face and covered it with kisses once more.

Upal grumbled under his breath, "More kisses?"

He directed his green envy toward that witless Crowboy. "You know you could have killed her?"

He stood up and flailed his arms wildly. "That was a Spee-eyeder in her eye you fool!"

Crawford was still confused by all the excitement and the kisses, not that he was about to start questioning the kisses. "A what?"

An animated Upal continued, "A Spee-Eyeder, you know? Everybody knows." He was wild and angry. "You could have killed her with your dim-witted eye blowing stunt Crowboy."

Crawford still had no idea what was going on. He decided to bluff his way through the moment until *he could* figure it out. Calmly he said to Upal. "Well, from where I stand, it looks more like I saved her life."

He smiled a proud smile for doing whatever it was he did. "You, on the other hand, seemed to be doing a great job at being dazed and confused."

Upal stood up and Crawford dug in his heels. "So, I think what you meant to say to me was, *thank you*." He took a gracious bow and waved his hand in Upal's direction.

"He's right, Upal" she said as she placed a hand on Crawford's shoulder.

"Oh, not the dazed and confused part." she said apologetically. "The saving my life part. That's what I meant."

"He does make a good point," said Preet.

Upal gave Preet a death stare.

"What? He's right Oop. She is alive after all. You'd think you'd be happy about that?" he giggled out as he made his way over to the pile of wood and tossed a fresh piece onto the fire.

Upal walked away.

"Where are you going?" asked Preet.

"None of your business. If that's alright with you?" said Upal.

"I'm happy that she's alive. Even if she is my sister. You big baby." Preet called him out on his sour mood.

Upal walked away ignoring Preet's comments and grumbled his way into the bush. "Buggeration... that dull-witted-half-wit. I can't believe she kissed him again." he said kicking debris around.

"He saved her by accident. At least when I save her I do it on purpose." he kicked up more leaves and shouted "*On purpose!*"

Upal was referencing the first he met up with them... It happened a few years earlier, before Preet's growth spurt. Upal had put himself in harm's way to protect Preet and Lashra. He stood up to a group of about twenty teenage boys and a few female zealots, who were walking the streets at night looking for loose girls and trouble. Once they set their sites on Lashra, things quickly escalated.

Preet had no choice but to try to protect her. Upal had watched the situation develop and could plainly see that these two strangers were outnumbered. Wanting to help or more likely impress the girl, he stepped in with an air of calm, ready to handle the tough situation with perfect aplomb. (Actually he was terrified. It was something he'd never admit to.)

He removed his shirt and handed it to one of the girls standing next to who he thought was the leader of the pack. "Do you mind holding this until I'm done?" he said to the girl as he made meaningful eye contact with her.

Stretching out his arms and cracking his neck, he stood as big and tall as his five foot six inch body would let him and said, "Ok boys, listen up, I'm only one man. So, if you guys don't mind, I'll only take on three or four of you at a time. The rest of you will just have to wait your turn."

"Ok, who's first?" The leader took a step forward. Upal raised his right leg and landed his foot squarely on his opponent's knee, breaking it. *Snap! Crack*! The sound of the break was made worse by the cries of "Ahhhhh @!#$!" coming from the boy.

"Ok, who's next?" Upal said, bouncing up and down on his toes. Needless to say, there were no takers.

"On purpose." he mumbled to himself.

He continued to walk and sulk. He turned around to glare at the threesome sitting by the fire only to realize he could no longer see the fire or its glowing light.

"Oh no!" His heart sank.

Chapter 45 A Step Too Far

Upal's eyes darted back and forth looking for any sign of life. How far did I go? Who knows how far this haunted forest has taken me? The thought nervously flashed through his mind. I could be halfway to who knows where. He raised himself onto his tiptoes, then squatted. He searched the blackness for something, anything that could guide him back to the camp.

He looked up, down, turned around, still nothing. The booms of his pounding heart drowned out all the other sounds of the forest. He stood silently, trying to calm himself. He forced himself to listen to the woods, hoping to hear the sound of Preet and Lashra talking or laughing. He was so distressed that even the sound of Crawford's annoying voice would have brought him relief.

He made his way back to the ground, straining, fighting, desperate to find a twinkle of firelight to guide him back to safety. He moved this way and that. Had he gone North or South? What did it matter? He didn't know where North or South were at this point. Which way should he go?

Out of nowhere something caught his eye. "Oh there it is." He saw a small sparkling light through the shrubs. He darted back concentrating and focusing on the sparkles and glitter making their way through the woods. He could hear voices. He was safe once more.

He stopped at the edge of the camp trying to compose himself. He could hear Lashra talking about how she feared that the joking might have gone a little too far. After all she pointed out to Crawford and Preet, they were all stressed out. She reminded the two and herself of their pledge.

"All for one." she said. "Maybe we should go look for Upal. He's been gone a while."

Upal was hiding at the edge of the rest area. Hearing Lashra worry about him put a smile on his face. "You can stop worrying about me Lashra." He tried sounding ceremonious, "I have returned safe and sound. As per usual."

"I wasn't worried." she said feeling her face go flush. "You were probably standing there the whole time." She casually stoked the fire.

"It's just that it's your turn to stay up first and we're all really tired."

"I'm not that tired," said Preet.

Lashra pursed her lips, widened her eyes, tilted her head and gave Preet a vivid expression.

"Oh yeah, I was just..." he stretched out his arms and gave a big fake yawn, "Yup tired and ready for bed."

He laid down and turned away from both Lashra and Upal. He gave Crawford a passing glance. Crawford smiled understandably while nodding his head in Lashra's direction. Preet simply raised his shoulders and closed his eyes. It was an easy way out and he was taking it.

"Wait a minute." Upal said, suddenly remembering that it was actually Preet's turn to keep the first guard.

Preet was already pretending to snore.

Upal kicked him in the but. "Nice try buddy, but you get first guard tonight."

"Lashra said I'm too tired." he responded sleepily. "And you know she's always right. Ask her yourself."

Upal wasn't tired, but he did want to hide and get away from everyone. He laid down and closed his eyes. Preet opened his eyes and knew it was a losing battle to argue with his comrade. He got up and threw a few more branches on the fire.

The night was moving forward and even though the day had been filled with climbing, crawling, walking, shoving, deadly

186

acid, a Spee-Eyeder and oh yeah, a witch that wasn't, they all quietly wondered if there was anything else waiting for them on such a glorious day.

Preet stoked the fire as the others lay on the ground hoping to find nothing more exciting then a good night's sleep.

Sleep did not come easy.

Preet continuously stoked the fire and stared up at the full moon. It seemed larger than usual, he thought to himself. Surely it was the forest playing tricks on his mind. It was all so beautiful being surrounded by billions of stars. The night sky was so bright that the contrast of the few dark clouds that were visible seemed like black holes in the universe.

The others simply laid on the ground with their eyes open staring up at the sky.

Crawford thought about his father. Had he even noticed that his son was truly gone? Was he out looking for him, worrying? "I doubt it." he said quietly. There's no way I'll ever be found in the Rubicon. Maybe... he fantasized, maybe someone saw me go in and word will get to my father. Then the almighty Councillor will regret his decision of choosing them over me.

He imagined his father's reaction upon hearing the tragic news. "My son, my son, I'll never see him again. How could I drive him into the Rubicon?" his father would cry out.

Yes, Crawford thought. If his father knew that he was now in the forest of death, he'd be regretting his decision to cast him out. Or, be grateful. "Finally, I'm rid of the burden." he would tell his friends.

He spoke to himself quietly, "If I make it out of here, I'll do things differently." All sorts of thoughts and scenarios ran through his head, until he fell asleep.

Lashra spent the first few minutes jotting down notes about what she'd discovered in the Rubicon that day. She put her things back in her bag and used it as a pillow. She stared up and spent time trying to count the stars. She moved on to finding star formations for the historic legends they were now trying to find.

Paladin with his shield, "There you are." she whispered to herself.

Patron with his helmet and Protag with her breastplate. She searched and searched the stars to find The Old Lady. "I know you're up there my teacher, my friend, my mother."

A tear drop silently found its way down her cheek and into her ear. She would swear to the others later, that she heard The Old Lady's voice in that drop. Every time she tried to re-imagine the moment, it would sound like a different word, but, all of them were words of encouragement. "I will find you up there." she replied to the tear.

Upal thought about his mother. He wondered how she'd feel about the man he had become. Maybe, if she was around he wouldn't be in his present situation? Maybe he wouldn't be this frightened and lonely little boy he knew he truly was.

Strangely, he also thought about Mrs. Nibbledent. He'd gladly take a beating from her old and wise slipper rather than being here, trying not to die. Oh, how he surprisingly missed the boredom of everyday life with his old bewitched Keeper. He smiled to himself when he realized that maybe Mrs. Nibbledent wasn't all that bad. That maybe he was partly responsible for her imbibing on such a frequent basis. "Nah." he quietly said, waving his hand in disbelief. (It was strange that his brother never came to mind.)

Preet sat alone listening to the sound of silence. He figured everyone was already asleep and so he thought about food.

"A growing boy needs to eat." he spoke to himself. He turned and saw Ray sleeping on a log. "Would it really be that bad if I ate the bird?" The thought made him giggle.

At one point that evening one common thought did run through all their minds. How was it possible that it felt like months, even years since they'd seen their home? It had only been a couple of days, and yet so much had happened. What would transpire tomorrow and the next day? Was Demorg truly alive? If so, what was he planning and how could they stop him?

And of course Lashra, Preet and Upal wondered what had become of Saudj.

Preet could hear them all snoring and breathing deeply. He also heard every crack, crickle, swish, rustle and scrunch in the forest. Tonight it seemed (at least to Preet), that the forest seemed more alive than usual. It was almost like the Rubicon was also having a hard time falling asleep.

His eyes were starting to get heavy. Thankfully his two hour shift was almost up. Just as he was about to get up to wake Upal, he noticed the temperature drop. A frosty wave of air suddenly filled their encampment. The iciness surrounded Preet. His body vibrated with cold and fear. He got up and looked to the others. The chill had not escaped them. He could see they were rolling around trying to find a warmer position.

Without warning the dark forest lit up. Preet turned back to glance at the woods. He saw a slow moving misty frost. The moon light was bouncing off the vapours creating a distinct but intangible glow.

Shaking and immobilized, he watched as the haze slowly rolled in.

Chapter 47 Sitting In A Tree

A ten foot wave of luminescence powered by a full moon approached the camp, bringing with it an eerie, frosty, calm of silence. Preet wasn't sure whether to enjoy the magic or wake everyone up.

The dense glowing cloud continued its slow, persistent trek toward him. Preet saw it was all around and closing in on them. All of a sudden he noticed a stinging, stinking smell that accompanied the fog. It was a pungent odor, much like the one found at the bottom of an old rotting bottle of glumvyn.

The smell left a bitter taste in his mouth. The bitterness made its way to his throat, irritating it and causing him to hack and cough. The fog continued its haunting crawl into the camp. A light haze covered his forearm; it was warm. No, it was hot. It quickly turned into a creeping, burning sensation.

Preet turned away from the fog to see his friends still asleep. How could they still be sleeping? He realized he hadn't said a word yet.

"Wake up!" he yelled.

Ray immediately woke up, cawed his warning and flew to higher ground.

"Wake up! It's an acid fog! It burns! He shouted as he ran around the firepit.

"Get up! Climb a tree, get off the ground, go go go!"

Preet continued screeching and bawling. He shook his friends, helping them up. He grabbed Lashra's arm, stood her up then moved over to Crawford, then Upal.

"Get up! Climb a tree! Get off the ground! It's an acid fog!" he repeated over and over.

He ran to Lashra and threw her up as high as he could manage. "Goodness me," he grunted. "You're heavy." he yelled at her.

"Ugh! I'm not heavy. You're weak!" she yelled back at him.

The ring of fog was drawing closer; Preet had only seconds left. He ran back to Crawford who was having a hard time getting a foothold. He bent down slightly and Crawford climbed on top of him and finally got off the ground.

"Ooop? Where are you?" He looked around in a panic.

Upal shouted from the tree next to Preet. "Start climbing you big oaf."

Preet reached up and tried to climb. Crawford reached down and grabbed hold of his arm and pulled with all his might. Choking and coughing, Preet clumsily tried to make his way up.

"Hurry!" Upal yelled.

"You've got to help me Preet." grunted Crawford, as he did his best to help the giant boy.

"It's burning my legs!" Preet cried out.

The fog had covered most of the camp. Preet was still struggling to get off the ground. "Don't let me die! I don't want to die! Please help!" His cries sounded like those of a small child.

Suddenly, as if by magic, he was lifted up off the ground and was able to find a firm footing. He climbed up high enough to get above the acid mist.

Below, Preet heard the sound of someone struggling for air. It was Upal. He'd jumped down to help rescue his best friend. Gagging and wheezing Upal made his way back to his tree and climbed until the acidic fog could not reach him.

"You saved my life Oop." Preet quietly called over to his friend.

Cough, cough, wheeze. Upal struggled to breathe. "I had no choice. If I let you die I'd never hear the end of it from your sister."

Upal's skin burned from the acid, but he didn't complain or let on of his pain.

"This must be the full moon fog," Lashra said. "I should have known." She was disappointed in herself.

"What are you babbling about Lash?" Preet said as he tried to make himself comfortable.

She continued. "The story goes that when this was the Forest of Eternals, the full moon fog's mist was collected by a certain fruit." She thought about it for a second. "The bromeliad fruit. Then from sunrise to sunset it would ripen. At sunset the people would harvest and eat it. The fruit was only edible that night. The next day it would go bad; it became unappetizing and uneatable."

"Hey, if we're lucky maybe we'll find some tomorrow." Preet's stomach was undeterred by the events of the night. "Lashra? Could you maybe try remembering stuff like that, before it almost kills us?"

Crawford started reciting a childhood rhyme.

> *"The full moon brings the sour smog,*
> *That wraps a fruit that brings agog.*
> *During daylight it comes of age,*
> *Then at sunset it's all the rage."*

"That's crazy," said Crawford. "I guess those foolish childhood nursery rhymes aren't so foolish are they? I wonder..."

"We'll have to wait for the sun to evaporate the acidic dew that's bound to be on the ground in the morning." Lashra cut Crawford off mid sentence. "Make yourselves as cozy as you can. It's going to be a long night."

They did their best to set themselves up in the trees. It wasn't going to be a night of rest after all. Preet had the hardest time. He simply sat on a thick limb stump and hugged the tree, hoping he wouldn't fall during the night.

Chapter 48 Coward

Saudj and his mother sat at the table with their heads down, quietly eating. Father on the other hand, was in the midst of a long glumvyn enduced rant.

"We are Demorgians." He slammed his fist on the table. "We are true descendants of the sword tribe."

He knocked his chair over as he rose from his seat, with some help from the table. He teetered from side to side, back and forth. "We!" he cried out as his hand landed on the table again and again. "Look at me!" he yelled at Saudj. The boy kept his head down.

"We are the true rulers of this gate. Umph..." He shook his head disappointedly and pointed to himself. "I... I... Me... I... I should be the true ruler of the West Gate... of all Eternal for that matter."

He did his best to stand up straight and proud. He ran his hands down his shirt to iron out the wrinkles.

"All I see is people quaking in their shoes. Cowards with heads hung low." He took a step back to keep himself upright. His eyes were getting heavy. He sloshed his way forward placing his hands on the table in an effort to keep his glumvyn-soaked body from tipping over. Drool and spit flew from his mouth as he continued his diatribe.

"Why should we feel shame? We have done nothing wrong... Nothing! Do you hear me? Nothing!"

In an eerily calm and clear tone he said, "Demorg, he tried to save our world, and this is how they repay him. How they repay us."

"You!" His paralytic hand tried to point at *one* of the Saudj's he saw. "Yes, you." His speech was getting more and more garbled.

"These fends of you... that gril... all her time at the witch's house. Ploding against me, plodden gen my people."

He attempted to restabilize himself but instead found himself laying across the table. He looked up to see Saudj still sitting at the table quietly. In a fit of rage he grabbed hold of the young boy and lifted him off his chair. He shook him like a rag doll, screaming and ranting. "Are you a spy? Do you spy against me with that girl? Do you plot against me?"

The acidulated and unsweetened smell of his father's glumvyn drenched breath was enough to make Saudj gag. He made quick contact with his father's bloodshot eyes and quickly looked down.

His father mumbled. "You're worse than a spy... You're a coward."

His father threw him into the corner. His head violently slammed against the wall. The boy did not move.

The old man was back on his feet. "You," he grumbled softly in his cock-eyed-glumvyn state. He forced himself and yet he still couldn't focus on his son. "You, you're weak like your mother, always hiding from me. Why do I even bother?"

He walked over to the boy huddled on the floor. He towered over him. "Why don't you do something to make me proud of you? Instead you sit there, cowering there, like... like..." He was too drunk to finish his thought. He steadied himself with the wall, raised his leg and crushed the boy with his foot. Then he spat on him for good measure.

"Coward." He managed to fumble out the word before taking a step and falling to the ground out cold.

Saudj's mother came to him and knelt down next to him. She wrapped her arms around the boy but he pushed her away. "Don't." He shouted. "Leave me alone." he said angrily. "It's too late."

He got up and sat on the floor next to his half dead father. He patted his head and whispered gently into his ear. "We will rule again one day soon father. Then you'll be happy."

He turned to look at his mother who was sitting on the floor crying. Next to her was The Old Lady's dead carcasse.

The image jolted him awake.

"I am not a coward." He crawled out of his hole. He stretched with the morning sun. "I am not a coward." he repeated to himself.

Again, he spent the day walking and going nowhere. He had no destination that he knew of. On his walk to nowhere he convinced himself that soon he would be inspired. Then he would set that plan, that inspiration into motion. Was he the chosen one, the one to find the armor and reunite Eternal? His father was no fool and neither was he.

"I am Demorgian! I am of the sword tribe!" he shouted at the top of his lungs. "No one will stand in our way." he encouraged himself. "If it is necessary, I'll kill anyone who tries." he told the trees. "*Anyone*. After all, peace can only come after war."

The forest seemed to be instantly filled with more darkness than light. He walked a little longer and as the day was nearing its end, he longed to find a resting place and some food to fill his belly. He'd now gone almost three full days without food or drink with the exception of licking morning dew from leaves he hoped were not poisonous.

The day was giving way to the gloaming that came with the beginning of nightfall. It had been another long, lonely and deprived day. He was tired and ached for a place of rest.

He continued for a short while. There, up ahead, he could see it. Even though it was the close of day he could see a bright spot in the woods. It must be a clearing, a wonderful, welcoming savanna. He made his way to it and cast his eyes across a field. His heart sank.

His wonderful, welcoming savanna could only be described as a disturbing, tortuous landscape and it warned its trespassers with an unambiguous message, "Visitors not welcomed." Saudj heard it with clarity.

As the full moon forced its way in, pushing out the daylight, the competing shadows and highlights being cast all around the orchard made it look as though the trees were dancing. It was a painful forced dance, that was both beautiful and distressing.

He wondered if he should turn back. Or maybe, should he attempt to get through now and get it over with? Perhaps, he thought, I'll make my way through in the morning.

As the moon took its rightful place in the sky, Saudj noticed a sound coming from the orchard. A soft plaintive cry. The more he listened, the more it seemed that it was a chorus of gentle whimpering wails. He was sure that when he focused on the sound he could almost make out words.

Were the tiredness, the nightmares, his lack of food and water, conspiring with the breeze to make him mad?

"Am I going mad?" he asked the dancers.

Lo and behold, across the field, flickering light.

Chapter 49 Fire Light

Sparks from a campfire, he was sure of it. He wanted to be sure of it. Someone on the other side. He questioned himself about whether he should cross. But what if there was someone over there? The question lingered in his mind.

His imagination raced. What if his friends had taken The Old Lady's words to heart? What if they had entered the Rubicon in search of the armor, in search of him?

"I could claim that I'd found the old woman lying dead." he spoke out loud, trying to figure out his plan. Yes of course he thought. "I came here after you. One of the kids told me you had all made your way into the Rubicon searching for the armor. Just like The Old Lady said we should. I'm so glad I finally found you." He heard his story and felt increasingly confident the more he ran the scenario through his mind.

A deep dark cloud covered the moon's light and the flickering of the fire had magnified. He decided to try. He could quietly make his way through and see who was on the other side. Once there, he could adjust his plan and take the next step.

The thought of being closer to another person, even an enemy gave him a strange sense of comfort. He just didn't want to feel alone.

He waited for the cloud to pass. He was about to step into this... this, Orchard of Souls. The moon's fullness had returned. He stepped into the foreboding orchard and began his trek through. A few steps in and he felt something grab at his leg. His heart exploded. His reflexive urge to jump was alarmingly halted.

Something has a hold of me. The fear of it filled his heart. I can't move my legs. The more he tried to pull his leg the tighter the grip got. Terrorized, he continued to fight, but to no avail. To make things worse, clouds were moving in to cover his only source of light. An obsessive fright filled his soul.

"Harder Saudj, pull harder!" he shouted. In total darkness he continued hysterically fighting for his life. He was being slowly sucked into the ground. His desperation seemed to have an effect; his attacker was loosening its grip on him. Saudj broke free.

He ran begging and pleading for the moon light to return. He focused all his energy on running and the sparkles of the campfire light.

He shouted at the darkness, "Leave me!" and to the clouds he yelled, "Move out of the way!" and as if by magic, the clouds heard his pleas and the moon reappeared.

When the moon fully showed itself he found himself once again stuck in his tracks. His aggressor had returned, gripping him once more. He pulled and pulled in desperation. He looked down for the first time and realized it was vines that had a hold of him. And now they had a hold of him past his knees; they were climbing and wrapping themselves around his waist. He was screaming for help, but his screams soon turned to muffles as the vines made their way around his chest and arms, gripping, climbing, conquering, fusing with him.

He could feel the vines wrapping themselves around his neck squeezing, clutching, compressing around his entire being. His screams were barely even whispers.

"I can't breathe. I can't breathe." It became just a thought, I can't breathe. He tried to cry out. His final hope was that whoever was on the other side would hear him and come to his rescue.

He looked to the sky and could see the clouds coming to cover his source of light. His mind screamed "NO!" He didn't want to be trapped like this in the blackness of night. No longer able to breathe, he closed his eyes and passed out.

He woke up a few minutes later in complete darkness. The Orchard had loosened its hold on him. He fought and fought and was finally able to move again. Exhausted and freed he crawled his way to the other side.

He laid on his back a few feet away from the orchard's exit. He was distressed, drained and exasperated. He stared into the sky watching the moonlight return in full force. After a brief rest he got up and looked around. The sparkles seemed to have moved deeper into the forest. His gut told him to turn around. He fearfully looked back at the orchard. Something dreadful was approaching.

The smell was somewhat familiar. It had a similar odor to the dirty glumvyn bottles he was made to clean, so that his father could refill them with his fresh poison. The moonlight mist burned his parched and dehydrated lungs. He turned away from it, to see the whole forest light up as in daytime.

He followed the light. As he approached its full force he saw giant insects gathered in a swarm. Their bodies radiated a brilliant fiery light that vanquished the darkness. Saudj was stuck between this horde of light flies and a giant wave of toxic fog. He looked around and thought that this was surely the end (again).

His surroundings grew darker, he turned back toward the light just in time to see the flying army pests flying high and away from the fog. Coughing and hacking he followed. He ran and ran and ran, right into a tree. He was knocked down but quickly picked himself up and climbed his way up as high as his weakened body would take him.

His whole body was aching, his heart was racing, he was filled with dread and anxiety. What had he got himself into? He was in no rush to come down. In fact he had found a large bed of moss. Finally something went his way. He stretched out and had no trouble deciding to stay there until the morning light returned.

He stared into the night sky and as if for the first time since entering the forest, he genuinely realized he was alone. It wasn't supposed to be this way. The Rubicon was playing tricks on his mind. He was angry, bitter, sad, lonely and hated everyone but didn't want to be without anyone.

He was going mad. Why had he killed The Old Lady? Those sparkles weren't from a fire. No one had come to find him. For all he knew the witch had survived her beating. He was sure of only one thing.

"I am in the Rubicon, the place from where no one ever returns." he whispered to the moon.

Unbeknownst to Saudj, Upal, Preet and Lashra were sharing the same night sky. A feeling came over him. They *were* here and they had come looking for him and the armor.

He was going to find them. "It belongs to me." he murmured to himself. Finally, he was inspired.

Chapter 50 Wake Up

"Uuuugh!" Preet greeted the morning light with an unending slew of grumbles. *Creak. Crack. Pop.* The sounds coming from his body added to his chorus of lamentations. "The pain!" he cried out. "In all my years…" he went on, "I have never had such a grinding, backbreaking, long-drawn-out-marathon of a night. Uuugh!" he repeated forcefully. "I need to stand up." He wiggled from side to side. "I think this branch is coming with me. It may be a permanent fixture in my caboose." he said with a groan.

Crawford sluggishly reported from his branch, "If I didn't hate this place before, I do now."

Preet looked at Crawford. "You didn't sleep a wink either?"

"Oh, my back." Lashra voiced wearily from the next tree.

Upal could be heard murmuring above everyone's heads. "That was the best night's sleep I've had in years." he said, still half asleep. Keep it down a little longer?" he said from the magical moss bed at the top of the tree.

They looked up to see him stretching out and yawning in what looked like, well, a soft and cozy moss bed.

"How did you manage to get all the way up there?" Preet cried up. "And why didn't you tell us about the sleeping arrangements up there?"

Upal ignored his question. He rolled over and closed his eyes to rest a little while longer.

Crawford did his best to move. "I'm getting down from here." He painstakingly worked his way to the ground.

"Hold on Crawford." Lashra called out. We need to make sure the dew has evaporated before we start moving again."

"I don't care. I can't sit another second." He hoped he wasn't being overly impetuous.

He carefully landed on the ground. It seemed to him that some good fortune was finally on their side.

This particular morning was much warmer than the previous two mornings, ergo the dew had vanished quickly.

Crawford walked around and gave everybody the thumbs up. Preet and Lashra laggardly made their way down.

Upal on the other hand had decided to take his sweet time. "I'll be down in a little while. Let me know when breakfast is ready." he chuckled to himself.

They spent a fair amount of the morning stretching and trying to get back some sense of feeling into their lower extremities. Lashra went over and observed the deadly drops from the Veuve-en-Colères. After some attentive studying, she was confident in her assumption that the petals were absorbing the entirety of the lethal beads and that none of the drops were making it to the ground.

She made note of her discoveries and shared them with the others. She suggested that the safest path would be underneath the Golden Flowers.

"I had that idea yesterday Lashra." Upal spoke up.

"Hey little-brain!" said Crawford to Upal. "Pushing me does not add up to an idea."

"I had to test my theory and uh… you volunteered. I'd say that's an idea." Upal quipped with a dirty smile.

"Well, I guess that makes me the hero again, doesn't it?" He turned and walked closer to the golden path.

"OK!" Lashra stepped in before another word could be spoken. "So we all agree. We crawl our way through."

Preet wasn't sure it was such a good idea, after all, his size made it all but impossible for him *not* to touch the flowers.

He questioned his sister's idea. "So you're saying we have to crawl on our hands and knees all the way?" He crouched down as he spoke.

He squinted as he eyed the path. "Hmm, I don't think it ends." he said nervously.

"Sorry to tell you Preet," Lashra answered disappointedly, "but we're all going to have to crawl through on our bellies and hope that the path is short." She shrugged her shoulders, "We have no choice."

Preet wasn't thrilled. "I have to be honest with you Lash, I'm not thrilled with the prospect of being eaten up by acid and fed to a plant."

"Plants." remarked Upal as he patted Preet on the shoulder. Preet gave him an inquisitive look. "You said *fed to a plant*, but we both know, *you'll be feeding plants*." He patted him again.

Lashra shook her head disappointedly. "Shut it Upal."

"We have no choice?" Preet paced the camp. "We have no choice." he said confidently. "We have no choice?" he was beginning to panic. Of course we have a choice. Let's find another way. For example: we can go around, or..." He tried hard to think of something else. "We can go around." he finally said.

"We can swing through the trees." Upal was not being helpful.

Preet excitedly pointed at Upal. "Yes! We can swing through the branches. We can..." Preet went on a fifteen minute anxiety driven tirade and no one said another word. They all just waited patiently for it to come to an end.

When Preet had ended his diatribe he was sufficiently calm and ready to face the reality that laid before him. "Ok," he said calmly, "I've made peace with the flood of poisonous acid that will very likely overtake my body." He looked at Upal who for some reason was smiling. "Plants Upal, I get it, plants."

He set his eyes on the path. "Bring on the curse. Bring on the affliction. Bring on the pestilence. Bring on..."

Upal interrupted, "Enough already!" he said exasperated, "If you don't stop you'll die of old age, before you die from the acid."

"Sure," Preet retorted, "I'd say the same if I was little people, but I'm not, am I?" He shook his head.

For some unexplainable reason or maybe he was just tired of hearing Preet go on, Ray entered beneath the golden path and led the way.

"I'll take that as a good omen." Crawford said.

"Ok, here we go." She breathed out a heavy sigh, laid down on the ground and started dragging herself along the floor with her elbows. "Move slow and stay safe everyone. Don't bump the leaves."

"Don't bump the leaves." Preet mumbled.

Chapter 51 And We're Crawling

Upal was eager to follow Lashra into the golden river. His efforts were hampered by Preet who sharply pulled him back. "Do you mind going last Oop? I don't want to be left behind." he spoke quietly.

Upal pulled away, "I'm going in now."

He turned to make his entrance, only to see Crowboy's feet vanishing under the large petals. "Ugh, foiled again." he mumbled.

Upal waited for Crowboy to make his way a fair distance down the path before entering. Preet stood back and questioned the situation once again. When he could no longer see Upal's feet, he realized he didn't really have a choice.

He laid on the ground and got on with dragging his giant torso through the latest nightmare, whispering to himself, "Forward, forward, cautiously forward. Bring on the virus. Bring on the outbreak. Bring on the plague…"

"Shut up!" Upal cried out.

"You shut up." he mumbled.

After an hour of seemingly endless dragging and pulling, Lashra's elbows were bruised, her legs tender and her back aching. She tried to find some hope ahead, but the path truly seemed endless. She was dog-tired, worn out, done for, kaput.

Lashra had no choice but to stop and rest. She spoke quietly to Crawford. "I need to stop and rest. Pass it on."

"We're going to stop for a break. Pass it on." said Crawford.

Upal passed the message on to Preet, "Crowboy's too weak to go on, so we're stopping to rest." and with that, the train came to a stop.

Lashra laid at the front of the line with her eyes closed and her head on her arm. She took notice of the surrounding sounds. She listened apprehensively to the acidic drops falling onto the petals above her head. *Drip*, she counted One, two, three, four, five, six, *drip* another six seconds, *drip* and another. They dropped every six seconds. She wondered why six seconds? Lashra questioned everything, even the rhythm of poisonous flesh eating pariah, like the ones dripping inches above her head.

Preet laboriously and awkwardly worked at turning over just enough, so that he could reach into his pocket for the few nuts he'd secretly stashed away. As Preet's luck would have it, his elbow lightly made contact with one of the petals. His ears perked. He heard it, *drip.* He held his breath. Frozen in fear that a drop might have slipped by, he waited and waited not saying a word about it to the others.

Thinking he was in the clear, he took a breather and felt a sense of relief. "That was too close for comfort." he thought to himself.

"What was too close for comfort?" Upal asked.

Caught by surprise and worried the others would scold him for not being cautious enough he said, "Uh, your feet and my face. *Way* too close for comfort."

Taking his time and being even more cautious, he brought the crunchy nutty fruit up to his mouth. "This will not keep me going all day." he mumbled to himself as he slowly chewed on his measly breakfast.

He quietly called to Upal, "Hey, ask Lashra how much farther? Pass it on."

Whispering he asked, "Hey, Crowboy, how much farth... Why am I whispering?" he asked quietly. Then he shouted to the locomotive driving the train, "Hey Lashra, how much farther?"

"I have no idea. It feels like we've been doing this for hours." she said disappointedly. "I don't know how much farther I can go."

She growled quietly and without warning she started shimmying herself forward. Crawford wiggled, Upal scooted, and Preet staying as close to the ground as possible, slinked and towed his mountain sized body forward.

As time went on Lashra was filled with questions. What if they had to crawl like this through the night? What if they had to sleep under the Golden Flowers? What if this went on for days?

The longer they dragged on, the more she questioned herself. She was responsible for this wearisome, drawn-out tour of the golden pathway. The deeper they went the more chances one of them had of making a false move. She thought about her brother trailing behind. *What if..?* She didn't want to finish the thought.

"Lashra?" Crawford called from behind. "There's something I just don't understand. If no one ever returns from here, how is it possible that our childhood nursery rhymes seem to know so much about this place?"

Lashra welcomed the chance to answer his question. Anything to get her mind off of her own questions.

"Well," she said, "The Old Lady had occasional visions. One day I asked about the visions. She said the Rubicon had gone through changes over her eight hundred years and so she would make note of those changes and write nursery rhymes in order to share what she'd seen with the children of the day. Those rhymes have been passed on from child to child ever since."

"So," Crawford interjected. "The Old Lady was able to return from here."

"I guess so." Lashra had never really thought of it that way. She continued. "All the Longevites traveled through the forest this way. For thousands of years they shared their stories about their visitations in the Rubicon. Over the years parents created rhymes to remember and pass on the stories to their children. These forewarnings were meant to instill fear in children and dissuade them from approaching the Rubicon."

"Hmmm." Crawford thought about all the nursery rhymes he knew. "I guess… if you think about it, the rhymes could be used as a guide for those who do enter it. If they can decipher their meaning."

"*If.*" she responded.

The rest stops became more frequent as the hours passed. Lashra was second guessing herself and she figured the silence behind her was a sure sign that the boys were also questioning her command of the situation.

Ray, who had really been leading the way, stayed quiet as he walked and pecked at the ground. He didn't seem to worry about anything. Not one squawk or gurgle was heard from him the entire day. Suddenly the path above their heads thinned. Ray took off.

Realizing the end must be near, Lashra yelled out, "We're through. I can see the end!" She shouted it again and again.

A few minutes later they were all out from the path.

"I am never laying down again." was Preet's first comment after exiting.

Their destination appeared to be a small opening just slightly bigger than Upal's cell at Mrs. Nibbledent's house. The walls were made of tightly intertwined roots, branches and trees going up like a deep well at least two hundred feet, straight up toward the sky.

They were completely surrounded except for one opening, a darkening channel, a tunnel-like shaft built in much the same fashion as the endlessly high walls that surrounded them.

"It looks like a mystical portal." commented Crawford as he looked inside. "Well? What are we waiting for?"

He stared back at the golden path. "I know I'm not crawling back." As he spoke he disappeared into the large tunnel.

Chapter 52 Uphill All The Way

One after another they disappeared into the tunnel. In no time at all, they were making their way up and deeper into it. Rather than being met with darkness, the lengthy straight was filled with thousands of ambient balloon vines giving off a soft tranquil glow. It was a calm, rhythmic, hypnotic pulse of ever changing light and it flowed like tongues of flames on the petals, gently encouraging them forward through the magical portal.

Hours of climbing, climbing, climbing. The rather steep and tiresome trek made their legs burn and ache.

"Is the air getting thinner?" questioned Upal. "It feels like we've been climbing straight up. We should be in the clouds by now."

Finally the trail flattened for a stretch. "I'm feeling kind of dizzy. I could almost use a nap and some food. Well, food for sure, then a nap." And with no care for the others, Preet stretched out on the ground and let out a tired and well deserved sigh of relief.

Upal looked back, "That's a good idea." and he followed suit.

Lashra quickly joined in and laid down closing her eyes. "I don't think I can do it for much longer." she said, yawning.

"I hope the path stays flat for a while." Crawford added.

After a few moments of rest Crawford encouraged them to get up and continue their march. "We can't stop too long or we'll be stuck in here all night."

Preet was curled up in a fetal position, trying to get as comfortable as possible. "We don't even know how long this tunnel is. We could walk all night and still be stuck here." he complained.

Upal and Lashra both agreed with Preet, but they knew that Crawford was probably right.

They half-heartedly resumed their walk at a much slower pace. As they progressed deeper into the shaft, the balloon vines' glowing lights increased their rhythm transforming into a bright orange stroboscopic effect. Preet's dizziness hadn't gone away and the show of lights only made things worse.

"Stop the lights." Preet said as he tried to cover his eyes. He stumbled and crashed into the side walls of the hollow shaking them. He was shocked by the unexpected showering of a liquid cascading from the large bucket-like flowers above his head.

Naturally, Preet panicked. "Ah! It burns! It burns!" he screamed out.

The others jumped back trying their best to avoid being splashed by the acid and being crushed by a frazzled and unhinged Preet.

"Do something Lashra!" shouted Upal.

But they could only look on as Preet uncontrollably bounced and slammed against the walls. One side and then the other, each time activating the shower of mysterious flowing fluid. His hair, face and neck were covered. He fell to the ground, screaming, squirming and writhing in agony. Then without warning, he stopped moving. The calm pulsing glow of the balloon flowers returned.

Lashra, Upal and Crawford hovered over Preet's body.

Preet opened his eyes, ""Oh, it doesn't burn." He gave a dumb smile and licked his lips. "It's actually a little sweet and sticky." He ran his hand along his face and collected the syrup. He put his whole hand in his mouth and licked his fingers clean. "Sorry about that."

Upal kicked him while he was down and let him have it, "What's wrong with you? We thought you were dying." He kicked him again for good measure.

They waited and watched to see if he would get sick or poisoned from the syrup he had eaten. Preet didn't seem too worried about being poisoned; he was just happy to have found something delicious to eat, or in this case drink. He stood up onto his tiptoes, reached up and removed a bucket shaped flower from the wall. He pulled it down carefully then paused for a moment as he looked at the sticky liquid inside.

"Whatever." he said to himself as he took a few large gulps.

The three watched as he drank.

"What?" he said quizzically. "I'd rather die drinking this, than starve to death." He returned to swigging the juice.

Upal agreed and jumped up to grab a flower, but alas it was too high for his littleness to reach. "Can we have some too?" he asked his bosom buddy and lifelong pal.

"Get your own." Preet laughed. "I'm kidding."

He reached up and gave each one a flower filled with the wonderful nectar. They sat for a few minutes enjoying the rest and the drink. After filling themselves they carried on and soon they were once again on an uphill journey.

A few more hours passed and their frustrations grew.

Crawford let out a sigh, "What if this thing really doesn't end? How much farther can we…"

Crawford was taken aback when Ray unexpectedly took off.

"Where's he going?" Lashra asked.

"Maybe we're getting closer." Crawford answered her.

Within a minute or two he returned with a beakful of berries.

"We must be approaching the end!" Lashra cried out.

Within minutes they were out in the fresh air. They walked through a few hundred feet of trees and shrubs and found themself in a somewhat open space. A few feet to their left was a lightly snow covered cliff that dropped down to an endless abyss. To their right was a narrow rock pathway covered with an impassable amount of thorn bushes filled with blue and black berries.

Directly in front of them was a large open mouth entrance to a cave. It was a giant monster-like creature. It had a growling furrowed brow and a mouth full of rotted and broken teeth that were ready to take a bite out of anyone who dared try to enter its jaws.

Tired and longing for rest they made a quick plan to best use the remaining sunlight. Seeing that Ray was feasting on the berries, they assumed they were safe to eat and so Crawford and Preet were put in charge of gathering food.

Lashra and Upal made their way around and gathered whatever they could find. They collected wood scraps from the floor and walls around the area.

"Do you think the armor is in the cave?" Upal asked Lashra.

"Retrieving in stone… it makes sense. I mean, we're not going to know unless we go in." she said.

They made their way back with some scraps and built a small fire by the tunnel's exit. Darkness soon arrived. They sat around the fire discussing their next step.

"I wonder what's waiting for us inside that cave?" Preet asked.

Lashra's eyes were fixed on the giant teeth of the structure. "If the entrance is any indication it doesn't bode well. What I'm wondering is what are we going to do with what we find?"

"If we find anything at all." Crawford whispered.

Lashra was feeling slightly nauseous and her back was beginning to ache. She got up and tried to walk it off. She made her way over to the pathway and started scraping and collecting moss from its walls. This moss is very oily, she thought. She gathered some up and figured they could use it to build torches. After all they would need light in the cave and this moss just might do the trick.

She made her way back to the fire, dropped off the incendiary lichen. Without saying a word, she made her way to the opening of the cave and stood at its entrance. Hopefully we won't have to go too deep inside to find what we're looking for, she thought. She peered into the darkness that awaited them.

The boys were sitting around, still eating everything they could get their hands on. Maybe it was the thought of finally finding something important, maybe it was tiredness, who knows, but, for the first time since coming into the Rubicon they seemed to be enjoying each other's company. Even Upal and Crawford were joking around.

Lashra could hear them laughing and for a moment it put a smile on her face, but it didn't last long. She started to well up as she thought about the pressures of leading this ragtag group of boys. She felt alone, sad and slightly depressed.

The nausea, cramps and back pain hadn't quelled. She wondered if it was all just a manifestation of the stress and anxiety she was feeling. At least that's what she hoped. I hope we didn't accidentally poison ourselves, she thought.

"Hey Lashra? You ok?" Crawford gently shouted to her.

"I'm fine." she said not turning around. "Just thinking." She wasn't ready to return.

She wasn't ready to talk to anyone about anything she was feeling. It wasn't easy always keeping everything inside, always looking like she knew what she was doing, always being in control. Sometimes she wished she could just be a girl, be herself, whatever or whoever that was. Maybe she just missed The Old Lady's companionship? Of course she did.

Crawford questioned getting up and making sure she was alright, but figured Preet and Upal would stop him and tell him that they should be the ones to check up on her.

Preet read the expression on Crawfords' face. "She'll be fine. It can't be easy hanging with us all day." he whispered.

"Speak for yourself Preet, I'm a blast to have around."
Upal made a motion to get up and both Preet and Crawford put
their hands on his shoulders and sat him back down. Upal
understood and did not protest.

A little while later all four were sitting around the fire.
Lashra had found a few sticks and they spent some of their
time making and testing Lashra's torch idea. Night came in full
force and no one mentioned the need to keep guard. They
huddled close together by the fire and soon the exhausted
brood fell asleep.

Chapter 53 Saudj And The Witch

Saudj stretched out and yawned. The pangs of hunger caused him terrible pain. He was desperate; he had to find some food. Anything to fill the hole and stop the misery. He climbed down from his resting place and laggardly made his way through the forest.

Head down, he looked around for a morsel, a tidbit, a bit of anything. His heart skipped a beat when he noticed footprints in the dirt. Someone had been here recently. Then his eye caught something miraculous. Was it possible? Food.

He fell to his knees and picked up a nut, one small, wonderful nut. His eyes darted back and forth. There under the leaf, another nut and behind that one, another. He didn't care about anything else at that moment. Food, food, food. He crawled the entire camp on his hands and knees laughing like a mad man who'd found gold. After about an hour of inching his way around the floor of the camp and when he was sure there was nothing left to find, he pondered where the creators of the footprints might have gone.

He sat back for a while and thought about his situation. "They have no idea where I am." he said to himself. "I have the upper hand."

He got up and carefully examined the area for signs of broken branches. Preet will have left a mess of broken branches, he thought. It didn't take long for Saudj to find indications.

The brush was full and it made his travels difficult, but if he was careful he could manage to retrace their trail. He was excited to be in control, to have an advantage over the three. This thought encouraged him and motivated him to keep moving. Without warning, Saudj was taken aback at the sight of a stranger.

Someone or something was just ahead of him. He realized it was an old witch sitting on a throne. He froze in place staring long and hard. It took him a while to figure out she wasn't real. He approached the statue and saw the remainder of a campfire. He was right, he nodded happily. "I've got them now." he said to the witch. He climbed onto her lap and held her face in his hands. He moved in until his nose was almost touching hers. He locked his wide eyes into hers and could see his own reflection in her emerald eyes. "I've got them now!" he cackled. "And there's nothing you can do about it."

Darkness was falling and he was tired. He sat by the pit and used a branch to tussle the coals. He noticed there were still a few small embers. He knelt down and blew on the coals. They lit up.

"Yes!" he shouted. A little fire would be great. He made his way around the camp and gathered up some debris for his soon to be fire. "Outstanding! Excellent behavior!" he cried out. Then, from out of nowhere his eye caught a few nuts he'd missed previously.

He fed himself as he went on scouring the entire area looking for any morsels he could find. He was delighted when he noticed a bunch of berries on the ground under a big leaf. He lifted the leaf and found a gold mine. He soon had a fire going and was eating and filling his belly for the first time in months, or at least that's how it felt.

He sat pretending to joke around with his three friends. How nice it would be if they were there with him. Someone other than himself to keep him company. But soon the joking turned to malice and he realized they were making fun of him and questioning him about The Old Lady. Accusing him of murder and deceit, he tried to defend himself but is was no good. Their constant attacks were infuriating him. They didn't understand he did it for them. His mind was racing and wandering under the effects of the hypnotizing fire light.

He woke up from his day dream and realized once again that he was the one. He would show them all. How dare they question him. In the darkness of the night he got up and made his way around the camp to gather more wood. It was nice to have a fire to keep him warm and to have light throughout his solitary night.

As he made his way around he was startled by a glowing bee. He turned and whacked it with a stick knocking it to the ground. That was the wrong thing to do. The dazed bee lit up brightly and swirled around on the ground and on it's way up stung him in the calf. The bee took off and Saudj jumped and howled in pain and surprise. He limped back to the fire, wailing and squealing in anguish.

The luciferine had taken a fair chunk of meat from the boy's leg. The sting's pain was piercing and biting. The abscess quickly inflamed. His calf expanded to triple its size. He was sure that the swelling would take over his entire body. It was undeniable, he was going to die. He sat in pain by the fire rocking and moaning, waiting for the pain to reach his heart.

The shooting sensations reminded him of his loneliness and solitude. No one was here to help care for him, to hold his hand and to tell him everything would be fine.

He thought of the time when he'd broken his leg jumping off one of the houses during a game of chase with the others. Lashra stopped running and turned when she heard him yell. She ran to him and coddled him.

"It'll be ok, just hold on. We'll take you to The Old Lady and she'll fix you up good as new." she said reassuringly.

The pain seemed to lessen just thinking about her comforting voice. He could barely move his leg, but the pain seemed to be easing a little. Yes, he was sure it was easing. He kept his mind focused on that day, when he broke his leg.

He replayed it in his mind over and over as he fell in and out of sleep.

It was a burden-filled night, stuffed with unsettling thoughts and sleeplessness. His only comfort sat in the belief that he would survive to see another *beautiful sunrise*.

And there it was.

Chapter 54 The cave

A bright yellow glow made its appearance from behind a distant mountain. Soft wisps of clouds were an explosion of bright red and orange flames. The far off mountains rolled their way down into a valley that was filled with an ocean of frosty vapours. Patches of giant trees popped up through the mist creating a magical contrast of colors.

Lashra looked to her left, and in the far off she could see the dreaded orchard. It seemed that the orchard of souls was never ending. Did it make its way through the entire forest? she questioned. "We haven't seen the last of that place." she murmured.

Crawford had been standing behind her within earshot. "I hope you're wrong," he murmured in response.

She turned to see him standing close. He did his best to move out of the way. "Sorry, it's a little cramped over here."

Lashra smiled politely as she squeezed by. Crawford nodded, then moved closer to the edge of the cliff and proceeded to enjoy the magic that was this beautiful sunrise. Lashra continued to the unlit firepit where Upal and Preet were sitting, staring into the entrance of the cave.

"It's a cave. How deep can it really be?" Upal's comment came from thin air.

Preet put his arm around his pal, "Ya, you're right buddy. Ten minutes or so, we'll be out of there in no time."

Lashra leaned in quietly and whispered in their ears. "After all, it has been pretty smooth and straightforward so far."

Preet stood up and faced her. "You think it could get worse?" he said nervously.

Upal stretched his arms out letting out a nice relaxing yawn. "We've done all the hard stuff already. We're here, let's just go in and get it."

"Your brain is about as big as your size." said Crawford. He could hear Upal's big mouth blaring away. "Think about it for a second." he continued as he made his way back to the cave.

"*Lore and vision are guides for your duty*. You can check that one off your list. *Anguish will grip you with sunlight's beauty*. Check that one too. *Safely guided through the golden path, hunting widows, you'll escape their wrath*. Yup, we did that too. *Retrieve from the rock what is incomplete*. We're about to embark on that." He took a long pause and whispered the final words (for dramatic effect). *Altruism bestows you death's defeat*."

"Hmm." Preet snorted. "That one doesn't sound good." He rubbed his chin. "Ya, death never sounds good."

"Death's defeat." He gave Preet a few friendly jabs in the ribs. "Come on... Ten minutes." He smiled at them all. "I say we fill up on breakfast, then we go." Lashra was probably the only one to notice a slight crack in his confident demeanor.

They ate, gathered their torches and prepared to enter the cave. Upal jumped into the mouth, looked up and screamed. The three jumped back in fear as the mouth closed in on... false alarm.

"Upal!" shouted Lashra, "You can't be doing things like that." she scolded him.

"Consider us even." he responded.

"Ok, so we're even." repeated Preet.

"No!" said Upal, "*We're even*." he pointed to himself and Lashra. "I'll get you two later."

"Hey!" Crawford put his hand up. "I had nothing to do with the kissing you, thing. You can kindly leave me out. That's their weird thing."

Lashra looked sideways at Crawford. "Thing?"

Crawford looked at her straight faced. "Ya, Preet likes kissing him," he pointed in Upal's direction. "And you like kissing me."

Lashra pushed her way past Upal and purposefully walked into the cave without looking back or saying a word.

"Speechless?" Preet chuckled, "I don't think I've ever seen that."

They were barely a few minutes into their travels when Preet who was trailing with Upal stopped and turned around to see if the opening of the cave was still visible or maybe he wanted to see if it was still available. It wasn't. He let out a long sigh and quickly caught up with Upal.

"Hey, Oop. Just to be clear, I don't like kissing you. I mean you are nice and all, but you're you know…"

Upal stopped. Preet stopped. "Preet." he said calmly, "Please stop talking." Upal resumed walking.

"Sorry."

"*Talking.*"

Each one had a makeshift torch and a pocket full of moss to replenish it a few times. The other pocket was filled with whatever food they had left over. Lashra was still leading the gang down the only available route. She noticed something shiny on the side of the cave wall and moved in to have a closer look.

"It's water." She held the side of her hand against the wall and soon her cup shaped palm was filled.

The water brought with it a faint sense of hope. With nothing to drink in almost a full day, this was a surprising welcome. They got their fill and continued their journey through the large deep crevasse. Lashra's torch was reaching its end. She gestured for Crawford's torch. She lit it and continued without a word.

Hours into their trek and having used up four torches so far, they stopped for a break and questioned whether they should continue. It was a short discussion. They continued.

Preet thought he noticed a dim light in the distance. "Hey, maybe we're through? I think I see light." he said pointing deeper into the cave.

"I think you're right." said Lashra. She picked up the pace. Before long they found themselves at the edge of a cliff. Looking down they could see thousands of different sized glowing mushrooms growing all around, up and down the sides of a deep hollow. Purple, green, red, yellow, it was a plethora of luminous colors each one more magical than the other and at the very bottom they could just make out a small halo of light that seemed to be constantly changing colors.

"I wonder if they're edible?" questioned Preet.

Upal circled the thin edge around the volcano shaped shaft. Once on the other side of the hole he investigated his surroundings. There was nothing but a solid wall.

"There's no way to get through. Looks to me like we're going down." he said.

He laid down on the edge and waved his torch in the dimly lit hole. "And there it is." he said to himself. He let the troop know he'd discovered a narrow path that started on his side.

"There's a narrow path about six or seven feet down that seems to circle this giant sinkhole's walls." Upal placed his torch down and hung himself over the edge. He gracefully dropped himself onto the path.

"It's not very big." he shouted back up. "We'll have to hug the wall on the way down."

It didn't take Lashra long. Soon she was hanging over the edge. Upal reached over and guided her down carefully. Crawford was a little more hesitant, but soon joined them.

Preet moved in closer and layed on the floor to investigate the situation a little closer. "Ya, I'm not sure that's an actual path."

He could see that the three had barely enough room for their feet on the narrow path. "Maybe I'll just wait up here?"

Preet did not want to make this trip. "If you guys make it down safely I'll probably join you." he said questionably.

"Come on Preet, we're not doing this without you." Lashra said firmly. "It's not that far down." She tried to encourage him.

"Not that far down?" *down, down, down*, his voice echoed in the tube.

"Looks like danger." croaked Ray.

The bird had been traveling quietly in the comfort of Preet's hair the whole time. "Are you still here? I thought you stayed back."

"Looks like danger."

"I heard you the first time." he mumbled to the bird.

Upal's voice came calling, "You're just wasting time buddy." He turned and started making his way down easily, but cautiously.

"That's easy for you to say." Preet shouted, "You have those little dwarf-like feet. You've got tons of room down there. I don't even think half of my foot will fit on the path."

Lashra looked to her right and could see Upal making his way at a steady pace. She looked up and could see Preet hadn't moved. Her patience was running low. "Come, down here, now!"

He begrudgingly rolled over and made his way down. "If I fall and die, I am never listening to you again." he said to his sister.

His feet touched down on the path and due to his height, his hair was still slightly over the floor of the cliff and his hands still had a tight grip on the top floor.

"You have to let go of the cliff." Crawford gently and encouragingly whispered to him. "I've got you. Let go and just hug the wall. I won't let you fall."

Preet followed Crawford's instructions and painstakingly started making his way down the constrictive pathway. Upal on the other hand, had been making his way the whole time and

225

was already a quarter of the way down. Lashra was not as confident as she had let on, but she still found a way to make good time.

"Oh no!" Upal shouted up the tube. "The path ends here."

There was a moment of silence, then Preet started making his way back up. "Oh well, we tried." he said happily reversing his course.

Lashra hadn't moved yet. She was contemplating the situation trying to think up a solution.

Strangely enough, it had taken Preet very little time to climb his way back out. "Ok, come on guys, I'll help you out." he said with some joy.

"Hey Preet?" Upal shouted up. "I was just kidding. The path goes all the way down." He laughed alone.

Lashra was not amused. "Why would you do that?"

"What?" Preet called down. "Why would you say that?"

Upal resumed making his way down. "*Now,* we're even." He nodded happily to himself.

After a short time Upal had made his way down the large corkscrewed structure. Lashra had carefully looped the long coiled cliffside path to its end. Preet was stuck with his hands, nose and toes scraping against the wall all the way down. He took slow, small and precise side steps.

Crawford calmly encouraged Preet as they made their way down the long pathway. "Everything will be fine as long as we keep moving." he said softly.

The two of them swirled and circled the giant vertical corridor. An hour later all four had reached solid ground.

Preet, who was slightly burnt-out and unnerved, squeaked, "That was a lot easier than it looked."

Having reached the ground safely, Preet was able to admire his surroundings. He found himself under a giant mushroom. Its cap covered almost the entirety of the well, leaving only a few inches between itself and the wall. Preet jumped up but could not reach the underside of this magical mushroom. Its gills gave off a radiant glow. It was constantly changing colors that moved in a rhythmic circular motion.

He watched the light dancing and was hypnotized by the wave of colors going round and round. "Wow." Preet uttered as his head began to spin.

"I know, it's so beautiful." said Lashra.

"No, I mean wow my neck is killing me." He rolled, stretched and rubbed his neck.

Upal had moved on to investigate a newly discovered fragment of their ongoing escapade through the never ending labyrinth. It was a moisture-laden path with a flat smooth surface and a low ceiling.

"In here!" he shouted out.

Lashra handed him a freshly lit torch. "I vote, we keep moving."

They were all in agreement. The sooner they found what they were looking for the sooner they could head back. The subterranean passage was leading them down a watery path.

"The water just seems to keep getting deeper." Upal stated plainly. "Do we keep going until we can't?"

No one answered his rhetorical question; they just kept walking.

Chapter 55 The Wall

"Do you hear that?" Upal stopped and turned his ear toward a sound. "Is that good or bad?"

It was the sound gurgling water and all of a sudden everyone heard it echoing throughout the cave.

"We're about to find out." said Crawford.

They continued pressing forward. The water continued to rise.

"Well, at least we know where the bubbling is coming from." Lashra said as she made her way past a large gushing jet of water.

Upal and Preet stayed back to investigate. Upal put his hand over the bubbling water. It came gushing up about the height of his waist. And being Upal, of course he couldn't resist trying to ride the jet stream.

"I think this jet of water is strong enough to hold me up." he said to Preet.

He bent over and placed himself on it and was amazed that it could hold his weight.

"This is so cool, you've got to try this!" he shouted in excitement as he tried to spin himself around in circles.

"I'll pass." Preet said as he squeezed by.

"You don't know what you're missing here." Upal said as he enjoyed the ride.

After a few minutes Upal caught up to the group and was unamused by their unwillingness *to be* amused.

"Walk, walk, walk." whined Preet. "Is the ceiling getting lower? Can we drink this water? Where did Ray go?"

No one paid attention to him. They continued their walk and the water kept getting deeper. After an hour's journey, they found themselves against a wall.

"Ok, so, where do we go from here?" Crawford commented as they stood about ten feet away from the end of the road.

Preet was quick to suggest his idea. "Let's turn back. I'm getting hungry."

They moved in closer to the wall but Upal wanted to get in even closer. He took one step and found no footing. He fell forward and almost got sucked down into the water. "Woah!" he exclaimed as he reached back. Trying not to get sucked in, he instinctively grabbed hold of Preet's pants.

Preet looked at him straight-faced, "Who's the pant-pulling-half-wit now Upal? When I pulled your pants down, it was just a reflex. I don't know what *this* is?"

Crawford and Lashra looked at each other with confusion, shrugged their shoulders and didn't say a word.

Upal did his best to ignore Preet's comment. "Look over here. There's a dull light shining through the water, and there's a huge gap between the wall and the floor. There's something down there giving off light, I'm sure of it."

Preet walked over and put his arm against the far wall and felt the gap with his foot. "It feels like it's about a five foot wide gap, and it's pulling down pretty hard."

Upal was exasperated, "Are you serious? Why can't we just find one easy thing to do?"

Without another word he took a deep breath and went underwater to investigate. Within a few seconds he came back up. "Preet's right. There's a good sized gap down there and the water's pulling down hard. It's going somewhere, and there is something glowing down there."

"What should we do?" said Lashra.

"We haven't come this far just to quit." said Upal. "I'm going down." No one argued.

He took a couple of deep breaths and... "No one is going to try to stop me?" he said disappointedly.

Crawford, Lashra and Preet just stared at him in silence with vacant looks on their faces.

"Of course no one is going to stop me. Why would I think anyone would try and stop me?" So, he mockingly did it himself, "Upal don't do it. You don't know what's down there. You could die." He put his hands up and shook his head, "At least one of you could fake a little concern?" he said in disbelief.

Preet put his hand on Upal's shoulder, "Oop, you don't know what's down there, don't do it."

"It's a little late for that now you nitwit." retorted Upal as he removed Preet's hand from his shoulder.

He took a couple of deep breaths and went under water to investigate one more time. As he made his way in he grabbed hold of the ledge with his toes, so as not to be dragged down by the water's pressure. He came up a minute later.

"It feels like some kind of underwater waterfall. If that makes any sense. It's pretty deep. I couldn't touch the ground."

"So we know it's at least four feet deep then?" joked Crawford.

"Hey!" shouted Preet, "I was gonna say that."

"Real funny. Either of you malaperts want to give it a shot?" Upal remarked. "I didn't think so."

"Focus kids." Lashra tried to calm things before they got out of hand. "Upal, do you think if we step into the current we could be pushed down to where the light is coming from?"

"Maybe," Crawford added, "There's an air pocket or another cave of some sort?"

"I could try going down a few feet." said Upal.

"Are you sure?" they asked in unison.

"No." he replied, "But what choice do we have? I'm going in. If I'm not back in five minutes I'm either dead... or hopefully alive." he smiled awkwardly.

"Feel free to join me in a few minutes."

Upal was scared. They could see it in his eyes.

Had this whole thing gone too far? Were they really going to risk their lives for this, this… what was it they were really doing? Stories, myths, legends. Lashra believed they were true. Preet and Upal wanted to believe they were true.

Crawford wasn't sure what to believe. Did any of them truly fathom the absoluteness of what they were asking of themselves at this very moment? Were they willing to lay their lives on the line for a hope, a dream, a vision? Were they going to follow through with this crazy plan? Crawford had been apprehensive about the *whole mission* from the beginning. He reached out and grabbed Upal. "Don't do it." he said nervously.

"Too late." Upal closed his eyes and disappeared into the unknown, with Saudj's final warning echoing through his mind.

"Leave with me now while you still have your lives and some of your sanity. Come with me that you might be free of all this. Come with me and live."

Chapter 56 Going Down

Upal was second guessing his decision. He really needed to work on thinking, *then* doing. Not the other way around.

He tried to slow his descent by bracing himself against the slimy walls of the crevasse. The space was a lot tighter than he imagined. He kept his arms and legs spread forcefully against both sides. It didn't seem to have much of an impact; he was still traveling downward at quite a hurried pace. The slithery, mucus-like coating on the walls made his efforts virtually useless.

The constant downward pressure of the water both pushed and pulled on him. The air in his lungs was getting stale. How long had he been underwater? It was long enough that he was aching for air. He tried hard to remain calm.

Don't breathe out, he thought to himself. Hold on.

Pressure was building in his head. His ears began aching. The pressure intensified. It hurt. He tried to focus on what he was supposed to be doing. What was he supposed to be doing? No longer able to resist, he let out a small air bubble hoping this would ease some of the pain he was feeling in his chest.

What am I doing? He had no plan. Should I let go and let the water carry me away? He stayed in control as much as possible. The walls suddenly felt coarse and less slippery. It slowed his rate of descent. Where does this end? he anxiously thought. He was becoming air hungry and his body was starving for fresh air.

Let go Upal, he heard himself say. Just as he did, a light passed by. A flash of brightness. He was sure of it. Instinctively he spread his arms and legs out as hard as he could and reversed his course.

Grasping both sides tightly he managed to climb. Desperate for oxygen he let out a little more air. He had only one breath left in his lungs. He was feeling light-headed and foggy.

You can't be much farther, he pleaded with the light. How could he have traveled so far in such a short time? He thought about just giving up and letting go. Maybe, that's what he was supposed to do, just let go and let the water take him.

Somehow he sensed the light. Yes, there it was. The soft glow; it was within reach. He extended one hand and found an edge. His fingers bonded to it in desperation. He released his final breath. He was about to pass out, his mind was cloudy and for the first time he noticed the thunderous sound of water pounding in his ears. He felt his grip loosening. It was too much, all of it, much too much.

No. Today is not my day to die. He persuaded himself. He reached up with his other hand and gripped the ledge. With all his might he pulled himself toward the beacon of hope. Using the last of his energy he dragged his body upwards and was able to get his head through an opening. He heaved and gulped for air. Large amounts of water were still pouring down on and over him causing him to gag and choke.

He worked himself onto a ledge. A beautiful life saving window of hope. His body was only half way inside the newly found cavity. Dizzy, exhausted and oxygen starved, he looked up. The glowing light of the bright sun, trees, green, blue, then everything went black.

Chapter 57 Light

Upal opened his eyes. Water was still tearing down on him. He wasn't sure how much time had passed; all he knew was that his body was still gasping and in need of air. He pulled himself through the breach in the wall and crashed down on a ledge a few feet below.

"Oh my goodness!" he tried shouting through the hacking and coughing. "Woohoo! I'm alive, I'm alive!" He couldn't believe it.

He made his way to his feet and braced himself against the large opening. He watched as an endless supply of water cascaded down with absolute power. How was it possible? Where was the water coming from? How did he manage to stay alive and make it this far? "Enough already!" he screamed.

At that moment, the most important question popped up. How was he going to get word to his friends? After all, he was alive. He began to question himself.

"How long have I been gone?" He was still breathing heavy. "It couldn't be more than five minutes." He thought about it. "Come on Upal, think."

He inserted his leg through the window into the falls. He stretched and felt the other side. "They couldn't have passed me, there's not enough room." he mumbled. Then the thought occurred to him. What if they thought he was dead? Crowboy warned him not to go. What if he talked them into leaving.

"I have to go back up." He thought about it. He was completely enervated. He might be able to make it back up, but he couldn't do it without resting a while first. However long he'd been gone, it took everything out of him. It would be impossible to go back up right now.

"Hold on." Upal tried to talk things out with himself.

"They think I'm dead. Now what?" He sat on the ground keeping a close eye on the rapids. "Will they come down if they think I'm dead? He kept talking to himself trying hard to organize his jumbled up thoughts. "One for all." He stood up and placed his hand in the waterfall. "Come on guys, I'm here." He tried hard to send them a thought transference.

He realized they might not make it. He was a good swimmer and he was barely able to make it. Now, he started to worry about their safety. He needed to let them know.

He shouted at the water pouring past the opening. "I made it, I made it!"

****

The trio waited and waited.

"It's been about ten minutes, what should we do?" Preet said worriedly.

"We're not leaving him alone. We know that. All for one." Lashra said quietly as she tried to evaluate the precarious situation.

Preet looked down at the water and said, "I'm going after him." and before Lashra could do anything, he'd stepped into the crevasse and was dragged down.

Preet hadn't thought about bracing himself against the wall to slow his descent. Be that as it may, his size hampered the water's efforts at dragging him down at a runaway speed. Eyes closed tightly he banged his way down from side to side.

From out of nowhere something grabbed hold of his hair. Preet tried to resist. It was Upal; he had both hands full of Preet's massive hairdo. Both of Upal's feet were braced against the wall. He pulled with every ounce of strength he had left in his tired body. At long last Preet's face made an appearance through the window. He dragged both arms into the room.

"You can let go now." Preet said calmly. Upal let go.

He shook his head to clear some of the water from his afro and made eye contact with his best friend. "Upal you're alive! He shouted excitedly. I'm alive?"

Upal smiled, "Yes you are!" and Preet could see that he was visibly moved. Upal hugged Preet's giant hair. "You risked your life for me?"

Preet reached around Upal's waist and hugged him in return.

Upal pushed himself away. "You almost broke my arms, you big lug." Upal had thrown his arms into the waterfall and braced himself in hopes of catching the next person to come down and of all the stupid luck, it worked.

Lashra and Crawford were still in shock. "He's gone." she said.

"Ok." said Lashra "I'm not waiting any longer." She turned to Crawford, "Count to a hundred and then come join us." she paused for a moment and thought about what she had just said.

"If you want to." she said to him. She took a few deep breaths and then let herself be taken in.

"I'm doing the same Ray." Crawford said to his feathered friend. "Sorry, buddy, but this is where we say goodbye."

"Looks like danger." Ray croaked out.

"This is a fine mess you've gotten me into Ray." Crawford was getting emotional. "Go, get out, go!" he shouted.

Upal had a hold of Preet's hands and was trying to pull him in. "What about the others?" he asked.

"You know how stubborn Lash... OUFFF!" he cried out. "Something's landed on me."

Lashra popped her head through the curtain of water and climbed off Preet who was eager to make his way into the cave.

"Way to put your body into that buddy." chuckled Upal. "That's one way to stop her."

"I can't believe we made it." she said.

"Come on, help me pull him out." Upal asked.

They each grabbed hold of one arm and pulled. "Careful!" cried Preet.

Then a thought popped into his head. "Actually, pull har... OUFFF!" Preet cried out. "Oh, come on already. Are you guys trying to kill me?"

"That wasn't so bad." Crawford said as soon as his head popped in the window.

"You were supposed to count to a hundred?" Lashra asked.

"I counted really fast?" Crawford said sheepishly as he finished climbing over Preet.

Preet reached out for a hand. "A little help please."

With a little teamwork they managed to pull Preet through the window.

They all sat on the ground facing the falls watching the water power by.

"I can't believe we just did that." said Crawford.

"I just hope it was worth it." commented Upal.

A bright blast of light flashed in the cave. Their shadows burst for a fleeting moment on the wall ahead of them. Silence filled the room.

They had been so distracted with recent events that they hadn't taken notice of their surroundings. They turned to see what had caused the blast and what was illuminating the dimly lit area.

They were frozen, wide-eyed, open-mouthed, awestruck and speechless.

Chapter 58 Paladin

Lashra stood up and took a few steps forward. She was so close. "Paladin..." her voice was filled with reverence. "the stories... they're all true." she mumbled out.

Thirteen steps led to a giant skeleton sitting on a throne, one very similar to the witch's. His left hand was firmly placed on a shield.

Lashra approached Paladin's throne with humility and respect. Her chest was tight, her hands were shaking, she hesitated for a moment and looked back.

The three boys couldn't decide whether to follow her or not. All three nodded their heads in harmony, silently encouraging her to keep going.

She swallowed hard. She forced her shaking body to move forward. Her heart was blasting, her hands were sweaty and her mind raced as she tried to process the situation.

She was mentally and physically exhausted. Step by step, she carefully moved forward until she reached the staircase that led up to Paladin's throne. She fell to her knees. The instant her hands landed on the first step, her mind was set on fire with ominous sounds and visions.

Sounds, smells, images. She was surrounded. Feelings, music, memory after memory, every moment of her life, past, present and future was being experienced at one and the same time. She bent her head down and closed her eyes trying to escape, *everything*.

At that very instant, Paladin's sanctom was filled with thousands of dead souls, chanting and singing his praises. She recognized some of the sounds as an almost prehistoric language. She couldn't describe them, but she could feel their song. Tears of joy, of sadness, anger and anguish were flowing like waterfalls from her eyes. It was too much for her to take in.

She lifted her hands and covered her eyes. The immediate silence was deafening. She opened her eyes and saw Paladin. To her amazement, he was no longer a dried up thousand year old carcasse.

He was a young man in his mid twenties (he was probably about two hundred years old). He had long flowing maroon colored dreadlocks. His pale white eyes clashed with his skin. It was the color of the blackest, darkest night. His face was rugged and chiselled. He was a magnificent and flawless creature. She was mesmerized by his exquisiteness. She was fully absorbed by the man, the legend, the myth.

His eyes made contact with hers. She looked down, afraid of what she was seeing, what she must be imagining.

"Set your faith in the power of the shield." Paladin's deep bass voice resonated and lingered in the air. "Remember Lashra, it is not with or without but within."

She jumped. A hand touched her shoulder.

"You ok Lash?"

"What?" she asked Paladin.

She heard the familiar voice again "Are you ok?" She turned back to see Preet.

"Are you ok?" he repeated.

Lashra nodded unconvincingly. She turned back to see that Paladin had returned to a skeletal figure. Did he have more to say? The thought flashed through her mind.

Preet helped her up. "We should probably go up."

She raised her foot slowly and carefully put it on the first step. She waited. Nothing happened.

Upal clapped his hands, "Let's go, let's go, let's go!" he shouted. "Pick up the pace."

Lashra led the way up and the three boys followed a few steps behind.

She stood just inches away from the historical artifact. Paladin's hand rested on the shield, his head was slightly tilted down as if he were looking at something on the ground in front of him. She looked down and looked around, then noticed his right hand was clenched and his index finger seemed to be pointing to the floor. Was something etched on the floor at the base of his feet? She knelt down and brushed away the dust and dirt from the area.

Her face went flush and her blood was haunted by the presence of what she saw. Words. Mystical, prophetic words. She recited the foreboding words quietly and apprehensively.

"Altruism bestows you, death's defeat." She turned and motioned to the others to come closer so they could read the words for themselves.

The three boys came close and looked over her shoulder. Preet was confused. "How do you know that language?" he asked.

She looked up at him bewildered. "What are you talking about?" She looked back down at the script and realized she could no longer read the strange hieroglyphs.

"I could read it plain as day a moment ago." she said a little rattled.

"It's ok," Crawford said. "This place is getting to all of us."

Lashra wasn't prepared to tell them everything she'd just seen and heard. It was all too much and so it would have to wait for another day.

"I can't believe we're this close to a piece of Pop's armor." Lashra took in a deep breath, "Aegis..." she said as she reached out and ran her hand around the contour of the magical piece.

It was a golden color and it felt like gold should feel. It was two feet high and eighteen inches wide. There were four symbols going down the center of the shield. Lashra extended her arm and traced the contour of the symbols.

The first three symbols were smaller than the fourth. Yet, all four symbols were similar in fashion. Each one was an unbroken Opal ring. In the center of each ring there was a vertical line made from the same Opal. It came up from the bottom and stopped half way up.

The first ring had one horizontal line attached at the top of the vertical one that went left. On its right, the line descended on a forty five degree angle.

The second ring had a line on its left going up at a forty five degree angle. Lashra's finger moved to the third symbol.

"She sure is taking her sweet time." Crawford cautiously mumbled.

Upal shrugged his shoulders.

Preet held the palm of his hand out. "It's getting pretty misty in here. I think it might rain."

Lashra was mesmerized and fell into a light trance. She was rounding the third symbol. Its vertical line went from top to bottom. From the center there was a forty five degree line ascending on its left.

The fourth stamp was four times the size of the others. Its ring radiated with glowing blue, green, orange, purple and red. It had one descending line on the left.

She removed her hand from the magical armor and studied her finger. In a strange way she envied it for having touched the precious armament. "I wonder what they stand for?" she uttered.

"How do you *not* know?" asked Crawford.

"I don't ever remember reading anything about symbols on the shield." she said.

"What should we do now?" Upal asked.

"I'm not sure? We need to take the shield with us but, I'm not sure how we'll make it out of here." she said. "Let's investigate this hole in the ground and see if we can find another way out."

"We should split up." Crawford said.

Upal was already working on it. He figured there had to be an easier way out of this catacomb. The giant walls were filled with greenery from floor to ceiling, colorful and exotic flowers were growing everywhere. He pulled on some vines and looked behind them. He found nothing.

Lashra stood in the middle of the colossal room and looked up and was sure she could see blue sky a mile above her head. In the distance she made out a large waterfall that seemed to be coming from the sky. "Look at that opening." she pointed up. "We must be standing in some kind of gargantuan volcano." She shouted out, "I wonder if we could somehow climb to the top?"

Upal joined her and looked up. "Even if the vines could hold our weight, it would take days to climb that high. We'd need to rest and what if we fell? The fall would kill us. I think our best chance is taking the shield and going through the window back up the falls."

"Let's keep that as our last option." she said.

Preet joined the two and looked up to see what was so interesting. There wasn't much to see. "There must be an exit somewhere." he said. "Look at how big he is." He pointed to Paladin. "There's no way he came in the same way we did."

They separated once more and continued looking. Lashra inspected the shrubs. Preet explored the greenery hanging on the walls. Upal inspected the rocks and Crawford pressed against the walls hoping to find a secret passageway, a door, a hole, anything. An hour later they were no closer to finding an exit.

Disappointedly Crawford said, "Seems like the water is our only way out."

"We should keep looking," Preet said nervously. "It might have been an easy trip for you two," he said all bug-eyed. "After all, all you had to do was land on me. It's a pretty tight fit for me in there." He was getting a little jittery.

"I think *I* can make it back up." Upal stated.

"That's nice." Preet chirped.

"I wasn't done." Upal hissed. "We can rip some of the vines off the walls and use them as ropes. I'll take one end up with me, then when I get to the top I'll pull up the shield then Lashra, then Crawford..."

"Wow, you called me Crawford."

"Sorry." Upal shot back. "Then *Crow Boy*, then Preet.

Preet quickly interjected, "Maybe we should go up in the same order we came down. Oh, look that would make me number two. I think that sounds fair doesn't it?"

Upal shrugged his shoulders, "If you think I can pull you up all by myself I'm all for it."

Preet reached over and squeezed Upal's bicep between his index and thumb. "I'll go last." he promptly changed his mind.

They gathered up the vines and pulled off all the flowers and leaves. Upal tied the ropes around his waist.

"If I run out of breath before I make it up, I'll just let go and you guys can pull me back in and we'll figure something else out."

"I have an idea." Preet suggested. "What if we just go out the window and let the falls take us, maybe it's not that deep, maybe *that's* our escape? The water has to lead somewhere."

"What if it's miles away?" said Lashra. "I think we try Upal's way first."

Upal put his hand in the water, "Here we go again." He jumped in and started his way up.

Preet and Crawford held tight to the other end of the rope. Upal's plan of escape seemed to be working, he forced his way up the falls. Using every ounce of strength he had he willed himself up inch by inch. Upal noticed how the walls were much less slimy since Preet had been through. It made his climb quicker than he'd expected. With his last breath of air escaping his lungs, he reached safety.

He was tired, his legs were burning and his arms were shaking from the stress of the climb. Even so, he wasted no time and pulled on the rope to let his friends know he had made it.

"He made it!" Preet exclaimed. "Ok, Lash, it's your turn."

She was just about to step in when she looked over at the throne. "The shield. I can't believe we almost forgot it."

Lashra ran back to Paladin's throne. She was actually going to do it, she was going to take hold of the shield. Her heart pounding, she leaned in toward Paladin and picked up the shield. Immediately after leaving his hand, water came gushing down from the top of the volcano down the walls. It came with such swiftness that by the time she was half way down the steps, she was already standing in water.

Preet and Crawford bayed in unison, "Put it back!"

Both boys had the same instant hope, that returning the shield to its owner would halt the alluvion, this niagara that was about to take all of their lives. The water was already up to the boys' ankles and within a few seconds would be covering their only means of escape.

Lashra ran back up the steps. The water was now up to Paladin's feet. She put the armament on the floor next to him and placed his skeletal hand onto the shield. Instantly the inundation ceased.

She waited to see if the water would recede and it did. The large symbol on the shield began to glow and light up. Its brightness was so great it turned the water crystal clear. The liquid became fully transparent and then it vanished. It was gone. Everything was dry, like it had never happened.

Lashra made her way back to the boys empty handed. "What was that?" she asked, shaking her head. "Did that just happen?"

Preet nudged Crawford, "I told you it was going to rain."

"There is no way we can take the shield with us." said Lashra.

Crawford hemmed and hawed while rubbing his chin. "That was a crazy amount of water in a very short time." His voice was filled with discouragement.

Lashra agreed. "We'll be lucky if one of us makes it."

"What if two of us go up now and one stays behind?" Preet suggested. "You said one of us could make it."

"I said we'd be lucky to make it."

Lashra felt heartsick. "Don't be crazy. The water would be ten feet over the window by the time any of us made it back with the shield. We were so close."

"We can't just leave it here!" Preet shouted in dismay.

Crawford took charge, "We'll have to come back. It's getting late, we're hungry, thirsty and tired. We know Upal survived the climb. Let's see if we can do the same. We need to get back up there and reassess our situation. There's no point in dying for nothing. We'll figure it out. Lashra, you said The Old Lady won't let you down and that we need to trust her."C

Crawford's words sounded reasonable, but Lashra was having a hard time accepting them. "Then trust her now. We'll come back tomorrow."

"He's right Lash, we need to rethink our plan. We can't stay in here. Let's see if we can even get out. We'll come up with something."

One by one they made their way back up the hammering waterfall and as they did they each filled Upal in with their side of the story. On the journey back to the outside world they discussed what could be done to rescue the shield. Each new idea was increasing in absurdity and zaniness. Half way through they fell into a tired silence. The four exhausted youths had only two things left on their minds, food and sleep.

"Looks like trouble." Ray's gargle echoed all around them. The bird flapped his large majestic wings with excitement. The orange light of dusk coming through the exit created a glowing halo around the beautiful bird.

They stepped out into the fresh night air.

"Look at that." Preet was the first to notice the pile of berries and nuts sitting next to the firepit. "You're quickly becoming my new best friend, buddy." He smiled at the bird as he ran to the food.

"Heyeh Hoop!" he said with a mouth full of everything available. He chewed once or twice then swallowed. "You should take notes. Ray could replace you soon."

"If I'm lucky." he retorted.

"You knew we'd make it back didn't you Ray?" Crawford said with a large smile.

They ate until they were full. Not long after that the four fell asleep where they sat. Preet fell asleep with his back against a large log. He was slightly curled around a stack of nuts he'd hoarded, *in case* he woke up hungry. Upal found a cozy spot just outside the entrance of the cave. Lashra had fallen asleep staring at the fire. She was half sitting and half laying. Crawford had not done much better. Somehow he'd fallen asleep leaning over a log, face first in the dirt.

The day had taken its toll on them.

Chapter 59 One More Night

"So soon?" Saudj mocked the sunrise.

"What the???" He was shocked by the size of his leg. The pain had steadied to a dull roar overnight. He hadn't noticed the swelling. "Can I even walk with this thing?" he said to himself.

He carefully worked his way to his feet and attempted to take a step. He swung his leg over and when it made contact with the ground an intense explosion of pain jetted through his body. He fell forward landing on the witch's lap.

He pushed himself up immediately and looked her square in the eyes. "This is all your doing isn't it?" He spit on the statue's face. He couldn't help but see The Old Lady's face mocking him. He bitterly turned away from her.

Not wanting to experience the shocking pain again, he literally dragged his foot around. Gently, slowly, he walked around the camp, hoping it would help reduce the blistering inflammation. "There's no way I'm going anywhere today." he said disappointedly.

He stopped next to the place where he'd found the berries the day before. He tried lowering himself to the ground carefully. His effort was futile. An excruciating, stabbing sensation brought him quickly to the ground.

"Ahh!" He screamed at the extreme and almost unendurable pain traveling through every nerve in his body. He lay motionless, jaw clenched, gripping tightly to his shirt. He groaned out in a momentary yet endless fit of agony. "I hate you!" he cried out to the Rubicon. His eyes closed. He passed out from sheer exhaustion.

Saudj slowly opened his eyes. The sun had moved up into the sky. He'd been out for a few hours. He was afraid to move. He turned his head to see an abundance of berries next to his corps. He reached over and picked at them.

After a few handfuls he worked up the courage to move. The swelling seemed to have gone down a bit. Although that could have been just wishful thinking.

"Ok." he said working up his fortitude. "I can't stay here all day. Here goes."

He cautiously inched his way into the sitting position. He stopped for a while to revel in his accomplishment. He wasn't going to make it back onto his feet. He'd have to wait a little longer for that. Instead, he dragged himself on the ground filling up his lap with berries and collecting bits and pieces of burnables.

Hauling his way back to a stump next to his dying fire, he managed to lift himself onto a stump. He grabbed a wooden poker and nudged a few pieces of dying coal. His foot itched and he instinctively used the edge of the poker to delicately scratch his foot.

"Great," he said sarcastically. "Now I'm covered in soot."

He heard a sound coming from behind. He turned. It was just a couple of hummingbirds feeding from the witch's cap. Was he crazy or had the expression on her changed?

"What are you smiling at?" he said with a stare. He turned his attention back to his blackened foot.

"Ah, what am I doing?" He attempted to clean it off but it wasn't worth the pain.

He noticed within a few minutes that areas covered in soot were itching less. He waited a little longer and noticed the swelling in those areas was also decreasing.

"What's the worst that can happen?" So, he spent the rest of the day covering his leg with charcoal. By sunset the itching had subsided and the swelling was all but gone. Saudj was not ungrateful.

"I'll sleep well tonight." He turned to the witch and scowled. "Tomorrow I will discover the path they've taken and there's nothing you can do to help them."

He laid down on the ground and threw what little pieces of wood he had left on the fire. He moved in close and closed his eyes for the night.

Chapter 60 Let's Go

Lashra forced her tired eyes open and attempted to stretch out the kinks and pinches created by a night of dreadful half-sleep. "Phooey." she hushed.

She soundlessly floundered her way to the cave's entrance. She peered into the darkness and questioned whether she'd really lived through the previous day's events. She watched her long shadow disappear into the cave. She rolled her shoulders, massaged her neck and rubbed her lower back.

"What are we going to do?" The question bounced off the walls.

She thought about Paladin's words. "Set your faith in the power the shield provides? It is not with or without but within?" Was it possible she had imagined his coming to life? Of course it was possible.

"What am I supposed to do with *Altruism bestows you, death's defeat*?" she whispered inside the cave, hoping her words would reach Paladin and that somehow he would whisper the answer in her ear.

Her mind swirled with ideas. She broke down every word from Crawford's vision. Yet, she still couldn't grasp how to unlock them. She desperately wanted to find their meaning.

Lashra stepped a few feet into the cave and stretched out her rusty body on a soft patch of dirt. Her lower back was aching again. The cramps in her abdomen had returned and the nausea that followed made her question her food choices. Something wasn't right. She figured she'd question the others about their wellness when they woke up.

She had no plans to disturb their sleep. Why wake them? She thought to herself. After all there's no rush to get things started. Rush into what? They knew what to do, but had no idea how to do what they knew they should do.

She stared at the ceiling. "Altruism bestows you, death's defeat. Altruism bestows you, death's defeat." The soft sound of her voice gently echoed back in a dreamy rhythmic fashion. "Altruism bestows you, death's defeat." She kept repeating the mantra. She enjoyed the effects the cave had on the words; it was a melodious and pleasing warble.

"Hey." Preet said quietly, trying not to startle her from her zen-like state. "Sorry, I was trying *not* to scare you." he said sleepily. He looked around the cave searchingly. "Where's Oop?"

"What?" She said in a dream-like state.

"I thought I'd find Oop in here with you."

"I'm pretty sure he's still out there sleeping?" She thought about it and realized she hadn't seen him.

"No, Crawford's out there alone. Oop passed out in that shrub by the entrance." He pointed to the area.

She bolted up and out of the cave. "Upal?" she shouted. "Upal!" She looked around. There was no trace of him. "Upal!" she cried out again. "Where could he have gone?"

"Quiet down, some of us are still trying to sleep." Crawford mumbled, still half asleep in still in the same awkward position.

Preet walked over and gently kicked him. "Get up, Upal's gone."

"What? There's nowhere to go." he said, closing his eyes.

Lashra and Preet went back into the cave. She cried out his name. The sound of her voice came echoing back, but this time the reverberations sounded urgent and despondent. A light flashed behind her. She turned toward the entrance.

"Upal you had us worried." She sounded like an upset mother.

It was Crawford. Her heart sank as she watched him laggardly making his way into the cave. He shook his head signaling that Upal was nowhere to be found.

Lashra's eyes grew wide. "He went back for the shield alone." She hung her head and shook it perturbedly. "Why would you do that?"

"Buggeration!" Preet angrily punched his fist into his hand.

"Always trying to be a hero." Crawford uttered. "He really is about as smart as he is tall." Neither paid attention to his remarks. "How long do you think he's been gone?" He grunted out.

"I was up a couple of hours before you two." She sounded worried. "It could be three hours or more. We need to go after him."

Chapter 61 Faster

"Grab what you can!" she shouted. "We need to get moving."

They ran out and gathered a pocket full of nuts, a couple of torches and some extra moss.

"We need to make up time. At least we know where we're going." Crawford said, trying to reassure the two. He might not have liked Upal much, but he knew Preet and Lashra would do anything for him and that was enough for him. He took the lead and made haste.

They arrived at the volcano shaft much sooner than they anticipated. This time, Preet didn't argue about going down. In fact, he descended first and was quick to encourage the others to pick up the pace.

From out of the blue they felt a tremor. "That's new." Preet said nervously.

The tremor was followed by a stronger shake and accompanied with a thick mist coming from below. "*This* does not feel right." Lashra's apprehensiveness was noticeable.

The earth convulsed again. Preet lost his grip. Lashra reached over to hold on to him but it was too late.

"Ahhhhhhhhh!" Preet was sucked down the crevasse.

"Preeeeet!" Lashra screamed. All she could do was watch as he dropped out of view. She braced herself against the wall. Crawford moved in close and put his arm around her, holding her against the wall.

The earth trembled again. Lashra was afraid to look down.

"Wooohooo!" she heard a scream coming from the pit.

"Preet?"

Yes, it was Preet. She was so happy.

While Preet descended the deep tube, the giant mushroom cap was making its way up it. As good fortune would have it, the hole was filling up with water, pushing the large fungus to the top.

"Jump on before it crushes you against the wall!" he shouted.

The ride was picking up speed. Lashra and Crawford jumped on the cap and within seconds the mushroom top came to a sudden stop. It threw the three travelers twenty feet into the air for a rough landing.

"Wooo! Hooo!" exclaimed Preet, "That definitely did not happen yesterday!"

They ran back to the hole in the ground. The cap was gone. A few seconds later it reappeared. "Here it comes!" Lashra yelled above the sound of rushing water.

It made a sudden stop, this time a little higher up the tube. The cap was beginning to warp and bow. Crawford realized what was about to happen. "The pressure's building." he said with a panic. "This thing is going to buckle under the pressure." His face went pale. "She's gonna blow. Run!"

Without hesitating they turned toward the exit and ran. Lashra and Crawford quickly outpaced Preet. The cave was now in a constant state of rumbling and shaking. The loudness of the reverberations were jarring and unnerving.

Lashra turned back to see Preet on the ground. She cried out above the sounds, "We have to move out! We need to leave! Get up!"

"I'm trying Lash!" he yelled at her.

Lashra hollered more warnings. "We need to get out of here, it's getting worse!"

He got up and ran past Lashra who was waiting for him. She followed him close. A thick mist unexpectedly covered the entire area. She peeked back to see a tsunami approaching. "Oh Buggeration!" she exclaimed.

When Preet heard her scream he knew not to look back. "This is no time to trip and fall." he said to himself.

The exit was within reach. They ran out and braced themselves against the wall outside the mouth of the cave. They watched and waited for the rush of water to end. But it didn't end. They covered their ears to block out some of the thunderous sounds escaping the cave. The cave spewed its water with a vengeance, jetting and gushing with an immeasurable force. The water made its way through the long tunneled path ripping through and dragging debris down the shaft.

When it reached the small opening with the tightly intertwined root walls, it climbed up to the sky with immense force and pressure until it exploded like a geyser.

In the distance they heard and saw a giant water volcano erupting. The water, the mist, the debris, it went up and up and up. It roared like a mythical beast with the sounds of a hundred thousand trumpets. It was so massive that it blocked out the sun's light. They watched in awe as day turned into night.

The mouth of the entrance vomited water, until it was completely eviscerated. As quickly as it started it stopped. A heavy and sustaining wind dispersed the heavenly waters and light returned.

Carefully turning their heads in to peek, they saw to their amazement barely a drop of water on the floor.

"What should we do?" asked Preet. He didn't wait for the others to respond. He made his way back in. There was no time to waste, they had to find him. They needed to find him and find him quickly.

After a distance, Preet was huffing and puffing. He slowed to a fast paced walk. "He must have tried to get the shield on his own. There's no way he could have survived this." His voice was filled with sorrow. "Lashra? What if Upal was the *one* to die?" he wiped tears from his eyes.

"What?" Crawford asked.

"The Old Lady said, *one* must die to save all. What if it was Upal?" Preet choked out.

Lashra growled at him. "Don't talk like that. He's alive. If anyone is stubborn enough to withstand something like this, it's him." She started running again. "Hurry!" she yelled back.

Filled with fear and sadness they accelerated their pace.

Chapter 62 Upal's In

Upal tossed and turned most of the night. He'd been stuck in a loop and kept reliving the same dream over and over. In the dream, he was running from Lashra, Crowboy and Preet. They were yelling but he couldn't make out what they were saying although it sounded familiar. He stopped and turned around just in time to see Preet disappear into a crack in the ground. Lashra and Crowboy followed Preet down and... Upal would wake up.

He looked up to the stars, "There's still a few hours before daylight." he said disappointedly. "I should try to get some more rest." he mumbled quietly to himself.

He closed his eyes and after a brief moment realized there was no way he could rest. There was a reason he couldn't sleep any longer. The dream, it was a sign. A couple of hours of broken up sleep would have to be enough. He knew there was no plan that could get the four of them out safely with the armour in tow. This was a one person job. Drawing to see who got the short straw? That was a bad idea. He knew he was the best person for this caper.

He grabbed a torch and made his way through the cave. "I can bring the shield back before they get up." he tried to convince himself. "With no one to slow me down, I can make my way in record time."

His mind raced as fast as he did. It felt like only minutes had passed, yet there he was soaking wet and standing at the bottom of the staircase, staring at Paladin.

"Hello my old friend." he spoke playfully to him.

He cautiously made his way up the staircase. His heart was a tight, painful beating drum. Upal stared back and forth from Paladin to the shield, the shield to Paladin. Was he really going to do this? He moved in a little closer to Paladin.

"*You* did it. You sacrificed your life so that my ancestors might live. That I might live. Your life is celebrated. As a small boy I often played the part of the great Paladin."

Upal raised his arm replaying the game. He protected himself from the fictional arrows, using his make believe shield. As he did he recited Paladin's Parnassus.

> *"Paladin had a vision*
> *Away from here to go*
> *Left with the shield, held it tight*
> *Arrows they did follow*
> *Defended us*
> *Imprisoned for me*
> *Now I'm filled with sorrow"*

"We all played the parts, we all wanted to be like the greats. But those were just games. Now look at us. Look at me." Upal was losing heart. "I need you to fill me with courage, help me get this done. How did you do it?"

He waited. Maybe, he thought, just maybe… but nothing.

"You know you could be a little more encouraging" he said to Paladin.

"Ok, what's my goal?" he asked Paladin. Upal answered himself. "Bring the shield to the surface." He tried to reach for it, but his body was frozen in place. "Come on Upal!" he shouted, trying to shake himself free of his fears. "All I have to do is make it to the surface. If worse comes to worse…" he didn't finish the thought.

"One must die to save all." The sound of The Old Lady's voice reverberated throughout the chamber.

"You're not helping!" he shouted out.

His hands were shaking as he reached out. Fear encompassed his entire being. "This is not the time to start thinking before you act." He let out a primitive "Yalp!"

True to himself, he proceeded without thinking, running as fast as possible, trying not to drop the shield; he kept his eyes glued on the hostile exit.

"Just make it to the window." he encouraged himself.

By the time he reached the bottom step, the water was almost waist high. He grunted, "One step at a time. One step at a time." as he struggled and trudged through the ever deepening waters.

He approached the raised floor that sat under the window. "Well, Lashra you were right." He shouted over the blasting sound of the falls, "I am now officially neck deep in trouble!"

By the time he reached the ledge, the water was over his head and only a few feet away from the overhang. The shield was weighing him down. He swam up toward the pocket of air hoping for a few final breaths of air. He was too late. He let the shield drag him down to the landing.

In a state of nerves he blindly hunted for the opening. One more puff of air, if only he could've gotten one more. He found the window in no time flat. He dragged himself and the armament through the hole.

He longed for air. Climb Upal, climb! his mind screamed.

A small volume of air escaped from his lungs. The downward pressure hadn't eased at all, in fact it seemed to be worse than before. The unrelenting force of the water pounded the shield. The burden was too great. The shield's size and weight made it difficult for him to move. The walls were closing in on him. He was suffocating.

Another bubble of air left his lips. He was sinking? Panic. Terror. He clawed the walls in vain. Yes, he was sinking.

Anxiety. Dread. Air, get to air, his mind could no longer hold a clear thought.

His mind conjured up images of dead bodies piling on top of his. They would all try. He blew out the remainder of the oxygen he had in his body. Exhaustion overtook him, he couldn't even slow himself down anymore. He accepted that he was sinking, the downward pressure from the falls was too much to bear. He was utterly depleted, and wanted nothing more than to close his eyes and sleep.

He needed to live. He wanted to live. He attempted to stop his downward motion but, he was wasted and sapped and the struggle was quick and futile. He stopped fighting. His arm was locked in the straps of the shield and it pulled him down.

Impressions of Preet filled his mind's eye, everything they had been through, across the years. Fantasies of Lashra, her smile, her eyes, their wedding day, their children, their life together. Images of his mother, his brother, his father. Even the likeness of Mrs. Nibbledent crossed his path. The Old Lady... her image stayed with him for the longest of moments. Then Paladin. Not the skeletal broken image he'd last seen but the young hero he'd always imagined. (The same Paladin Lashra saw the day before.)

Paladin put his hand on Upal's shoulder, looked him in the eyes and said, "Altruism will bring death's defeat."

Upal had a moment of lucidity. He realized at that moment that he was fulfilling both prophecies: *One must die to save all, and altruism brings death's defeat. They were really the same prophecy.* His death would save them from having to die. He finally understood. No longer able to resist, his lungs and mind gasped for air. Upal inhaled water.

The pain of being smothered by water was excruciating. His body clenched and all the suffering that was being inflicted on him was gone. He smiled in that moment and letting go of everything, Upal accepted his fate. Everything went white, the brightest purest white light one has ever seen or could ever imagine. It brought with it a sense of peace. He sent out a prayer for his friends. Then he was gone.

As if knowing he was dead, the current grabbed hold of Upal's body and dragged it downward until it slammed his limp body against the stone foundation. With all the vengeance it could muster, it whipped the boy back and forth, using his lifeless corpse to sweep the base of the catacomb.

Chapter 63 Lost And Found

Upal and the shield were transported through a long dark conduit that abruptly came to a dead end. The two slammed against the wall coming to a blunt stop.

Instantly, he was sucked up by its powerful force. The two objects went straight up twenty, possibly thirty feet. With great vigor the water spewed him up from a hole in the floor. It had done it with such intense authority that, had he been alive, this alone would surely have killed him. The mighty jet of the water kept Upal's body cornered against the ceiling and a protruding wall.

Water was flowing from everywhere. It breathed out from all surfaces of the cavern. It bled from every nook and cranny; the discharge was unstoppable. Floodwaters pounded every inch of the cave. It was an overwhelming, unconquerable and irreversible deluge.

If the magical substance had been put there to protect the shield, it was fulfilling its duty with apocalyptic might.

The cataclysmic event came to a sudden stop and as if possessed, the cavern resolved to rid itself of every drop of water. Upal's ragdoll body dropped to the floor. In its single-minded effort to bleed the enchanted cavern of every drop of water, it took, even from Upal's lifeless body. He began to have violent seizures. His body spewed out every last drop.

****

"There he is!" Lashra screamed as she ran toward Upal. She fell to her knees and rolled him over. His arms were still wound in the straps of the shield and it covered him like a blanket. She lifted his head and gently placed it on her lap. She wept.

Overflowing with emotions she erupted in anguish and anger. She pounded his chest and berated him. "You dimwitted fool!" she cried out. "Why did you do this?" Her scream turned into a whimpering sob. "All for one Upal, all for one." She continued to beat his chest.

Preet seized her arm. "Stop it." he said, tears streaming down his face. "Stop it." He fell next to his sister. "He did this for us." The shield let off a soft glow. "He knew we had to continue. He knew what he was doing."

Crawford stood at Upal's feet looking down at him. He shook his head in disbelief. "The last line of the poem," he whispered. "Altruism bestows you…"

"Death's defeat." a very hoarse whisper cut Crowboy off in mid sentence.

"You're alive!" Lashra and Preet shouted.

Upal attempted to open his eyes and speak again but his tired, battered body was fighting for air. After a few minutes of Lashra and Preet fussing over Upal, Crawford made his way to Upal. He smiled as he reached down and tousled his hair.

"You really are as smart as you are tall." he said, shaking his head in wonder. "But I do have to admit," he paused, as a large grin took over his face. "You're also as brave as you are short." he laughed. "You did it!"

"We did it." Upal forced out the words with a hack. "Well, mostly me." he said. "Mostly I did it." He closed his eyes and his head fell to the side.

Lashra shook him in a panic, "Upal wake up, wake up."

"Stop it, I'm just really tired and sore. Let me just rest here a little bit longer." he said with a weak smile. Even half dead, Upal could still find a way to enjoy resting his head on Lashra's lap.

As if reading his best friend's mind, "Only because you're too weak to try anything." Preet interjected.

Lashra smiled. She was happy to be holding him, happy that he was alive. She couldn't imagine life without both Preet and Upal. Holding him like this, stroking his hair, she felt something. She wasn't sure what it was, so she passed it off as cramps and indigestion. The thought made her laugh on the inside and her smile grew wider.

"Another crazy day in the Rubicon." Preet muttered. "You were dead Upal. Did you know that?" He nudged him gently with his foot.

"Dead?" he looked up to meet Lashra's eyes. "But I'm alive."

All of a sudden, looking into his eyes made her feel self-conscious. She quickly got up and Upal's head hit the ground. "Ahhh!" he grunted.

"Come on Preet help me get him up." she said slightly flustered.

They reached down and took him by the arms, gently lifting him up. His legs were weak and unstable. Crawford walked over and placed himself between Preet and Upal. Preet lifted Upal's arm and tenderly placed it around Crawford's neck.

"I'll help you until you get your feet under you." He placed his arm around Upal's waist and held him up.

"I'll be fine." Upal said as he attempted to remove his arm from Crawford's shoulder but he found the task to be quite challenging. "Well, maybe the first few feet."

Preet picked up the shield and placed his arms through the leather straps. *Clang,* the armour hit the wall.

"Be careful with that Preet, I had to die to get that thing."

"But not really, because you are alive." Crawford was more than happy to point out that fact.

Miraculously Upal had no broken bones, although he was severely battered and bruised. The long trek back to the outside world took a considerable amount of time. Preet, Lashra and Crawford all took turns assisting Upal on his journey. They stopped multiple times along the way to allow him to rest and recover.

"Light," Upal nodded toward the exit. "Finally. I can make it out on my own."

"Two and half steps away and *now* he can do it on his own." Crawford laughed rhetorically.

Thankfully Preet caught Upal just outside the exit. Two and a half steps was almost unbearable. He delicately helped his friend to the ground and made him as comfortable as he could.

Crawford stretched out and kicked back near the edge of the cliff. He saw a beautiful canopy of green; the morning fog had long lifted. They were so high up that the tops of the trees below looked like rolling grass.

He turned toward the gang and quipped, "I have to say, after everything we've gone through in the last few days, salvaging Paladin's shield was rather anticlimactic."

"What? Need I remind you I died for that shield?" Upal uttered out in dismay.

"I'm just saying, if that's the best that the Rubicon can throw at us, I think we'll be fine." Crawford had a faint smile as he continued with his erroneous comments.

"Preet." Upal wanted a little help from his best friend. "Can you remind this guy" he said as he exhaustedly nodded his head in Crawford's direction, "of my tragic death?"

"But Oop, you're still alive." He chuckled and gently shoved Upal, who was too weak to hold himself up and just fell over.

"I guess *dying* is just another thing you're not good at Upal." Crawford said as he turned away laughing.

"Leave him alone guys. He's been through enough today." Lashra said in a disapproving tone.

Upal moaned out, "A couple of momes, that's what you are. Just a couple of momes." He closed his eyes and fell asleep.

Preet was about to shake him awake when Lashra stopped him. "Leave him alone. He needs to rest. He's going to need all day and night to have any chance of making it back tomorrow."

"Back to where?" asked Preet.

"Back to the witch, I guess?" she responded. "Upal's in no shape to climb down a cliff and that's about the only other choice we have. Now that we have the shield…" she stopped in mid sentence.

She wasn't sure what to do and neither Crawford nor Preet were offering up suggestions. "Maybe we wait for another vision?" She was weary and sore and feeling grumpy. "I'm getting a little sick and tired of this whole situation. What was The Old Lady thinking sending us in here?"

Preet could hear her exasperation. "You're right." He opened his arms wide and embraced her in a giant hug. "There's no point going farther. He needs his rest and we can all use a few hours without excitement."

They took their turns admiring the shield. The shape, the metal, the colors, the symbols. It was all so surreal.

Nightfall was approaching and they decided to take no chances, someone had to stay awake just in case. Crawford drew the short straw and therefore he would keep first guard. Upal, who had spent the entire day sleeping, would continue his well deserved rest and get the night off.

"My eyes are starting to burn, I need to shut them for a while." said Preet. "Three hours comes quickly."

Within seconds they were asleep. Crawford sat with Ray warming his back with the fire. "Thanks for always being there little buddy. You truly are my best friend." He smiled and petted the raven. "Well, at least now you're not my only friend."

Crack, the sound was jarring in the silence of the night.

Crawford held his breath and turned his ear toward the sound. He got up without delay and lit a moss torch. Waving it high above his head he lit up as much of the area as possible.

"Did you hear that? he whispered loudly to Ray. He looked over at the bird. Ray's back was hunched over, his beak pointing at the ground; he too was fast asleep. "Great. Forget everything I said about being my best friend."

With trepidation he made his way quietly and slowly toward the sound he thought he heard. I hope nothing jumps out at me, he thought to himself. A sense of horror began to fill him. He moved the flame around to see if he could see anything or hopefully scare away anything that could possibly be out there. He stopped and listened for a minute. He breathed a sigh of relief. It must have been my imagination. He peered to his left and his right and could see nothing out of sorts, although his heart and stomach said something completely different.

Content with the fact that he found nothing out there, he retraced his steps backwards when suddenly something grabbed his foot and dragged him to the ground. His heart raced. He looked around in a panic and realized he'd tripped over the log he'd been sitting on. Crawford was feeling quite flustered.

He put his hand over his heart and massaged the aching muscle. He wondered if the sound was loud enough to wake the others. It wasn't.

"I won't have to worry about falling asleep tonight." He spoke quietly but, also loudly enough to be heard by whoever or whatever was out there listening. He did whatever he could to comfort himself.

He held his breath and turned his ear to a soft sound coming from the tunnel's direction. What was murmuring out there? Was it the wind or a large flying insect that glows? No, it was just his overworked and tired imagination. He thought about waking up the others but he could already hear Upal's voice lamenting.

"I died and you woke us up because you heard a noise?"

That was enough incentive to let them sleep.

He sat for a short time in silence, thinking of the most horrible things that might happen to him if he didn't stay alert. Then he tried hard to think of comforting thoughts. He would have taken a comforting thought.

"Ahh yes," he said, trying hard to forget the self-perceived horror of his situation. "What was Lashra saying earlier about the Scrolls of Tralatitious? What was it she said? They were never seen from again?" He felt discouraged.

"She could've ended that lesson on a more positive note. Maybe I should wake her up and ask her what happened next?"

Chapter 64 Saudj's End

"Where am I?" Saudj's voice echoed. He was in the unknown, surrounded by the purest blackness he'd ever experienced. A strange yet delicate buzzing sound surrounded him. He carefully stretched out his arms and spun slowly in place trying to feel for something, anything that might help him figure out where he'd landed. "Where am I?" he repeated.

He took a small step to one side and his hand felt a monstrous slimy something. He quickly removed his hand and wiped it on his shirt. "That was creepy." he muttered softly. Carefully waving his arms in front of himself he took a step. Suddenly a light went off in his face. He instinctively flailed his arms and struck an object. The light started blinking on and off a few times then the glow remained permanent. It was a Luciferin.

"Not this again?!" He waited for a moment preparing himself for the imminent attack. But it never came. Why was it here? Why was he? The insect regained flight and moved forward on some kind of path. Saudj squinted, trying to see where it was going. The creature's light was only able to illuminate a small area at a time. "Where are you leading me?" he questioned the Luciferin. It stopped in mid flight and turned around. Saudj jumped back in terror. He tripped over his own feet and fell to the ground. He looked up at its sinister face as it approached him. He couldn't fully make it out in the darkness. The glow became so intense it lit up the entire area. It couldn't be?

"I must be dreaming. This has to be a dream." he cried out. "No, not you?" He tried to convince himself it was all a dream. Saudj closed his eyes but it only bore down on him. It stopped and hovered only inches from his face. He could feel the breath of air created by the flying nightmare. He uncovered his eyes and came face to face with him.

It was Upal. He was forcefully staring into his eyes. Saudj was dumbfounded. He could see the shield in the glint of Upal's eyes. Like a shot, Upal the Luciferin repeatedly stung his nemesis. Saudj was defenceless and screamed in agony.

"Ahh, uhh?! Saudj was jolted from his nightmare. He sat up batting his arms, trying to rid himself of the monster. He looked around in a state of shock, slowly coming to the realization that it had been a nightmare.

"He did it, He found the shield." Saudj was still stunned by the trauma.

He looked to the sky. The sun would be up in a matter of an hour or so. He wasn't going back to sleep. He got up and was grateful for the lack of pain. He hobbled around the camp for fuel. He made his way back and threw a few pieces onto the coals. He bent down and blew. After a few puffs the fire was going. He got up and fell back from the dizziness.

He sat and stoked the fire a little. The flames had disappeared. Just as he was about to bend down and resume blowing, a gentle zephyr came through the camp and reignited the flames. "Shield." the wind whispered. It was scarcely perceptible and Saudj was sure he had imagined it.

The clear sky brought with it a rather warm start to his day. He sat staring into the fire; he couldn't seem to shake the image of Luciferin Upal from his mind's eye. "Something strange is going on, I can feel it in my bones."

He rose and walked the camp again. He gathered whatever goodies he could find to fill the hole in his belly. The sun beamed its light into the camp hitting the scrolls that lay by the fire. He'd had them all this time and didn't bother to read them.

He struggled to remember why he'd even grabbed them. There were thousands of pages in The Old Lady's library. Why was she holding these that fateful night? He held them up and was about to throw them in the fire. He unrolled them and grabbed a page and read a random passage.

They vanished into the Rubicon and the remaining Longevites called out to everyone. "Today we start a new chapter in the history of Eternal. Let us never forget all the tragedies that we have withstood in the recent past. Our brothers, sisters, mothers, fathers and children, yes, even our own selves have been damaged and destroyed, because of our lawlessness.

Our transgressions have doomed three blameless souls to the Rubicon. This day in our history should never be disregarded. Every year at this time, we shall celebrate for three days the lives of those who died for us. Today and for the next two, we shall unite in peace and friendship in the Celebration of Liberation."

Saudj was convinced that some things in the scrolls had to be true. After all, there were days ordained to commemorate the historical events. But the magic and myths of Demorg and his blasphemies? Those stories were added to keep his people down, to enslave their minds and their souls. That he was sure of.

"I should've burned the whole place down." he said as he threw the scrolls on the ground; at that moment the earth shook. Saudj braced himself. The rumbling only lasted a few seconds. He immediately grabbed the scrolls and tucked them away.

Unharmed, he toured the camp once more. He looked high and low, trying to figure out where those darn kids could've gone. "There's got to be a trace of them somewhere."

He stopped in mid step, the same soft buzzing sound from his dream had returned. No, it wasn't a buzz, it was more of a *purr, a hiss.* He forced himself to focus and to listen attentively. It was an indistinct continuous whispering sound.

"What is that?" He turned his ear to the sound and closed his eyes to help reduce the distractions. Whatever was causing the sound, he was sure that it wasn't good.

Saudj was standing directly in front of the Angry Widows. The sound seemed to be coming from somewhere in that direction. He looked down and noticed a bit of a rut under the flowers. "Hmmf. I knew I'd find you." He bent down to take a look under the Golden Flowers and sure enough, there was the trail he was looking for. "Trying to sneak out of here are you?"

He started to question why they would choose to crawl out. Did they know they were being followed? It didn't make any sense. He peered deep into the underbrush and then noticed the hissing sound had turned into a rushing sound. A wave of water appeared and it was close-at-hand. He turned and ran with a painful limp.

He fell to the ground a short distance away. He watched in awe as the wave destroyed the path. It crashed up against the witch's throne shattering it to bits and pieces. Saudj was completely covered with debris and seemed to be out of danger. He thought it remarkable that the wave magically stopped where the throne once sat. In that same instant the sky grew dark and the day had turned to night. Then out of the blue the light returned, bringing with it a heavy mist.

And just like that the water was gone and a clear path lay ahead of him. "If I had to guess… I'd say they went this way."

He made his way through and soon found himself climbing up and up and up. About half way through the tunnel he was exhausted and decided to rest. He closed his eyes and soon he was asleep.

He woke up and wasn't sure how long he'd been asleep. The tunnel seemed much darker and the flowers hanging from the walls were losing their luster. He needed to get a move on. A few hours later he found himself walking out of the tunnel in the dead of night.

He looked up and could just make out the moon through the canopy. He decided to move forward with hopes of finding a good resting place for the night. A few feet into his journey he spotted twinkling lights. Was it more of those futile glowing bugs? He quietly moved in for a closer look.

Saudj heard an unfamiliar sound by the twinkling lights. He was too close. He stepped back and...

Crack... Saudj stopped and took in a deep breath. The sound of the snapping branch under his foot echoed throughout the Rubicon and it paralyzed him with fear. Oh no, I've been exposed; his thoughts were barely audible over the blasts of his pounding heart.

He saw a light in the not too far distance, it was high and it was moving back and forth. Then he saw a large dark shadowy figure that seemed to grow and shrink with every move. It held light and it was coming for him.

What have I done? Why did I get so close? The thoughts were screaming in his head. He didn't dare move or even exhale. Somehow he had been lulled into a false sense of security brought on by the flickering firelight and the faint crackling and snapping sounds of the fire. His aloneness had gotten to him, and now it had drawn him in. He was dangerously close. If only he could get out of this situation, he swore he would not be this careless again.

"Did you hear that?" A strange sense of relief fell over Saudj, as he heard the voice.

It's human, he thought to himself, at least I have a chance. He realized it wasn't Preet or Upal's voice that he'd heard. Could there be survivors like himself roaming the forest? Did this stranger know that his friends were in here? Was he working with them, plotting against him?

Saudj heard the footsteps moving away from him. The man hadn't traveled far and Saudj realized how close he was to their camp. I need to see it. I need to see who's there. "Be

273

careful Saudj, move slowly, thoughtfully. Don't make a sound." he unknowingly mumbled to himself.

He moved deliberately and without a sound. He approached the clearing and could see the stranger warming his hands by the fire. He took another step needing to get a closer look. *Crack...* not again. He stopped.

Saudj could see them. Preet and Upal, one on each side of the fire. Where was Lashra? She must be on the backside, he thought. Then, as if by magic he laid his eyes on the shield.

"They did it. They found the shield, they really did it." he mumbled quietly.

Then he heard the stranger's voice again.

"What was Lashra saying earlier about the Scrolls of Tralatitious? What was it she said? They were never seen from again? She could've ended that lesson on a more positive note. Maybe I should wake her up and ask her what happened next?"

Saudj did everything he could not to move. He was stuck. Now he had to figure out how much time he would have to stand there before he could make his move and leave.

It was going to be a long night.

Chapter 65 Upal's Window

Mrs. Nibbledent sat on the large trunk darning the mattress covers. It was hard to imagine that the children had been with her less than a week. The thought brought a smile to her face. She could not recall a time she'd felt more fulfilled or satisfied.

She paused from her task at hand for a moment and peacefully listened to the voices coming from the street below. She listened as the children sang and skipped rope in time with their rhymes.

> *"Paladin had a vision*
> *Away from here to go*
> *Left with the shield, held it tight*
> *Arrows they did follow*
> *Defended us*
> *Imprisoned for me*
> *Now I'm filled with sorrow"*

The song brought back memories of another Longevite. It was so surreal that The Old Lady was dead. She'd been murdered, it was so surreal. Mrs. Nibbledent was unexpectedly shaken off the trunk by a powerful tremor. Luckily she'd fallen on the mattress next to the trunk. She rolled off as quickly as her old body would let her. She scrambled to her feet and she stumbled her way to Upal's window (as the children had come to know it).

She looked down and was relieved to see that the children were safe and sound.

"What's going on?" the oldest child (her name was Culy) cried up from the street below.

Mrs. Nibbledent's eyes were gaping and unblinking, her mouth wide open and her arm was stretched out pointing westward. Something must be happening near the Rubicon, thought Culy.

The woman tried to utter a sound that would convey what she was seeing but nothing came out. A brobdingnagian waterspout was jetting out from Mount Paladin. It flowed endlessly up, filling the sky with all types of debris. As it reached its pinnacle it spread out like a giant mushroom. Day turned to night.

Everyone in Eternal who could witness the event, did. The daylight slowly returned with the help of a breeze coming from the Rubicon. Soon the entire city was covered with a thick murky mist. Everyone recognized the moment as a fulfillment of some kind of prophecy. Most likely one that involved the murder of the last living Longevite.

Without a second of delay people began explicating the sign of the times.

The North Gate untangled the event and told it's people that it was The Old Lady sending a message to the world. She had found her murderer and had passed judgement on him. The release of water was a sign. She was free and not even the Rubicon could hold her back. The dark mist that fell over the city was a remnant of his burial.

The South Gate instructed its people that they should see it as a sign that the return of Demorg was imminent. The Old Lady was the only thing stopping his return. With her murder (obviously planned by Demorg), he was now able to return and finish what he'd started thousands of years ago. The earthquake and the explosion of water was a warning to them that Demorg had retrieved the shield and murdered a second Longevite. The thick mist that covered the city was symbolic of Paladin's blood.

The East Gate counselled their people in this way. "There will be more signs to come." their mentors preached. "It is the fulfillment of the *One*'s prophecy. The Old Lady's murder was the turning point. The unfettered display of water was a celebration of life, freedom and joy. The opaque mist that traveled from the Rubicon and covered the city was a sign that everything will be ours again."

The West Gate leaders with their long history of being outcasts, soon spread stories of a soon coming war. One that would bring redemption to its long enslaved people. The Old Lady was displeased with the descendants of Demorg. Not only had they murdered her, but they let her murderer go unpunished.

Saudj's father preached to his neighbours. "The Old Lady has joined forces with Paladin. She seeks to punish us for our supposed betrayal."

People were quick to gather around and listen. "The battle for the Rubicon and all of Eternal has begun. You cannot deny the signs. Demorg is *The One* and he has returned to avenge our years of torment. We will no longer be oppressed." The gathered mob nodded and cheered him on.

"The dark muddy mist that has fallen on us, is a sign to us that these walls will be destroyed and washed away. Rejoice! We will soon be free. Go and share the good news with your neighbours." He released the pack and they swarmed the West Gate spreading their message.

"Mrs. Nibbledent!" Culy cried up from the street below. "Mrs. Nibbledent?"

She couldn't take her eyes off the vision. What does this mean? she thought to herself. In that moment she traveled back to the last time she saw Upal. He had been staring out this very window, *his* arm extending out to the Rubicon, shouting impulsively.

Oh my precious Upal, she thought. You said one word and it was prophecy.

Culy shouted and waved her arms, trying everything to shake the woman from her trance. "Mrs. Nibbledent!"

Culy read her lips and seemed to understand when Mrs. Nibbledent whispered in the wind "Murder."

Made in the USA
Monee, IL
27 May 2021